*"Lightning and ~~sage and desert rain,~~
Holly whispered. "I've tasted you
in my dreams, Linc."*

His breath drew in sharply.

"Holly," Linc said huskily. "Are you sure you're not a dream?"

Before she could answer, his tongue probed the hollow at the base of her throat, then moved slowly up her neck until he found her ear. His teeth closed delicately on her earlobe.

When the tip of Linc's tongue traced the curves of her ear, Holly began to tremble. With eyes half-closed, she rubbed her palms over his back.

His skin stretched smoothly over muscles hardened by work. Silk and steel, the taste of Linc on her lips, dream come true.

"Which is better—this or dreams?" he asked.

ELIZABETH LOWELL

"A LAW UNTO HERSELF IN THE WORLD OF ROMANCE."
Amanda Quick

Books by Elizabeth Lowell

Contemporary

DEATH ECHO • BLUE SMOKE AND MURDER • INNOCENT AS SIN
THE WRONG HOSTAGE • WHIRLPOOL • THE SECRET SISTER
ALWAYS TIME TO DIE • THE COLOR OF DEATH
DEATH IS FOREVER • DIE IN PLAIN SIGHT
RUNNING SCARED • MOVING TARGET
MIDNIGHT IN RUBY BAYOU • PEARL COVE
THE RUBY • JADE ISLAND
AMBER BEACH • DIAMOND TIGER

Historical

THIS TIME LOVE • EDEN BURNING
REMEMBER SUMMER • TO THE ENDS OF THE EARTH
WHERE THE HEART IS • WINTER FIRE
DESERT RAIN • AUTUMN LOVER
A WOMAN WITHOUT LIES • ONLY LOVE
FORGET ME NOT • ENCHANTED
BEAUTIFUL DREAMER • LOVER IN THE ROUGH
FORBIDDEN • UNTAMED
ONLY YOU • ONLY MINE • ONLY HIS

ELIZABETH LOWELL

DESERT RAIN

AVON

An Imprint of HarperCollinsPublishers

Desert Rain was previously published in an altered form entitled *Summer Thunder* by Silhouette Books in 1983.

Re-published

AVON BOOKS
An Imprint of HarperCollins*Publishers*
10 East 53rd Street
New York, New York 10022-5299

Copyright © 1983 by Ann Maxwell; 1996 by Two of a Kind, Inc.
Excerpt from *Death Echo* copyright © 2010 by Two of a Kind, Inc.
ISBN 978-0-380-76762-5
www.avonromance.com

First Avon Books mass market printing: September 1996

Avon Trademark Reg. U.S. Pat. Off. and in Other Countries,
Marca Registrada, Hecho en U.S.A.
HarperCollins® is a registered trademark of HarperCollins Publishers.

Printed in the U.S.A.

20 19 18 17 16 15

One

"Come on, Shannon, smile like I'm your lover. You do know what a lover is, don't you, sweetie?"

Holly Shannon North bit back what she wanted to say and smiled as she had been trained to do.

Jerry was the hottest fashion photographer outside of Paris, but he had a mouth like a razor blade. Since Holly had refused to sleep with him, he had become nearly impossible to work with.

The flash that burst in Holly's face was reflected in flexible metal shields held by sweating technicians.

"Better, but not good enough," Jerry said. "I know you're ice from the neck down, but let's keep it our secret, lovey."

Holly lowered her eyelids until her unusual sherry-colored eyes were only glints beneath thick black lashes. Long hair fell like black water over her bare shoulders and upper arms. Her smile widened without becoming a bit softer.

1

Jerry grunted.

Motionless, Holly waited. Perspiration made fine tendrils of hair curl over the high temples and slanted cheekbones that had transformed a young girl called Holly North into Shannon, an internationally famous model.

"Now give me a pout," Jerry ordered. "Lots of lip just begging to be bitten."

Holly pouted.

"Turn left," Jerry said harshly. "Make that hair fly. Make every man who looks at you want to feel it sliding over his naked skin."

Holly turned with the grace that was as much a part of her as her long legs and lithe body.

The heat that had everyone else short-tempered and sweating was like wine to her. She had been raised in Palm Springs' scorching, brilliant, endless summers. The desert sun that bleached out most people made her bloom.

A delicate rose flush glowed beneath her skin, hinting at the heat within, a heat that only one man had ever touched.

Lincoln McKenzie.

Don't think about him, Holly told herself automatically. *It only hurts you.*

Though she tried not to think of Linc, she couldn't help herself. The feel of Palm Springs in the summer was too unique. She couldn't make herself believe that she was in New York or Paris, Hong Kong or London or Rome, and Lincoln McKenzie was half a world away.

Holly knew that Linc lived here, near enough

to touch. He was part of the desert, as strong as the mountains rising in stark grandeur beyond the city.

Memories of Linc, like the sun, fired her skin.

She had worshipped Linc since she was nine years old and he was seventeen, riding one of the Arabian horses his family raised. The first time she saw him was a moment so vivid Holly could still smell the sage and dust, see Linc's slow smile and hazel eyes, feel the velvet flutter of the horse's nostrils and her own heart as she stood in the path of his mount and smiled up at him.

"Lovely!" Jerry said. "Keep it up! Over the shoulder now. Turn. Faster! Again. Again! Again!"

Feeling like a leaf caught in the winds of time, Holly turned and spun, giving herself to the desert heat and her memories of one man.

She couldn't mark the day or even the month when her young girl's crush on Linc had changed into something deeper, hotter, more consuming. Although their ranches shared a common boundary, the two families did not socialize.

Yet as Holly grew older, she saw Linc frequently at horse shows and auctions and training rings. With each meeting she fell more completely under his spell.

Each time, it crushed her that Linc didn't notice her.

"Yeah, good," Jerry muttered. "Now a little

brighter, less pout. Big smile, baby. Gimme teeth."

Holly smiled at the camera, but her eyes were focused on the past.

On her sixteenth birthday she had been baby-sitting Beth McKenzie, Linc's half-sister, who was only nine. The McKenzies came home very late, arguing and more than a little drunk. Holly had never heard people swear at each other like that.

When Linc showed up unexpectedly, Holly ran to him. He drove her home, talking softly to her until she stopped shaking. When he learned that she had turned sixteen at midnight, he teased her gently about "sweet sixteen and never been kissed."

What began as a comforting gesture became different, deeper, the timeless kiss of a man holding a woman he desired. Holly responded with an innocent abandon that had all but destroyed Linc's control.

After a long time he had taken her face between his hands and looked at her, memorizing the moment and the moonlight pouring over her dazed face. The smile she gave him had been that of Eve newly awakened to the possibilities of being a woman.

"That's the smile I want!" said Jerry triumphantly. "My God, babe, if you were only half as hot as you look. Left shoulder. Gimme some heat. Yeah. Yeah! Turn on for me, babe!"

Holly barely noticed the photographer's chatter or the battery of flashes going off around her. She was sixteen again, smiling up at the man she had always loved.

Linc had wanted to take her out the following night, but Holly had promised to baby-sit for her father's foreman. That was where she had been when Linc came and told her there had been an accident, a head-on crash along a twisting county road.

He had driven Holly to the hospital where doctors were trying to save her parents. He had held her through the long night while first her mother and then her father died.

Linc had held Holly while she screamed and wept, held her while her world shattered, held her until she fell into an exhausted sleep in his arms.

When Holly woke up, she was in a hospital bed and her mother's sister, Sandra, was there. Holly knew her aunt only from a few faded photographs in a shoebox full of family pictures.

Within a few days Sandra had taken Holly back to Manhattan, where Sandra owned an agency that specialized in high-fashion models.

By the time Holly was eighteen, she was working full time as a model. By the time she was nineteen, she had been on the cover of every major American and European magazine. By the time she was twenty, she was the Royce Reflection, the woman chosen by Europe's foremost designer to represent his total line of products, from perfumes to clothes, from negligees to cosmetics.

Holly used only her middle name, Shannon, when she worked. It was her way of separating herself from the alien, glamorous creature who stared back at her from the pages of magazines and spoke seductively about negligees and sex on millions of television screens.

Shannon was sensual, beautiful, extraordinary.

Holly was not.

After years of seeing herself as an awkward duckling, she wasn't at all comfortable with what makeup and lighting magicians did to her face and what fashion sorcerers did to her slender body.

Most of all, Holly resented the males who groped after her carefully applied beauty in expensive cars and penthouse suites. She knew that the men were really making love to a four-color magazine spread.

And that was how she responded—cool, sophisticated.

Flat.

Men had called her many names, frigid being the most polite.

At twenty-two, Holly was a virgin who looked like every man's dream of a sexy, very experienced lover.

"Lift your arms," Jerry said.

Dreamily she did, remembering what it had been like to slide her hands up Linc's shoulders and comb her fingers through his thick, chestnut hair.

"Higher," Jerry ordered. "Good. Now arch

your back and shake out your hair."

Holly hesitated. Acting like that wasn't part of her memories. She hadn't flaunted herself and teased Linc.

She had loved him.

"C'mon, sweetie," Jerry said impatiently. "Give it a little sex. Think of your lover."

Caught between the innocent past and the empty present, Holly tensed.

"No, no, no," Jerry snapped.

Forcing herself to relax, she tried again.

"Not good enough," he said. Then, sarcastically Jerry added, "Oh, yeah. I forgot. You're not into lovers. So put your hands on those lovely, useless hips and pretend, damn you!"

A toss of Holly's head sent black hair rippling down the center of her back. She moved her body into a taunting stance and looked sidelong at the camera.

Memory stabbed through Holly as her hair slid over her skin. She wished her hair had been long when Linc's fingers had tugged playfully at her chin-length curls.

Why couldn't I have been beautiful then, when I was sixteen and in love?

On the heels of that thought came another, one that had haunted her for six years.

I wish I was sixteen now, in Linc's arms, his mouth warm against my throat and his taste on my lips. . . .

The memory was hot and sweet at the same time. It transformed her body with a tidal wave of yearning so strong that the camera couldn't miss it.

"Beautiful!" crowed Jerry. "Babe, I'm gonna put you up for an Oscar. If I didn't know better, I'd swear you liked sex."

His words were meaningless noise to Holly. She was six years in the past, smiling, lost in her memories of Linc and her first taste of passion.

Turning, hair swirling, she held her arms out to the only man she had ever loved. She could see him so vividly, chestnut hair shot through with gold, taller than other men, stronger. His eyes changed with the light, first hazel, then green, now dark with an emotion she couldn't name.

Past and present collided, throwing Holly off-balance.

She wasn't holding out her arms to a dream, but to the real man.

Linc.

She couldn't believe that she wasn't seeing her dream. Linc was here, now, towering over the crouched, muttering photographer.

Abruptly Holly believed it was the present, not the past. The look Linc was giving her was one of absolute contempt, not of gentleness or of rising passion.

His cold hazel glance swept the crowd of technicians and gawkers. Then he returned to an examination of her that was so intimate she blushed.

Instinctively she crossed her arms over her

breasts and shook her hair forward until it was a veil concealing her from Linc's icy scrutiny.

"That's a new one," Jerry said, shifting for a better angle. "It has possibilities."

The motor drive on his camera raced like a mechanical heart, pumping frame after frame of film through the camera.

"Not bad, lovey," Jerry said grudgingly. "Now shoot out that right hip and give me the hungry little girl bit you do so well."

Motionless, Holly stood frozen in Linc's contempt. She didn't know why Linc hated her, but the look on his face left no doubt that he did.

Her dream of love, of Linc, exploded like glass inside her, cutting her, hurting her so much it was hard to breathe.

"Wake up, Shannon," Jerry snapped. "We don't have all day."

Shannon.

Holly's professional name echoed in her mind, breaking the grip of pain. She remembered that she was twenty-two, a top international model. She was no longer a plain, love-struck girl of sixteen.

Not Holly, she reminded herself harshly.

Shannon.

Shannon wouldn't let a man's contempt strip her nerves raw. She would give as good as she got.

Or better.

Holly assumed a provocative stance, hand on hip, chin lifted, as graceful as a lily swaying on a long stem. She bared her teeth at the camera in a mockery of a smile.

"You call that a come-on?" Jerry demanded.

Turning away, Holly let out a breath and narrowed her eyes. She tried to forget the present and recall the dream that had sustained her through the empty years since her aunt had dragged her from the land—and the man—she loved.

It was the dream of Linc that had made Holly come alive for the camera. It was the dream of Linc that made her radiate a leashed sensuality that fairly shimmered through the magazine pages and TV commercials.

"Over your right shoulder," Jerry ordered. "Gimme some teeth and a hint of tongue."

Holly turned again.

Linc hadn't moved. He was still there, watching her.

Hating her.

Why? Holly asked herself painfully. *What did I do to make him so angry that he never answered my letters?*

Why is he here, now, hating me?

Abruptly Holly realized that the silk dress she wore was molded to her body by heat and static electricity. The clinging cloth told anyone with eyes that Royce designs, as the ads purred, "are made to be worn over nothing but a woman's perfumed skin."

For an instant Holly was motionless, caught in Linc's consuming glance. Embarrassment and something else shot through her, something she hadn't felt since she was sixteen.

Her body changed, hot and cold at once. The tips of her breasts tightened, pressing in intimate detail against the thin silk.

The sardonic twist to Linc's mouth told Holly that he hadn't missed her body's response to him.

She wanted to run from him, but that was something Holly would do. She wasn't Holly at the moment. She was Shannon and she ran from nothing, certainly not a man's contempt.

Shannon would return that contempt with interest.

Fine silk clung to Holly's hips as she spun away from Linc, from the camera, from everything. She walked through the battery of lights and reflectors without a backward look.

"Shannon?" called Jerry. "Where are you going? I'm just getting started!"

"Too bad," she retorted. "I'm just getting finished."

The words came out in the brittle, East Coast accent Holly used on difficult men.

Shannon's voice.

Without a backward look, Holly kept on going, walking away from Linc McKenzie, the only man she had ever loved.

Two

Holly grabbed sunglasses and a bottle of mineral water from the catering van that followed her to every location, whether it was mountaintop, sea, or desert. The van was just one of the fringe benefits of being the Royce Reflection.

Holly put on the darkly rose-tinted glasses and sipped at the cold water. With a sigh, she rolled the bubbly liquid around on her tongue and rubbed the icy bottle over the pulse that beat hotly in her wrists.

"What the hell do you think you're doing?" Jerry shouted. "We're in the middle of a shoot and you're sitting on your tight ass like Queen Elizabeth!"

Holly ignored him and concentrated on her hands. They showed an alarming tendency to shake.

Jerry began yelling names.

Holly ignored that, too. Grimly she reminded herself that Jerry was a great fashion photographer as well as a miserable human being.

Roger Royce's clipped British voice cut across Jerry's tirade.

13

"Belt up, Jerry. You've been working Shannon like a donkey for hours in this heat. Any other model would have told you to get stuffed long ago."

Slowly Holly turned and faced her boss. He was blond, elegantly masculine, and almost six inches taller than her own five feet eight inches. Roger was a genius with shapes, textures, colors, and women's bodies. He was also that rarity in the fashion business—a gentleman.

"You okay?" Roger asked.

"Working on it," Holly said tightly.

Roger touched her forehead with his palm.

"You're pale underneath all that makeup," he said.

"I'm fine."

"You don't look it."

Holly smiled thinly.

"I didn't realize Jerry had been at me for three hours," she said. "It caught up with me all at once."

"You're certain?"

"Sure."

Roger turned Holly so that her face was not in shadow.

"You *are* pale," he said, alarmed.

She shrugged.

"I shouldn't have trusted Jerry," Roger said. "He's beastly with models who won't sleep with him."

"It's not all Jerry's fault that I'm pale."

Roger said something contradictory under his breath.

"But it's true," Holly said.

As far as she was concerned, if anyone was to blame for her wan state, it was a man called Lincoln McKenzie, not Jerry.

No, that's not fair either, Holly told herself. *I'm to blame. I was the one who let memories and dreams seduce me.*

Sweet memories.

Sweet dreams.

Bitter reality.

Holly didn't know why Linc hated her now. She only knew that he did.

"I get wrapped up in what I'm doing and forget about time," Holly added carelessly.

"I know. It's one of the things that makes you such a fantastic model."

Roger's blue eyes narrowed as he took in the lines of strain around Holly's eyes and lips. He stroked her hair away from her elegant face.

"You look positively transparent, love," he said in a low voice. "Go back to the hotel and lie out by the pool. Not too long, or—"

"—I'll get tan lines and won't be able to wear half your designs," finished Holly, smiling crookedly.

Roger laughed and gave her a quick hug.

"That's why I love you," he said. "You understand me so well."

"You love every model who looks good in your clothes," Holly pointed out.

"Ah, but you look the best so I love you the best."

Holly smiled even as she shook her head. She

took Roger seriously as a designer and as a friend, not as a potential lover.

Roger would have liked it otherwise, but he was wise enough to know that if he insisted on seducing her, he risked losing her. If he settled for friendship, he would continue to have Shannon's unique, incandescent presence to grace his products.

For her part, Holly felt no more physical attraction toward Roger than she had felt for any man since Linc. Roger's kindness and his quick wit, however, had made him one of her favorite people. She needed his friendship in the cold, slick world that Shannon inhabited.

"Sorry to break up this little love feast," said a man's hard voice, "but I was told I'd find Roger Royce here."

Even as Holly turned, she knew she would find Linc. She could no more forget his voice than she could forget the feel of his skin beneath her palms.

"I'm Royce," Roger said.

"Lincoln McKenzie."

Linc's voice was flat. He didn't offer his hand or add anything to his clipped statement.

Roger looked Linc over from the top of his curly chestnut hair to the dusty soles of his cowboy boots. Like a race announcer, Roger gave a running description of what he saw.

"Six four, maybe five," Roger said. "Good muscle development. Well defined but not overdone. Dreadful cowboy clothes, but you won't be wearing them if I use you."

Holly held her breath, wondering what Linc would do in response to being looked over like a thoroughbred on the auction block.

"Clean hands," Roger continued. "Good legs, lean but still powerful. Expensive boots. All in all, not bad. Quite good, actually. Except for the face. Too . . . dangerous. Husbands would take one look at you and decide *not* to buy Royce products. Can you smile, Lincoln McKenzie?"

Linc's smile made a chill move down Holly's arms. She didn't know what game Roger was playing, but she knew he was playing it with the wrong man.

"No," Roger said, shaking his head. "You won't do at all. Tell your agency to send out someone pretty. And tell them to be quick about it. We shoot at Hidden Springs on Monday."

Linc's smile vanished, leaving nothing to soften the hard planes of his face.

"No," Linc said.

Holly couldn't help staring at him. This was not the Lincoln McKenzie she remembered. This man didn't look capable of tenderness. His mouth was too unyielding to have the warmth and sweetness she remembered.

"No what?" Roger asked. "No, your agency doesn't have anyone pretty, or no, they can't be quick about sending another male model out?"

"No. Period."

"Come, come," Roger said, his British accent increasing along with his impatience. "One can carry the tight-lipped western man act too far, you know."

Linc laughed with genuine amusement.

"I'm male, but not a model," Linc said. "I don't have an agency, but I've seen men prettier than me. You, for instance. A nicely civilized Viking."

Surprised, Roger smiled in return. He cocked his head to one side, reassessing the tall man in front of him.

"Not a model?" Roger asked.

"No."

"Pity. You have possibilities. And brains."

"I also have control of Hidden Springs."

"Oh. That's where we're going to shoot on Monday."

"No. That's where you're *not* going to shoot on Monday or any other day."

Roger frowned and released the lock of Holly's hair that he had been absently playing with.

"Would you mind explaining that?" Roger asked.

"Not at all."

Linc's smile made Holly wince, though he was not looking at her, had not looked at her since he had found her in Roger's arms.

"I don't like jet-set parasites and their prostitutes," Linc said clearly. "I won't have them on my ranch."

If Holly had been pale before, being called a prostitute made her go white. She was too shocked by Linc's words to defend herself or to say anything about who really owned Hidden Springs.

Roger looked sideways at Holly. He knew that Hidden Springs was on land owned by Sandra Productions. In fact, it was Holly who had suggested that Hidden Springs would make an ideal backdrop for Roger's new line of products.

He put his arm around Holly in a protective gesture and turned to confront Linc.

"I sell style, period," Roger said in a clipped voice.

Linc shrugged and looked at Holly.

"You may be selling style," he said, "but she's selling something more basic."

Linc's cool appraisal of Holly's body was more insulting than any man's touch had ever been.

"Apologize to Shannon," Roger said, "and then leave."

"I don't apologize for telling the truth. If she can't stand the name, she should get out of the game."

Anger flared in Holly, burning away the pain that had frozen her. She stepped out of the protective curve of Roger's arm and confronted Linc with a flashing, professional smile.

"I'm going to enjoy the shoot at Hidden Springs," she said in a husky voice. "Knowing that you don't want us there will make every minute . . . special."

"No one steps on that land without my permission."

"Really?"

"Bet on it."

Holly's smile vanished.

"You lose, Lincoln McKenzie," she said. "We have a little piece of paper from the owner of Hidden Springs that says we can camp there all summer if we like."

Linc's face changed, showing surprise and some other emotion that was too complex to be easily labeled.

"Holly?" he asked incredulously. "Do you mean that Holly North gave you permission to use Hidden Springs?"

For a moment she was too stunned to speak. The fact that Linc hadn't recognized her brought both relief and unexpected pain.

In the wake of pain came the realization that she shouldn't have been surprised that Linc didn't recognize her. The only thing about her that hadn't changed in the last six years was the unusual color of her eyes, and that was concealed behind sunglasses.

Fortunately, Roger was also too surprised to say that Holly North and Shannon were one and the same woman. Before he could find his tongue, she did.

"Yes," she said. "Holly North gave us permission to use Hidden Springs."

"I don't believe it," said Linc. "Holly wouldn't associate with people like you."

She put a restraining hand on Roger's arm, afraid he would reveal who she was.

"Let me defend Holly," she murmured to

Roger. "After all, she's my best friend."

She turned to Linc again.

"Do you know Holly very, very well?" she asked.

Her voice was pure Shannon, bright and cold.

Roger snickered.

"I knew Holly." Linc's voice was as hard as the line of his mouth. "It's been six years since I saw her."

"People change," she suggested lightly. "They must. The Holly I know would never have put up with a dirty-minded boor."

"The Holly I knew would never hang around with prostitutes."

"On that, we are in perfect agreement," she snapped, dropping her brittle accent for a tone closer to outright anger.

Surprisingly, Linc smiled.

"Maybe you do know her after all," he conceded.

"Better than you ever did," Holly retorted.

Instantly she regretted it. She didn't want Linc to investigate how close her relationship was to Holly.

She couldn't bear to know that the contempt in his eyes was directed at herself rather than the high-fashion creation called Shannon.

"I know Holly well enough to guarantee that we'll shoot at Hidden Springs on Monday," she said.

"I'm managing that land for Holly. If I say no, she'll say no."

"You'll have to get to her first," Roger pointed out, suppressing a smile. "I think she's on a desert safari."

"That's right," Holly said quickly. "She won't be back in Manhattan for weeks. I'm afraid that you lose both this battle and the whole bloody war."

"You've spoiled her," Linc said lazily to Roger. "Mongrels like that one need a firm hand if you want them to show well in the Companion Class."

Wind whipped Holly's hair across Linc's face as she leaned forward. He flinched as though her hair were black fire.

"I'll bet you're one of those tall, tight-lipped men who is only good with dogs and horses," she murmured.

Roger moved uneasily. "Shannon—"

Holly shook off his warning and gave Linc her most seductive smile. Through the tinted glasses her eyes were dark, nearly brown, brilliant with anger and pain.

To be so close to Linc again and see only contempt in his look was almost more than Holly could bear. She had hoped he would be drawn to her beauty, that he would see her and return her love, a love that hadn't wavered in all the long years of their separation.

"Dogs," Linc drawled, "are docile, obedient and *loyal*, unlike beautiful women."

"You noticed," Holly murmured, lowering her thick lashes.

"That you're beautiful?" Linc shrugged.

"Lightning's beautiful, too, but only a fool wants to touch it."

"Then crawl back under your rock, tall man," Holly said between her teeth. "Lightning won't reach you there."

For a moment there was only charged silence beneath the awning of the catering truck. Then a pouting, breathless voice spoke from behind Linc's back.

"There you are, Linc, honey. I've been looking all over for you."

Numbly Holly watched as the stranger rubbed against Linc's arm like a hungry cat. The woman was everything that Holly was not—tiny, blond, and lushly built.

Next to Linc's hard body she looked delicate and delicious. If her figure had a fault, it lay in her ample bottom. Few men would have noticed the flaw, or objected if they did.

Linc smiled down at the woman. Even though she was wearing very high heels, the top of her head barely reached to his breastbone.

"Hi, Cyn," Linc said. "Tired of shopping already?"

Cyn gave Linc a pout that Jerry would have loved to photograph. Fingernails as pink as the tip of her tongue scratched lightly down Linc's arm.

"I picked out three dresses and the cutest little negligee you ever saw," she said.

Then Cyn glanced sideways at Holly. Her blue eyes were as hard as glass.

"The negligee is meant for a woman, not a giraffe," Cyn added sweetly.

Linc laughed and wound a lock of her fine blond hair around his finger.

"Sharpened your claws, too, didn't you?" he asked.

The last of Holly's dream broke around her as she watched the easy intimacy between the man she loved and the lush, beautiful woman called Cyn.

Well, now I know why he never wrote me, Holly thought starkly. *He was too busy with his busty blond.*

Holly felt like running away and hiding, but her face showed nothing at all. She was every inch the professional model posing for the most important assignment of her career.

Life had taught Holly that you either fought back or went under. She hadn't gone under when her parents died. She would survive the death of her childish dreams, too.

At least, Shannon would survive.

"You bought only dresses?" Holly murmured, glancing at Cyn's hips with a knowing smile. "Roger could design a pair of pants for you. I'm sure we have some cloth around here somewhere, don't we, Roger?"

Roger cleared his throat.

"Oh, I forgot," Holly said, her eyes wide and innocent and cold. "The material is only forty-four inches wide. That won't quite get the job done, will it?"

Cyn's mouth sagged, then snapped shut. Her full lips flattened into a line.

Before she could think of anything appropriately cutting to say, Holly dismissed her with a small smile. She turned and spoke to Linc in a voice that was both cool and oddly intimate.

"Now I see why you were so nasty on the subject of parasites and prostitutes," Holly said. "I'd sympathize, except you have only your own bad taste to blame."

She turned her back on the pair and spoke only to Roger.

"I'll be at the hotel if you need me," she said.

With outward calm Holly sauntered across the burning asphalt street to her hotel. The sun was unbearably hot, scorching her body to the soles of her feet.

But nothing was as hot as the tears she could no longer hold back. She swallowed convulsively and prayed that no one could see the evidence of her lack of control spilling down her cheeks.

Now, too late, Holly realized that she had come back to Palm Springs hoping to see Linc again. She had wanted to bask in his admiration and love when he saw the graceful butterfly that had come out of such a plain cocoon.

Instead, she had found a taunting stranger whose contempt was a knife turning in her, cutting her to pieces.

I was a fool to come back, Holly thought bitterly.

And I was an even bigger fool for believing that dreams come true.

Three

Holly tossed her canteen into the back of the open Jeep. She checked that the sleeping bag and various tarps were securely tied down before she turned to face Roger.

"Quit worrying about me," Holly said, forcing a smile. "I've camped at Hidden Springs since I was four years old."

"Alone?" Roger challenged.

Holly ignored him.

Roger made a sweeping gesture toward the barren, rugged mountains looming on the horizon.

"It's not exactly Central Park out there," he said. "It's a ruddy wilderness."

"If it were Central Park, I'd take a sawed-off shotgun with me," Holly retorted.

Roger almost smiled.

"Up there," she said, "all I need to worry about is water, and the springs have plenty of that."

With that, Holly turned back to the Jeep. She shook the five-gallon gas can to make sure that it was both full and secure in its bracket. Years of experience with rental cars had taught her to check everything herself.

"Shannon," Roger began.

Holly ignored him. She pulled a screwdriver from the hip pocket of her jeans and tightened one of the bracket screws holding the gas can in place.

Roger's pale eyebrows rose.

"You're not Shannon now, are you?" he asked quietly.

"I'm off duty."

Shaking his head, Roger looked at Holly's severely French-braided hair. Her face was innocent of makeup. Her clothes were loose, unassuming, and durable. Her shoes could most kindly be described as sturdy.

"Holly Shannon North," Roger said. "You're the most amazing creature. If it weren't for your eyes, I swear I wouldn't recognize you. No wonder the photographers love you."

"Sure," Holly said, her tone icy. "I'm the perfect blank canvas for men to paint their sexual fantasies on."

With that, she grabbed a carton of food and cooking gear and stowed it in the front of the Jeep.

Roger put his hand on Holly's arm and squeezed gently.

"I didn't mean that the way you took it," he said.

"I know." Holly sighed. "I suppose I didn't mean it the way I said it, either."

She lifted the final carton of supplies and turned toward the Jeep.

"Let me come with you," Roger said.

She was so surprised that she nearly dropped the carton.

"You? Camping?" Holly smiled and shook her head.

"I mean it."

"So do I. Camping isn't your style. We both know it."

"You're my style," Roger said. "Let me come with you. I promise I won't get in the way."

Holly simply stared at him.

Level blue eyes looked back at her.

"You're serious," she said after a moment.

"Quite."

Holly felt a familiar sinking in her stomach at what she saw in Roger's eyes. After yesterday, she needed to think about old dreams, broken dreams. She needed to sit alone in the middle of the vast silence of the high desert and know that no one was going to demand anything of her, not even a smile.

She needed the peace she could find only in the desert.

She most certainly didn't need to spend the next three days evading Roger Royce's propositions, no matter how gently and elegantly they would be put.

Roger was neither insensitive nor stupid. He read Holly's refusal in her tight lips and silence.

"That bad?" he asked, his tone wry, "I just

thought . . . you were so upset at what that rude cowboy said. It worried me. Are you all right now?"

"Of course."

"You don't act like it."

Saying nothing, Holly shifted the carton in her arms and turned back toward the Jeep.

Roger continued talking like a man exploring hostile country—wary and ready to retreat instantly.

"There's something between you and Lincoln McKenzie, isn't there?" Roger probed.

"No," Holly said curtly.

Not any more, she thought. *Probably there never was. Just a dream, that's all.*

And now a nightmare.

"Shannon?" Roger asked softly.

Holly dumped the carton of supplies in the front of the Jeep with unnecessary force before she turned to face Roger. She owed him more than the cool, abrupt facade that was Shannon.

If nothing else, Roger was her friend as well as the man who had literally invested millions of dollars in her career.

But Holly couldn't talk to the very sophisticated Roger Royce about her childish dreams of love and Lincoln McKenzie. So she told Roger about the rest of the truth, the part she could talk about without feeling like a juvenile fool.

"This is the first time I've been back since my parents died," Holly said. "There are . . . memories."

"I realize that," Roger said. "It will be worse at Hidden Springs, won't it? You shouldn't be alone, Shannon."

As always, Roger's kindness touched Holly.

"I'll be all right," she said.

Roger's expression said he didn't believe it.

"Really," she said.

Holly went to Roger and kissed his cheek quickly.

"But thanks for caring," she said.

Roger caught her shoulders, holding her only inches from his lips.

"I'd care more, if you'd let me," he said.

Holly felt herself freeze up inside. She knew she had to stop this now, before she lost one of the few people in the world who mattered to her.

"It wouldn't be worth your time," she said stiffly. "I'm frigid."

There was a moment of shocked silence.

"Jerry is a bloody swine," Roger said finally, his voice harsh.

Holly's laugh was short and humorless.

"I won't argue that," she said. "But he's right. I'm just not a sensual woman."

"Rubbish! Do you think I haven't watched you? You're always touching things, tasting textures with your fingertips. Hot, cold, rough, smooth, whatever is within reach. You drink sensations."

"That's not the same."

"The hell it isn't," Roger said in a husky voice. "Your body changes when silk slides over it, Shannon. You need a silken lover, not a selfish swine like Jerry."

Memories of Linc washed over Holly. His body had felt exciting beneath her hands, silk over steel. She needed both the silk and the steel, the unique combination that was Linc.

Silk alone, Roger alone, just wasn't enough.

"I wish silk was all I needed," Holly whispered, surprised by the weight of tears in her lashes.

"Don't cry," Roger said gently, releasing her.

She gave him a wan smile.

"I'm so sorry," he said. "The last thing I wanted was to upset you. I just thought that maybe this time . . ."

Silently Holly shook her head.

Roger looked at her closely.

"You aren't angry, are you?" he asked.

"No," she whispered. "You?"

"It's not the first time you've said no to me," he answered with a rueful smile.

Then his smile vanished, leaving behind an intent, intense, very male expression.

"If you change your mind," Roger said, "don't be shy about telling me. Any time. I mean it."

Holly nodded, but looked away from him.

"I'll meet you at the Hidden Springs gate on Monday," she said, quickly sliding behind the wheel of the Jeep. "And be sure that all the vehicles have four-wheel drive. Anything less won't make it to the springs."

Roger nodded.

The vinyl seat of the open Jeep was brutally hot beneath Holly's legs. Before she even put the key in the ignition, her jeans felt scorched. She pulled a pair of driving gloves out of her purse, knowing that the steering wheel would be too hot to touch.

When Holly looked up, Roger was watching her. She grabbed a battered straw cowboy hat, pulled it firmly over her head, and drew the chin cord up. Sunglasses followed. The lenses were so dark that her eyes were invisible behind the ovals of blue-green plastic.

Leaning forward slightly, Holly turned the ignition key. The Jeep surprised her by starting the first time. She shifted smoothly, backed out of the hotel parking lot, and waved at Roger as she turned onto the palm-lined street.

During the white-hot days of summer, Palm Springs was a quiet place. Most of the wealthy people migrated to more gentle climates. The rest of the populace either embraced the rhythms of the desert—laze away the hottest hours and emerge at twilight—or they huddled inside air-conditioned cocoons and didn't come out at all.

Holly waited at a stoplight, impatient for the signal to change and allow her to create her own breeze again. She needed the illusion of movement as much as she needed the cooling wind.

She needed to get away.

It was hotter than it had been yesterday,

when Linc had appeared like a mirage, ruining her day and her dreams.

Stop thinking about it, Holly advised herself curtly. *Think about the weather. Everyone else does.*

Finally the light changed, releasing her. She sped off toward her beloved mountains, her mind firmly set on the weather.

Not only was it hot today, it was also humid, an unusual thing in the western desert. The humidity was caused by moist air slowly sweeping north from the Sea of Cortez. As the hot, thick air met the mountains, it was lifted up and transformed into clouds.

By the end of the day, summer thunder would peal through dry mountain canyons, shaking the land down to its granite bones. If there were enough clouds, it might even rain, cooling the incandescent country for a few sweet hours.

Such cloudbursts were rare. But then, water in a desert was always rare.

Now, in the flatlands between the mountains, even the thought of cool rain was impossible.

Holly drove quickly, unconsciously trying to escape her uncomfortable thoughts as well as the heat.

She could no more outrun herself than a sky empty of clouds could rain. The memories came at her in waves, called up by the sound of the Jeep and the smell of metal baking beneath a relentless summer sun.

Holly had first learned to drive her father's

battered Jeep when she was a long-legged, shy fourteen-year-old begging to help feed the horses that were held in a Garner Valley pasture eight miles from the North's ranch. That particular pasture bordered on Linc's ranch.

She used to go there as often as she could, hoping to see him as he rode the fence line, looking for breaks.

Don't think about it, Holly raged silently at herself. *Think about driving. Think about mountains. Think about Hidden Springs.*

Think about anything but Linc, who didn't recognize me, hates what I've become, and never cared enough to remember me in any case.

After the first miles Holly drove the Jeep automatically, confidently. The familiar feel of the vehicle helped to calm her as she took the Palms to Pines Highway, speeding toward the land she had not seen for six years.

When Holly had refused to sell Hidden Springs, Sandra had turned over the management of the ranch to the McKenzies. It had seemed like a good solution to Holly six years ago, for she couldn't bear to auction off the home and land that were all she had left of her childhood.

And there was always her dream, hidden under layers of logic and excuses, that someday she would go back and Linc would be there, waiting for her.

The gap between dreams-then and reality-now was a slicing pain that left Holly bleeding no matter how she tried to deny or ignore it.

By the time she reached the unmarked dirt road leading to Hidden Springs, clouds had condensed around the purple peaks of the San Jacinto Mountains.

The air was visibly thicker, unbearably humid, clinging to Holly's skin like clouds to the mountaintops. A breeze moved restlessly across the dry land, rubbing over the brittle sage with a distant, secret sound.

The gate to Hidden Springs was locked, but the combination hadn't been changed since Holly left. Well oiled, painfully hot to the touch even through her gloves, the lock opened with a metallic click.

She drove the Jeep through and locked the gate again behind her. A tantalizing hint of coolness curled down from the mountains, riding the fitful wind.

As she drove ever higher, clouds changed color and density, going from oyster to blue-tinged slate. The road dwindled to nothing more than twin ruts winding up rocky ridges and over dry riverbeds.

Holly watched the clouds constantly, looking for the first sign of rain in the mountain peaks rising above the road. She was relieved to see that despite the growing heaviness of the clouds, they hadn't yet frayed into sheets of rain.

Even so, she wasted no time when the road dipped down to cross one of the many dry washes that radiated down the steep, rugged mountain slopes.

Normally the ravines held nothing more than sand and rocks and wind. Any moisture that existed was well beneath the surface, beyond the reach of even the hottest summer sun.

But Holly knew that a storm higher in the mountains could change that very quickly, even if it never rained at the lower elevations. A hard rain ran off the baked land rather than soaking in. Soon every crack, every crevice, every crease in the dry land overflowed with water.

Then rain spilled down rocky slopes in tiny streams that met and joined into walls of water that roared like muddy avalanches down formerly dry ravines.

Such flash floods usually lasted only a few hours before they outran the high-altitude rainstorms that had created them. The floods left behind tangles of muddy brush, rapidly drying puddles, and riverbeds that would know no water until the next storm came.

To anyone who understood that mountain rains could mean desert floods, the sudden appearance of rivers in a dry land was more exciting than dangerous.

Still, Holly breathed a silent sigh of relief as the Jeep churned up out of Antelope Wash, the last big ravine between her and Hidden Springs. She was well above the desert floor now, into the chaparral zone. A few thousand feet higher would bring her to the first pines.

But the Hidden Springs road didn't go that high into the mountains. The twisting, rock-strewn ruts ended less than a mile away, where water welled silently from the base of a shattered cliff.

Above Holly thunder rolled across the peaks, pursuing fickle lightning, never quite catching up. Clouds veiled the mountains, bathing granite peaks in mist. Though the wind was stronger now, cooler, there was still no smell of rain. For all their tossing and flirting, the clouds weren't yet ready to embrace the land.

Holly unloaded her gear before she drove the Jeep a hundred yards from the place she had chosen for her camp. If lightning danced over the land, she didn't want to be sleeping near the only metal on the mountainside.

Nor did she pitch her tent too close to the five rocky pools that glittered like gemstones along the cliff's base. As much as she liked water, she liked the desert animals better. Bighorn sheep drank at Hidden Springs. If she crowded too close to the water, the animals would stay back among the dry rocks, waiting and thirsting until the thoughtless intruder left.

Holly started making a trench around her tent to carry off any rain that might come. Just as she finished, thunder rumbled down the granite face of Hidden Springs.

Straightening, she measured the sky. The sun was no more than a pale disc burning behind clouds that thickened and changed as she watched. Streamers of mist flowed down the flanks of stone peaks, softening their masculine angles.

Lightning flickered too fast to be seen clearly in the late-afternoon light. Thunder came again, closer now, carried on a rising wind.

The sudden coolness of the air was more intoxicating to Holly than any wine. She laughed aloud and stretched her arms out as though to hold both clouds and mountains.

Later, when she was cold and wet and water overflowed her careful trench, Holly knew she would rue the moment she had greeted the storm with laughter and open arms.

Yet at this instant she was like the land itself, hot and dry, waiting for the pouring instant of release.

Sunset was as sudden as thunder. Light drained out of the sky between one moment and the next. Needles of lightning stitched randomly through the lid of clouds.

Holly smelled rain on the wind, but no drops fell nearby. Somewhere above her on the mountainside clouds were pouring themselves into the land. Somewhere water was brawling down dry ravines, playfully juggling boulders as big as her Jeep.

Somewhere the waiting had ended and the storm had begun.

But not here, not yet. Here there was only her and the silence between bursts of thunder.

Even when Holly lay within the tent trying to fall asleep, the rain hadn't yet come. It was cooler, though, almost cold. Lightning flared randomly over the rocky land, pulling thunder behind like another color of darkness.

Then came a different noise, hoofbeats pounding down the mountainside.

Holly couldn't tell the exact direction the horse was coming from. The rocky cliffs and ravines baffled hoofbeats, adding echoes that overlapped and faded and changed directions until she wondered if she had imagined the sounds in the first place.

White light blazed directly over the tent, followed instantly by an explosion of noise so great she didn't immediately identify it as thunder. Blinding light and black sound alternated with dazzling speed.

Wild hoofbeats rattled in the silence between thunderclaps. A horse screamed in fear. Somewhere near Holly's camp a horse was running over the rugged land mindlessly, terrified by the storm.

She came out of the tent at a run. She knew there was little chance of helping the panicked animal, but she couldn't simply cower in her tent and listen to the horse's terrified scream.

She ran to the shelter of a boulder field just up the slope from her tent. Crouched with her back to the wind, Holly stared into the night, trying to find the horse.

An explosion of sheet lightning lit up the sky from horizon to horizon, freezing time into a black-and-silver portrait of a horse rearing wildly on the low ridge just above her camp. Nearly lost in the horse's long, flying mane, a rider fought to control his crazed mount.

For an instant it seemed the rider would win. Then thunder came again, breaking apart the world. Black sound and white sky melded into light so fierce that the eye couldn't see, sound so brutal that the ear heard only silence.

Lightning continued in an incandescent barrage, outlining the plunging horse. Holly knew the ridge, knew it was impossible for a wildly running horse to keep its feet.

With each new stroke of white light, she expected to see the horse go down, smashing itself and its rider against granite boulders, killing them both.

And then a chill greater than the rain swept over Holly as she realized who the rider was.

"Linc!"

Four

Holly called Linc's name again and again, screaming at him to jump and save himself.

She kept on screaming even though she knew he couldn't possibly hear her. The thunder was so loud and continuous now that she couldn't even hear herself, though her throat was tearing apart with the force of her cries.

Yet still Holly screamed at Linc to jump off, because that was the only way he could save himself from the mindless terror that drove his horse.

Horse and rider kept plunging together down the dangerous, boulder-strewn slope.

Holly made an anguished sound when she realized that Linc had no intention of abandoning the horse to its own terror. He was sitting deep in the saddle, using all his strength and skill to keep the horse from going down, riding a whirlwind with a savage determination to save both of them.

Though Holly screamed with fear for Linc, she didn't blame him for wanting to save the horse from its own folly. Even in the grip of panic, the Arabian was magnificent. Its body rippled with muscular beauty. It moved with a cat's quickness and grace.

Linc, too, was magnificent to watch, so extraordinary in his skill and strength that Holly forgot to be afraid for him. He was part of the horse, shifting his weight from instant to instant, braced in the stirrups, using his powerful shoulders to drag up the horse's head whenever the animal stumbled.

Holly began to believe that horse and rider would survive the wild plunge down the boulder field.

Then the world turned inside out and an ocean poured out of the sky.

Instantly she was up and running toward the ridge. She knew that no skill, no strength, nothing but a miracle could prevent the Arabian from going down in the greasy mud that would be created during the first instants of the cloudburst.

The inevitable fall came during a burst of lightning. The horse twisted and turned wildly, trying to keep its feet where nothing could walk, much less run.

At the last possible instant Linc kicked free of the somersaulting animal. He fell like the trained horseman he was, head tucked in, body relaxed, ready to roll and absorb the worst of the impact.

Linc did everything possible, but there was

nothing he could do about the boulders in his path.

Holly ran through the rain, crying soundlessly. The ground turned to grease beneath her feet, sending her staggering and sliding. A river of rain poured over her, choking her.

She found the horse first. It was lying on its side, trembling all over, drenched with rain and lather.

As Holly ran toward the horse, it groaned and heaved itself to its feet. The animal took a few tentative steps, then stood docilely, not even flinching when lightning sizzled across the ridge. For the moment, the Arabian was too stunned by its fall to be afraid of anything.

Holly clawed up the last few feet of the slope to the boulder that had so brutally stopped Linc's fall.

Lightning forked across the sky, revealing Linc. He lay on his back, motionless.

She skidded to her knees beside him, shaking with fear.

"Linc!"

Her voice was hoarse, no match for the thunder boiling through the night. She crouched over him, sheltering his face from the downpour.

Bursts of lightning outlined him harshly. A cut beneath his hair was bleeding. The blood looked black in the white light. His shirt was shredded down his right side, but beneath the ribbons of cloth his chest rose and fell in even rhythms.

Alive.

For a moment Holly was too dizzy with relief to do anything but put her hand on Linc's chest and savor the strong beat of his heart. Then she shook herself and looked around.

Linc was alive but far from safe. If he was injured, she wasn't strong enough to carry him to the tent. Yet she had to get him out of the chilling rain.

Lightning came again, followed slowly by thunder. The center of the storm was moving away. Rain still fell hard and steady, but it no longer qualified as a cloudburst. The first, most violent minutes of the storm were over.

Gently, very carefully, Holly ran her hands over Linc's arms and legs, searching for obvious injuries.

She felt nothing but the resilience of his muscles beneath his soaked clothes. She moved her fingertips lightly over his chest, searching for any swelling that might tell of cracked or broken ribs.

Linc groaned, startling her.

Holly snatched back her hand before she realized that her light touch wasn't what had caused him to groan. It was the pain he felt as his body returned to awareness.

While Linc struggled out of unconsciousness, his head moved slowly from side to side. Holly let out a sigh. The motions eased a fear she had been afraid even to acknowledge.

Thank God, Holly thought fervently. *His neck isn't broken.*

Suddenly Linc rolled onto his side and tried to sit up. He grabbed his head and groaned again.

"Take it easy," Holly said quickly. "You've had a fall."

He shuddered.

"Linc?"

As he turned toward the sound of Holly's voice, lightning burst. His eyes were dark, dazed.

"What . . . ?" he asked, then said no more.

"Your horse fell," Holly answered loudly, trying to make Linc understand between bouts of thunder. "Your. Horse. Fell."

Linc started to nod in acknowledgment, then grimaced and held his head again. When his right hand dropped, it was streaked with blood.

Holly stared anxiously into the darkness that divided violent bursts of lightning. The worst of the storm might be letting up, but it was far from over.

"Can you move?" she shouted.

His only answer was a stifled groan and an attempt to get up.

"Just sit up at first," Holly said.

Painfully Linc pulled himself into a sitting position, helped by Holly.

She touched the right side of his head with gentle fingertips. There was a small swelling at the base of his skull. Blood seeped slowly.

Holly had no way of knowing whether Linc had a concussion or simply a cut.

"Do you hurt anywhere else?" she asked.

She had to repeat the question several times before Linc's head moved in a slow negative gesture.

"Then you must stand up," Holly said urgently. "I'll help you, but I can't carry you. Please, Linc. Stand up!"

Using the boulder and Holly, Linc managed to lever himself to his feet. When he stood, dizziness nearly overwhelmed him. Anxiously she supported him.

Then Linc started to walk with the same grim determination and strength he had used to save his horse.

After a few false starts, Holly adjusted to Linc's uneven stride. Together they reeled and staggered down the slope toward her tent.

A small battery-powered lamp filled the tent's interior with yellow light. For the moment at least, everything was still dry.

As Holly eased Linc onto the floor, she realized that he was shivering uncontrollably. She had to get him warm, quickly.

She tore off what was left of his shirt. His soaked boots and jeans were harder to remove. As she struggled to drag the denim down his legs, she was divided between frustration at the stubborn cloth and admiration for the powerful lines of Linc's body.

The sleeping bag Holly had rented was large, loose, and lightweight. It would not radiate back body heat very efficiently, but it was all she had. She unzipped the slippery nylon bag with three quick strokes, rolled Linc inside, and zipped the bag shut again.

Linc's eyes opened. When he realized that he was inside a tent, he started to sit up.

"No," Holly said firmly. "Don't try to get up."

He ignored her.

She held him down with her hands on his shoulders and the force of her whole body.

"Lie down," she commanded. "You have to get warm."

"Horse." Linc's voice was barely a whisper. "My horse."

"It was on its feet before you were."

Lightning bleached the interior of the tent. Thunder came like a falling mountain.

Linc sat up, sweeping aside Holly's hands with a strength that frightened her. Even dazed and injured, he was far stronger than she was.

Dizziness struck Linc again, chaining him for a moment. Holly knew that he was too stunned to realize his own danger and not rational enough to argue with.

Linc was a horseman through and through. He would see that his horse was cared for and to hell with the consequences to himself.

"I'll take care of your horse," Holly said urgently. "But you must stay here. Do you understand? Stay here!"

With an effort, Linc nodded.

She helped him lie down again, grabbed a

pocket flashlight, and went back out into the storm. For the first time she really noticed the rain. The drops were almost icy, for they had condensed at high altitudes.

The Arabian was standing where Holly had last seen it. The horse's head was held low. It was still breathing rapidly. The animal's body heat steamed outward, draining warmth into the chill air.

Holly shivered repeatedly as she worked over the horse, checking for injuries. Other than a few scrapes, she found nothing. She led the Arabian down to the partial shelter of boulders and chaparral. The horse followed without limping.

A barrage of lightning made the Arabian shy violently, jerking Holly off her feet. She scrambled upright again, tore off her blouse, and blindfolded the animal.

After that, the horse stood absolutely still, ignoring lightning and thunder alike. Holly loosened the cinch and rummaged in the saddlebags, hoping to find a hobble. There was only a hatchet, a large folding knife, and a ball of rough twine.

"Not good enough," Holly muttered. "At the first yank, twine will either give way or cut the horse's legs to the bone."

She took a deep breath, peeled off the blindfold and quickly twisted it into something that resembled a hobble.

As Holly bound the horse's front legs with her blouse, the Arabian sniffed her wet hair.

Then the animal snorted wearily and gave up all thought of fear and flight. The horse didn't even object when Holly threw a flapping tarp over its back. She laced the waterproof cloth onto the animal as best she could with twine.

By the time Holly got back inside the tent, she was shaking with cold. Her chilled fingers were clumsy, making hard work of peeling off her own wet clothes.

Finally she managed to get rid of the last cold, dripping piece of cloth. She dug out dry jeans and a jacket, yanked them on, and crawled over to check Linc.

He was neither awake nor quite asleep. His skin was cold.

Holly knew just enough about hypothermia and shock to be afraid for Linc. Yet there was nothing more she could do to help him. Even if she could get him to the Jeep, Antelope Wash would be in full flood.

"Linc," Holly whispered. "What can I do?"

She looked at the dark hair curling down over his forehead, framing the strong face that had haunted her dreams. His eyebrows were thick, dark arches spiked with gold. His mouth, usually generous with laughter, was drawn with cold and pain. Drops of water gleamed in his mustache.

How many times Holly had dreamed of seeing him again, touching him and feeling his touch, hearing his laughter and tasting him on her lips. Helplessly she wondered what had changed him from the gentle, passionate man of her memories.

What did I do to Linc that I deserved being cut off from him all these years?

Only silence answered Holly's painful question. Despite Cyn's appearance with Linc yesterday, Holly knew that he hadn't been dating anyone six years ago. His motives for not keeping in touch with Holly at first were as much of a mystery to her now as they had been when she had wept over unanswered letters.

Why did Linc become cruel and sarcastic, his cold eyes watching me, his words slicing me?

No answer came to that question, either.

Slowly Holly bent to brush her mouth over Linc's. For a long moment she kissed him, warming his cool lips, tasting the raindrops beaded in his mustache, trembling with memories.

Part of Holly was ashamed of stealing back a piece of her dream while Linc slept, unable to protest the caress. Yet she couldn't help herself.

Nor did she really want to. It was little enough to warm the emptiness in her.

When Holly lifted her head, there were tears caught in her lashes. She watched Linc for long moments, forgetting her own chilled body. The strong heartbeat and the easy rise and fall of his chest beneath her hand reassured her.

Then she began to dread the coming morning, when he would wake up, realize she was

Shannon, and stare at her with cold-eyed contempt.

But there was nothing Holly could do about that. Tonight she and Linc needed each other on the most primitive level.

Sheer animal warmth.

Without hesitating any longer, Holly unzipped the sleeping bag and crawled in. There was barely room inside to breathe, for the bag hadn't been designed to hold two people. Especially when one of them was the size of Lincoln McKenzie.

Shaking with cold, she switched off the lamp and managed to zip up the sleeping bag once more. After a long time, their shared warmth heated the bag enough for both of them to sink into troubled sleep.

Holly dreamed that she woke up in Linc's arms, his lips against her neck, her body pressed along his. The tip of his tongue teased her mouth until she sighed and smiled, giving herself to his kiss with the sensual abandon that only he had ever drawn out of her.

She felt his breath against her ear and shivered with delight. His hand slid over her thin jacket, caressing her breasts. The touch was more vivid than any dream of him she had ever had before.

Then Holly realized that she wasn't dreaming.

Her eyes flew open. Daylight glowed in the

tent, but not half so warmly as Linc's eyes.

"Holly," he murmured, tracing her lips with his tongue. "My sweet Holly. I thought I had only dreamed you."

Five

"You recognize me," Holly said, suddenly nervous.

Linc smiled.

"It would take more than a rap on the head to make me forget you, Holly."

"But yesterday—" she began.

"All I remember about last night," he interrupted, "is that it was dark and a mountain fell on me."

Linc's tongue slid between Holly's lips and moved slowly. She made a small sound as she touched the tip of her tongue against his, tasting him delicately, hungrily.

"If you had kissed me before you dragged me into your bed," Linc said, "I'd have known you no matter how dark it was."

Holly couldn't speak. His eyes were golden, passionate, tender . . . her dream made whole and radiant again.

"Linc," she whispered.

He kissed Holly again, thoroughly, drinking her response. When he finally lifted his head, his pulse was beating visibly in his throat.

"You taste the same as you did six years ago," Linc murmured, "sweet as a desert spring."

His voice had changed with the long kiss. The tone was husky, intimate, as male as the powerful arms wrapped around Holly.

She drew a shaky breath, remembering the stolen kiss last night and the kisses before that, six long years before. She looked into Linc's eyes again, studying him in a silence that shimmered with dreams and possibilities.

Nowhere did she see the harsh contempt that had been on his face yesterday.

A relief as intense as last night's storm swept through her, shaking her. She reached up and kissed Linc again with lips that trembled.

"You taste the same, too," Holly whispered against his mouth.

He lifted his head and smiled down at her.

"Like water?" he asked whimsically.

"Half right," she teased.

"What's the other half?"

"Fire."

Linc's arms tightened until Holly couldn't breathe. She had forgotten how strong he was, strength enough to make or break a world.

Her world.

"Firewater, huh?" Linc teased.

He laughed against Holly's neck, sending shivers of delight over her skin.

"From an illegal still, no doubt?" Linc asked.

Holly nodded her head solemnly, like a small child.

"The still is hidden way, way up in the mountains," she whispered.

"What goes into it—cactus and pine cones?"

"Nope."

Holly smiled and tickled her lips against Linc's mustache.

"Rocks and ice?" he guessed again.

She laughed. Then she looked at the man she loved and laughter vanished, replaced by an intense emotion that only Linc had ever been able to call from her.

"Lightning and sage and desert rain," Holly whispered. "I've tasted you in my dreams, Linc."

His breath drew in sharply.

"Holly," Linc said huskily. "Are you sure you're not a dream?"

Before she could answer, his tongue probed the hollow at the base of her throat, then moved slowly up her neck until he found her ear. His teeth closed delicately on her earlobe.

When the tip of Linc's tongue traced the curves of her ear, Holly began to tremble. With eyes half-closed, she rubbed her palms over his back.

His skin stretched smoothly over muscles hardened by work. Silk and steel, the taste of Linc on her lips, dream come true.

"Which is better—this or dreams?" he asked.

"This," Holly murmured. "This is better than any dream."

As she spoke, she moved slowly against Linc, savoring his skin with her fingertips and lips.

Holly felt a tremor go through him. Belatedly she remembered how chilled he had been last night.

"Are you cold?" she asked quickly.

"Hardly."

"But—"

Linc nibbled on Holly's lips, distracting her from doubts about his health. When he spoke, laughter curled in his voice.

"If you don't believe that I'm plenty warm," he said, "run your hands down my front instead of my back."

Abruptly Holly remembered that Linc was naked. She jerked her hands away from his skin.

"I forgot I'd undressed you," she said, embarrassed, "but you were wet and—I'm sorry."

"I'm not," Linc murmured, rubbing his lips over Holly's mouth. "In fact"—his hand slid up to her jacket zipper—"I'm going to return the favor."

"But I'm not wearing a blouse," she said frantically.

Linc's only answer was the ragged sound of his swift, indrawn breath when the zipper slid down to her waist and the jacket fell open.

Holly was so shocked she couldn't say a word. Linc had kissed her before, even touched her breasts lightly, but it had been nothing like this.

She had never been naked, skin against skin.

Slowly Linc's dark head vanished beneath the sleeping bag as his mouth slid down Holly's neck. The tongue that had teased her lips stroked slowly over one of her breasts. As he blew gently, her nipple hardened in a tingling rush.

Holly made a low sound, gripped by feelings she had neither the experience nor the words to describe.

By the time Linc's mouth melted over her other breast, she was no longer shocked. Pleasure shivered through her repeatedly. Her fingers kneaded his back with sensuous, hungry motions that encouraged his caresses.

Holly had no realization of what she was doing, no thoughts that weren't as wild and hot as Linc's mouth. Her body didn't feel like it was her own. Sensations lanced through her, fine wires tightening her with each caress, each hot movement of his tongue, her whole body tightening until she felt like twisting and moaning beneath his knowing mouth.

"I've got to see you," Linc said huskily.

He reached across Holly, unzipped the sleeping bag halfway down, and pushed it away from her body.

No bathing suit lines marred the smooth flow of her golden skin. Her breasts were swollen with desire and her taut nipples were the same dark rose as her lips.

A slow flush bloomed beneath Holly's skin as she realized that she was lying half-naked while Linc looked at her, his hazel eyes smoky with desire. She pulled her hands away from his back and tried to zip up her jacket.

He laced his fingers through hers, holding her hands in a gentle vise.

"If I had undressed you six years ago," he whispered, "I never would have let Sandra take you away."

Linc's head lowered again, and again Holly felt his tongue set fire to her skin. Instinctively she arched against him, all thought of shyness or embarrassment consumed by his caresses.

All she wanted was to be closer to him. She needed to feel more of his body covering her, to bury her fingers in his hair and hold his mouth against her forever.

As though Linc knew what Holly wanted, he released her hands. Her fingers raked up his back, then burrowed into his hair. In the instant before he flinched, she remembered his injury.

"I'm sorry," Holly said breathlessly. "Does it hurt?"

"Only when you stop touching me."

She looked at Linc's eyes. Her breath filled her throat. Even in her dreams he had not wanted her so much.

Very gently Holly turned Linc's head so that she could see the swelling just beneath his ear. Her own breath hissed out.

The bruise was darker than it had been last night. Its center was a crust of blood.

"You must have a terrible headache," she said.

Linc smiled crookedly.

"Isn't that the woman's line?" he asked dryly.

Holly laughed despite her concern.

"I've got some aspirin in my kit that will help the ache," she said.

His hands closed over her arms, gently holding her when she would have left the sleeping bag.

"There are other kinds of aches," he said in a low voice. "Aspirin won't do a damn thing about them."

"Take two aspirin—" Holly began.

"—and call you in the morning," Linc finished, covering his face with a groan. "That's nearly as old as the line about headaches."

"Serves you right," she said impishly.

With that Holly slipped out of the bag.

Linc could have stopped her, but decided to watch her instead. Wearing only an open jacket and old jeans, she was worth looking at.

When Holly tried to close her jacket, the zipper jammed at the bottom. She fussed with it for a moment, then gave up. She overlapped the front and stuffed the jacket into her pants like a blouse.

"I'll get the aspirin," she said.

Linc simply smiled. The gap in the jacket offered intriguing glimpses of the breasts beneath.

Holly sat down, dragged her large seaman's

duffel onto her lap, and jammed her arm into the open end. Frowning, she fished blindly through the deep bag, trying to find her first-aid kit by a combination of memory and touch.

As Holly worked, her jacket slowly pulled open, revealing and then concealing her breasts in a display that was as unintentional as it was arousing.

Linc watched with half-closed eyes. If Holly's reaction to him hadn't been so plainly a combination of embarrassment and passion, he would have reached out and dragged her back into the sleeping bag. But she looked—and acted—as innocent as she had six years ago.

The thought was both staggering and violently arousing to him.

Holly made an exasperated sound and shook the bag. Her breasts swayed in echo of her movements.

With a stifled groan, Linc looked away.

Her head snapped up. A worried expression pinched her face.

"Lie down, Linc. Please."

Without a word, he put his arm over his eyes and laid back on the rumpled bag.

Finally Holly's fingers felt a smooth plastic bottle. She yanked it out, shook two aspirin into one hand, hesitated, then added two more. She grabbed the canteen from under a pile of Linc's soggy clothing and went back to him.

"Here," Holly said. "Take these."

Cautiously he opened his eyes. She was kneeling in front of him, holding out aspirin in one hand and a canteen in the other.

Holly's breasts were mostly covered. Linc told himself that was an improvement.

He didn't believe it.

"Four?" Linc asked.

"I usually take two and you're twice as big as I am."

Linc's glance moved from Holly's unique slanted eyes to the well-shaped nails on her bare feet. His hand curled around her foot and his thumb caressed her arch.

"How about if I take you twice and to hell with calling the doctor?" Linc suggested huskily.

A tremor of desire moved over Holly. Mutely, she held out the aspirin and water.

He leaned forward, but not to take the aspirin. He eased the jacket off her shoulders until it settled around her elbows, softly binding her arms to her sides. Slowly, deliberately, he caressed her with tongue and teeth until she forgot to breathe.

Holly's eyes glowed nearly gold as she looked down at the dark head bent over her breasts. She saw Linc's tongue touch her, saw herself respond, saw him look up at her.

She knew her feelings must be as naked as his tongue and she didn't care. Since she was eighteen, men had been telling her how gorgeous she was.

This was the first time she believed it, and Linc hadn't said a word.

"You make me feel so beautiful," Holly whispered.

Linc made a sound that could have been her name. Then he kissed her with a fierce possession that she met and matched. He rolled onto his back, pulling her with him until she lay half across him.

His hands kneaded down her back to her hips, silently demanding another kind of caress. She molded to him, stretching against his hard body, feeling weak and strong at the same time. The blunt length of his arousal startled her. Then it made her even more hungry to blend her body with his.

The repeated neighing of Linc's horse finally penetrated Holly's sensual daze, and his. The unhappy sounds told both of them that the horse was working itself into a frenzy.

Reluctantly Holly shifted her weight and began a slow slide off Linc's body.

"Hold still," he said urgently.

He pressed her face between his hands and fought to control his breathing. After a few moments, he succeeded.

"Holly North," he said through his teeth, "you are the only thing on God's earth that could make me forget to take care of my horse. You're dangerous, woman."

"Me?"

She sat up slowly. She tried to laugh, but her breath kept catching in her throat.

"If I'm dangerous," she said, "you're outright lethal."

Linc admired the flush spreading up from Holly's breasts and her eyes brilliant with desire. He leaned toward her.

"Let's argue about it," he suggested, teasing her with his tongue. "Two falls out of three?"

The horse neighed again. It was a shrill, frightened sound.

"Damn!" groaned Linc.

"I'll check him while you take your aspirin."

"What aspirin?" Linc asked innocently.

A startled look came over Holly's face. She held her hands open in front of her, palms up.

No aspirin.

She looked at the rumpled sleeping bag that covered Linc like an oversized pair of pants. She quickly spotted one aspirin, caught in the same fold of cloth as the canteen. The second and third weren't hard to find, but the fourth eluded her.

Linc washed down the three powdery pills with water from the canteen.

"Maybe the last aspirin is inside the sleeping bag," he suggested with a slow smile.

"You look for it, then," she retorted.

"It would be more fun if you did. Who knows what you'd find?"

Holly felt the heat of a blush and something more spread over her skin, yet she couldn't help laughing at Linc's outrageous teasing.

"I found the other pills at the top of the bag, not the bottom," she pointed out.

"I was hoping you hadn't noticed." He

laughed suddenly. "Bet I can find the fourth aspirin before you do."

Holly turned to look behind her, assuming that he had spotted the pill on the tent floor. Then she felt his fingertips brush beneath her breast. Startled, she looked back.

In Linc's hand was a white pill that looked a bit wilted around the edges.

Holly realized that the aspirin must have been caught beneath her breast, held to her body by the fine mist of desire that suffused her.

"An aspirin after my own heart," Linc said, his voice rich with laughter and sensuality.

She shook her head in helpless embarrassment.

"I'll get you another one," she muttered.

His hand closed gently on her thigh, holding her in place.

"No," he said softly. "I want this one."

Linc's eyes held Holly's as he put the aspirin on his tongue. When the pill vanished behind his lips, it was as though he had taken part of her into himself.

He leaned forward, nuzzling under her breast, his tongue licking up the last of the fine powder that clung to her skin. Then his hand slid between her thighs, caressing upward until he cupped around her intimately. His palm moved in slow circular motions, savoring the special heat of her desire.

The wires of sensation that had been tightening in Holly exploded into a network of fire that raced from the pit of her stomach throughout her body. Her fingers dug convulsively into the hard muscles of Linc's arms as she moaned.

"What are you doing?" she asked.

"Taking my medicine."

Gently Linc bit the taut flesh of Holly's stomach.

The horse neighed, a high, wild sound.

"Linc—"

"Yes, I hear him."

Linc's tongue moving across Holly's navel, lingering, probing. He lifted his head with a groan as the horse's cry ascended into a scream.

"Why did I have to raise horses?" he asked, his voice thick with passion and exasperation. "Why couldn't I have chosen something nice and quiet?"

Holly laughed raggedly.

"Like plants?" she suggested.

"Like rocks."

After a moment Linc's hand slowly slid from between Holly's legs. Even as he withdrew, he caressed her. She tried to bite back a sound of hunger and desire, but couldn't.

"Don't," Linc whispered hoarsely. "When you make that sound I want to take off all your clothes and taste every bit of you until you scream."

Suddenly he buried his face in the warmth that lay between Holly's thighs.

The heat of his breath and the wild intimacy of his caress shocked Holly. She stiffened.

"Linc—"

When he saw her face, he swore silently at his own lack of control. Holly indeed must be as innocent as she looked.

"You're right," Linc said, slowly releasing her. "Sand Dancer sounds like he's in trouble or planning to get that way real soon."

Numbly she nodded.

But despite Holly's shock, she was empty when Linc didn't touch her. She wanted nothing more than to feel him pressed against her again, to hold him until the burning in her body consumed them both.

Then Holly sensed Linc's eyes watching her and knew that her thoughts were as plain to him as if she had spoken them aloud.

Very carefully she eased her hands out of his hair, feeling each crisp lock sliding between her sensitive fingers. With hands that shook so much she was clumsy, she tucked in her jacket once more.

Linc didn't offer to help her.

Holly didn't ask.

Both knew that if he touched her again, he wouldn't let her go.

Six

Moving quickly, Holly jammed her feet into her shoes and untied the tent flap. A bright triangle of sunlight swept into the tent, nearly blinding her.

Blinking, she turned back to Linc to ask if he was sure he was all right. Her mouth opened, but no words came out.

A single look at Linc and Holly forgot what she was going to ask.

He was reaching for his clothes. Sunlight poured over his skin, turning it into polished bronze. The dark hairs on his body burned like molten amber, shimmering and shifting with each move he made. Muscles coiled and shifted smoothly, powerfully, telling of a strength he accepted as casually as he accepted the number of fingers on his hands.

Then Linc turned onto his side and the sleeping bag fell off his hips, leaving him completely naked.

Distantly Holly thought that she should be embarrassed or appalled, but she was neither.

Linc's male beauty transcended narrow defini-
tions of right and wrong, wise and foolish,
proper and improper.

When she finally looked up from his fully
aroused body, she found herself caught and
held by his eyes.

He had been watching her even as she
watched him.

Slowly Linc smiled.

Holly's heart turned over. Desire shivered
visibly through her. She remembered how it
had felt to be nearly naked in his arms, his
breath hot against her body, his mouth separated from her softness by a single thickness of
cloth.

"Come here, Holly."

Linc's voice was husky, as urgent as his
aroused, vibrant flesh.

The Arabian neighed frantically, repeatedly.

With a harsh, frustrated sound, Holly turned
and fled from the tent.

After the intimate twilight of the tent, the sun
was almost overwhelming. Though the damp
ground sent tendrils of vapor into the air, there
were only a few puddles left. Once softened,
the land drank water like a tawny sponge.

Holly pushed her way through clumps of
brush. Branches shaken by her passage
drenched her with water and the pungent smell
of sage.

The Arabian stood with his head up, ears
pricked forward until their tips almost touched.
The tarp Holly had tied onto him last night had

slipped to one side. Her blouse was still in place around the horse's front legs, hobbling him.

The animal snorted as she approached. He watched her with dark, wary eyes.

Holly spoke in low, comforting tones. Her movements were the same, measured and reassuring.

"Good morning, Sand Dancer," she said. "You look like a mess, what with your grubby white hobble and your pea-soup tarp. The twine doesn't do much for the ensemble, either, does it?"

Sand Dancer snorted and stretched his nose toward the strange human.

Holly stood quietly while the horse whuffed over her, drinking her scent. After a minute the animal's velvet nose bumped her gently, accepting her as a friend.

She rubbed the horse's ears, admiring their expressive elegance.

Sand Dancer's nose bumped Holly again, less gently.

"Friendly beast, aren't you?" she said, laughing.

"Like his owner," Linc said.

Startled, Holly turned and looked over her shoulder.

Linc was standing just out of reach. He wore no shirt because it had been shredded in his fall. His jeans were still wet.

They fitted his body the way Holly wanted to, an unbroken line of intimacy.

"Sand Dancer's all right," she said quickly. "Are you?"

Holly winced at the breathless, husky quality of her own voice. She might as well have shouted Linc's effect on her.

His right eyebrow lifted in a wry arc.

"Cold wet shower, cold wet jeans," he said. "Either one gets the job done. For a time."

"I meant—" Holly felt herself blushing and groaned. "Good Lord, you have me acting like I'm nine again."

"You must have been a very advanced nine," Linc teased.

Her blush deepened.

He smiled and relented.

"My head aches," he admitted. "My shoulder is stiff. My knee is tender."

"Oh," Holly said unhappily.

"Don't look so stricken, honey. I've been hurt worse tripping over my own big feet."

"Somehow I can't see you as clumsy," she said, shaking her head. "I've been jealous of the way you move since the first time I saw you."

Linc looked surprised, but before he could say anything, Holly was talking again.

"And those eyelashes of yours," she added. "My God. Do you have any idea just how devastating your coordination and thick lashes were to this nine-year-old? And you never even noticed me for seven years."

"Don't bet on it. The thoughts that crossed my mind after you were fourteen would have gotten me arrested."

At first Holly thought Link was joking.

The look in his eyes convinced her that he wasn't.

"I wish you'd told me," she whispered.

"Great," he retorted. "You could have visited me in jail on alternate Thursdays."

She laughed.

Dancer bumped her with his nose, demanding her attention.

"Duty calls," Linc said.

"Looks more like a horse to me."

Holly turned around and began to work on Sand Dancer.

Linc walked up behind her. He stood so close she could feel the heat of his body radiating through the back of her jacket.

"My hands are cold," Linc lied. "Let me warm them on you."

He rubbed his palms over Holly's arms. Slowly he cupped her breasts. The nipples instantly hardened between his fingers.

She made an odd sound, surprise and passion combined.

With a soft curse he put his hands behind his back.

Holly went to work on the wet, knotted twine that held the tarp on Sand Dancer. The job was made worse because her fingers refused to stop trembling.

"I'm not to be trusted this morning," Linc muttered. "Sorry."

"Put your hands in your pockets," Holly suggested.

"My hands won't fit in my pockets," he admitted wryly.

His hands eased into the front pockets of her jeans.

"Can I use yours?" he asked.

Inside Holly's pockets, his hands moved in sensual rhythms.

"Linc," she said raggedly, feeling herself melt with each touch. "Linc . . ."

He shuddered and pulled his hands out of her pockets.

"The things you do to my self-control," Linc said ruefully. "I thought I was long past the age when I couldn't keep my hands to myself."

Holly turned toward him.

"I wasn't complaining," she said.

"I know. We'll make a deal, though. I won't touch you until poor Sand Dancer is taken care of."

Holly thought of all the tight little knots and wondered if she could last that long.

"Shake on it?" Linc asked, holding out his hand.

At the same moment they both realized that he was waiting to feel the warmth of her hand sliding across his palm.

Quickly Linc dropped his hand.

"I'll take your word for it," he said. "Safer that way. Not as much fun, but safer."

Holly didn't disagree.

Together they attacked the twine knots holding the tarp on the horse. After a night of being soaked by rain and pulled tight by the horse's restless movements, the knots were as hard and stubborn as wood.

"Are you getting anywhere?" she asked after a few minutes.

"Nope."

Automatically Holly reached into her pocket for the jackknife she always carried when she was in the desert. Belatedly she remembered that her knife was in her wet jeans.

Then she thought of the saddlebags tied on behind Sand Dancer's saddle.

Holly reached underneath the tarp, groped for a saddlebag—and found Linc's hand. Startled, she looked over the horse's back.

Linc was watching her, smiling. His fingernails curled across her sensitive palm as his hand withdrew from both saddlebag and tarp.

With a deft motion he opened the knife he had taken from the saddlebag. The long blade glittered as he went to work on the stubborn twine.

Suddenly Linc stopped, frowning.

"I don't remember fixing up this tarp for Sand Dancer," he said, puzzled.

"You didn't."

Holly pulled twine out of the tarp's metal-ringed eyelets and waited for Linc to get back to cutting knots.

"You tied the tarp on Sand Dancer?" he asked.

She laughed.

"Can't you tell?" she asked. "No matter how

many times you scolded me, I still tie granny knots in a pinch."

"In a pinch, getting the job done is all that counts."

He cut away the last of the twine and peeled off the tarp. Sand Dancer's bridle was neatly tied to the saddle horn. The cinch had been loosened enough for the horse's comfort but not enough to let the saddle slide or turn.

Linc glanced around. With approving eyes he measured the shelter provided by the tall boulders and chaparral.

Then the muddy hobble caught Linc's eye. He knelt and fingered the cloth. Like the cinch, the hobble was neither too tight nor too loose.

"Sand Dancer is all right, isn't he?" Holly asked anxiously.

"Sand Dancer is better than he deserves after his performance last night."

She let out a sigh of relief.

"He was calling so frantically that I was afraid he was hurt somehow," she admitted.

"He's spoiled. He was just yelling because he was alone."

Linc stood up with casual grace. He looked at Holly intently.

"What happened last night?" he asked. "I don't remember much after Sand Dancer went down."

"I saw you up on the ridge. Your horse was crazy with fear."

Linc smiled wryly. "I remember that much."

"You should have jumped," Holly said

tightly. "I screamed and screamed for you to jump, but you didn't hear me. Then it began to pour. . . ."

Her voice frayed into silence as she remembered her terrible fear for Linc.

"Sand Dancer went down," she said finally. "You threw yourself clear. You rolled twice and then the boulder . . . oh, Linc, I was so afraid!"

Gently Holly's fingers touched Linc's mouth as though to feel his breath and reassure herself that he was alive.

He kissed her fingertips and whispered her name.

"When I finally got to you," Holly said raggedly, "your face was turned up to that awful rain and you weren't moving. I thought you were dead."

She tried to smile.

Linc's expression told her that it wasn't a success.

"I was glad to hear you groan," she admitted. "After a while we got you on your feet and staggered to the tent."

This time her smile succeeded.

"I wish I had a movie of that," Holly said, "thunder and lightning and rain like the end of the world, and the two of us slip-sliding down the ridge. I felt like a tugboat with a runaway ocean liner."

Linc didn't smile in return. He was remembering the shattering violence of the lightning that had sent Sand Dancer into a frenzy.

"We're lucky we didn't get cooked by lightning," he said.

"Amen," Holly said. "After we got to the tent, I took off your wet clothes and stuffed you into the sleeping bag."

Linc smiled crookedly. "Made you blush, I'll bet."

"I was too busy," she retorted. "Suddenly you decided that you had to go and take care of Sand Dancer."

"Glad to hear I hadn't lost my senses entirely."

"You weren't in any shape for it, so . . ."

"So?"

Holly shrugged and waved her hand at the scraps of twine scattered around their feet.

"So I made a lot of granny knots in the rain," she said.

"You should have waited until the storm let up."

"You're a lot stronger than I am, even when you're half dead from cold and getting rapped on the skull by a boulder. You didn't want to wait."

"You mean I sent you back out into that storm to take care of Sand Dancer?" Linc asked tightly.

"It was you or me, and I was in better shape at the time."

"My God, Holly." He pulled her roughly against him. "You should have let me go. You could have been hurt."

"You already were hurt," she pointed out.

"Still—"

"Linc," Holly interrupted, exasperated. "What kind of person do you think I am? You were hurt!"

"And you were alone in a wild storm with a stallion that went crazy every time the sky lit up."

"I blindfolded him," she said simply.

Linc's hands framed her face as he studied her deceptively fragile face. His thumbs stroked her cheekbones.

"You're incredible," he whispered. "Clever and long legged and wild, with eyes like gold coins . . ."

Suddenly Holly was acutely conscious of the sunlight glinting in Linc's hair and mustache and eyes, of the tempting line of his lips, of his tongue so quick and moist.

A muscle moved and tightened along his jaw. He struggled to control the impulse to kiss Holly until they were both breathless. Very carefully he let go of her and turned his attention to Sand Dancer's hobble.

"Where did you get this?" Linc asked as he worked over the knot. "I don't remember having a spare shirt in the saddlebag."

"It's my blouse. That's why I wasn't wearing anything under my jacket when you—"

Abruptly, Holly stopped talking. The thought of the moment Linc had unzipped her jacket and looked at her naked breasts made heat tremble deep inside her body.

Linc saw her betraying shiver.

"Holly," he said wonderingly, "it's a miracle I can keep my hands off you from one minute to the next. But I'm trying. God knows I'm trying."

Linc removed the hobble and untwisted the fabric of Holly's blouse. The material was stained. Fine sorrel hairs stuck to it in random patches.

He held up the blouse and shook his head.

"I'd stick with the jacket if I were you," he said.

"I've got another blouse."

"Too bad. I like the way the jacket fastens."

"It doesn't. The zipper is jammed."

"Like I said. . . ."

Linc's eyes lit with silent laughter as he untied the bridle and slipped it over Sand Dancer's head.

"Come on, boy," Linc said. "Let's see how thirsty you are."

He tugged on the rains. Obediently Sand Dancer stepped forward.

Holly and Linc both watched the horse move until they were sure that the animal suffered from nothing more serious than a few stiff muscles.

Linc nodded, smiled approvingly at Holly and took her hand.

"Seems like old times," he said. "Hidden Springs, the smell of sage, a horse and"—he gave Holly a teasing sideways look—"a rumpled munchkin watching me with gold eyes."

Suddenly Linc's glance changed, probing

Holly's face as a new thought came to him.

"Why are you here?" he asked. "And why didn't you call and tell me you were back in California?"

Seven

For an instant Holly went cold. She had forgotten that she was the Royce Reflection rather than the innocent sixteen-year-old of her memories.

And Linc's.

Holly remembered all too well how he had reacted to "Shannon" in Palm Springs.

I don't like jet-setters and their prostitutes.

Holly walked the short distance to the springs in silence. With every step she felt Linc's watchful eyes on her face. She didn't want to tell him that she was Shannon, yet she couldn't bring herself to lie.

"I didn't call," she said, "because I didn't know if you'd want to see me."

"What?" Linc demanded in shock and disbelief.

"You never wrote to me," she said simply. "Not even a Christmas card."

Holly's voice and her expression showed the hurt she had felt when her own cards had gone unanswered.

"I wrote three times," he said flatly.

She made an odd sound and turned to look at his face.

"You did?" she whispered.

"The third time I wrote, I got back a note from Sandra," Linc said. "She told me to stop writing, that my letters upset you. I gave up then. I assumed Sandra had taught you to hate me."

"Hate you?" Holly stopped and stared at him. "Why on earth would I hate you?"

Without answering, Linc looped the reins around Sand Dancer's neck. He gave the animal a swat on his gleaming haunch. The horse started forward eagerly, thirsty for the liquid wealth of Hidden Springs.

When Linc turned back to face Holly again, his face was impassive.

"My father was driving the car that hit your parents," Linc said calmly.

His tone was as blunt as his words. He was utterly still, watching Holly's response.

When he saw neither surprise nor revulsion on her face, he let out his breath in soundless relief.

"You knew," he said.

"Sandra told me."

"Figures," Linc said grimly.

"But what does that have to do with hating you?" Holly asked. "It was an accident. A rainy night and a rotten mountain road and a car that went out of control."

Holly's lips trembled for a moment. She took

a ragged breath and wondered if she would ever get over the pain of losing her parents.

"I found out later that your stepmother died, too," Holly whispered. "An accident. That's all. Nobody was to blame. Certainly not you."

Linc lifted Holly's hand and kissed her palm.

"Not everyone would be so forgiving of the McKenzie family," he said. "Sandra sure wasn't."

"I could never hate you," Holly said simply.

Linc looked into her eyes.

"Did you write to me?" he asked.

"Yes." Her voice broke. "Oh, Linc, I wanted to see you so much, to hear your voice, to have you hold me when I woke up in the middle of the night cold and shaking and frightened. I was so alone."

Linc folded Holly into his arms, holding her as though he would make the lonely years vanish with the sheer warmth and strength of his body.

"I never should have let you go," he said savagely. "I wanted to keep you so badly."

"Why didn't you?" Holly asked in a muffled voice.

"Sandra. She couldn't believe that I felt anything more than lust for you."

"She thought that of every man," Holly said curtly. "She was right most of the time, but she was wrong about you."

Linc smiled and kissed Holly's nose.

"I wanted your tender little body," he said huskily. "But that wasn't all I wanted. I'd watched you, watched your parents. They loved each other and they loved you."

"Of course."

Linc almost smiled.

"There's no 'of course' about it," he said. "Living together doesn't necessarily mean loving together."

Holly remembered the rumors she had heard about Linc's mother and stepmother—and Linc's father, who drank far too much before he finally died.

Then she realized something else.

"Sandra never showed your letters to me," Holly said.

Linc wasn't surprised.

Holly was. She and Sandra had never grown close, but Holly hadn't thought her aunt would lie to her.

"Sandra has a lot to answer for," she said in a clipped voice.

Linc looked at Holly's eyes. They were hard and narrow, showing an anger that was repeated in the tight line of her mouth.

"Don't blame her too much," he said after a moment.

"Why not? She has it coming."

"When she first saw you with me, your face was swollen from crying, your hair was every which way and you were curled up in my arms asleep. You looked no more than thirteen."

"So?"

"If you were my daughter or niece," Linc said, "and some hard-looking man said he was going to marry you, I'd have done the same thing Sandra did—scream and swear and generally raise enough hell to get my ass hustled right out of the hospital."

"Maybe," Holly said. "But you wouldn't steal somebody else's mail. And neither would I."

Linc's lips flattened.

"No, but I'm not surprised that Sandra did," he said bluntly.

"Did you know her?" Holly asked.

"I didn't have to. If there's one thing Dad taught me, it's that you can't trust beautiful women."

The leashed savagery in Linc's voice sent a chill over Holly's skin.

"That isn't true," she said.

"The hell it isn't. Take it from an expert." Linc smiled sardonically. "Sandra's a bitch, but no one can say she isn't beautiful."

Ice condensed in Holly's stomach as she looked at Linc's face. It was the cruel face of the stranger who had watched Shannon the way a cat watches a butterfly hovering over a blossom.

Predatory. Ruthless.

"Beauty doesn't have anything to do with it," Holly said tightly. "I know ugly women who are mean right to the marrow of their bones, and beautiful women who are kind."

Linc's hand stroked Holly's face tenderly.

"You'd see kindness in a rattlesnake, *niña*," he said in a soft voice.

Holly felt a curious melting in her bones. Once she had hated it when Linc called her *niña*, "little one," but now the word was as sweet and warm to her as his lips.

"Kind Sandra," Linc continued, his voice different now, raw with remembered rage, "*kind* Sandra swore she wasn't going to let her sister's baby girl marry the son of an alcoholic and a whore. She called me a savage bastard who knew nothing about love."

Holly flinched at the hatred in Linc's voice.

"So Sandra waited until I was at my stepmother's funeral," Linc said, "and then she stole away the only person who might have taught me how to love. You, Holly. Very *kind* of Sandra, wouldn't you say? And so like a beautiful woman."

His voice was like a whip, and like a whip it stung. He looked as unyielding as he sounded.

When Holly spoke, her voice was ragged with Linc's pain and her own fear.

"It's all in the past," Holly said, her voice almost pleading. "I'm not sixteen any more. Sandra can't take me away again."

Linc's arms tightened, holding Holly against his body with a strength that left her aching.

"She'd better not even try," he said flatly. "Did she come here with you?"

"She stayed in Manhattan. Summer is a busy season for Sandra Productions. Everyone is shooting the spring line."

Holly smiled at Linc's blank look.

"Clothes," she explained succinctly. "In order to have all the ad campaigns ready for spring, they have to shoot in the summer."

Comprehension came. Linc's face drew into lines of distaste.

"Yeah, I remember now," he said. "Sandra makes her living selling tits and ass to magazines."

"Linc!"

He saw the horrified look on Holly's face.

"Sorry," he muttered.

Holly was too shaken to say anything.

My God, she thought frantically. *What am I going to do? How can I convince Linc that I'm not what he thinks Shannon is?*

Linc saw Holly's pallor, sighed, and ran his hand roughly through his hair. Sunlight gleamed off his naked arm.

"I don't like models," he said finally. "My mother and stepmother were both models. At least, that's what they called it. Looked like something else to me. And it was."

Holly closed her eyes. She wished she didn't have to open her mouth and see her dream die again.

But she couldn't lie to Linc, not even in silence.

"I'm a model," she said starkly.

"What?"

"I'm a model."

Holly opened her eyes, expecting to see Linc's contempt.

Instead, she saw disbelief and amusement.

"A model," he said neutrally.

"Yes."

Linc laughed softly. Then he looked Holly over from her rumpled braid to her jacket stuffed into wrinkled cotton pants. His eyes lingered on her sturdy, dirty shoes.

"What do you model?" he asked. "Teddy bears? Swing sets? All-day suckers?"

Anger snaked through Holly.

"I didn't realize I was so unattractive," she retorted in a clipped voice.

His laughter vanished. He looked at Holly again, but this time his eyes remembered her as she had been in his arms, her body changing with caresses, her naked skin glowing with desire.

"If you were any more beautiful to me," Linc said tightly, "I would be afraid to trust myself. Or you."

"Being beautiful doesn't mean being untrustworthy. Beauty is just something done with mirrors and makeup. I can be beautiful and still be worth loving!"

"Hey, hey," Linc said, hugging Holly against his chest. "I wasn't talking about you."

"But I was! I'm—"

Holly's words were lost beneath the sweetness of Linc's tongue inside her mouth. His kiss told her of gentleness and caring and the passion for her that infused his every breath.

Unconsciously she moved against him, fitting herself to his powerful body until there was nothing between them but clothes and the words he hadn't let her speak.

"You're more than beautiful enough for me," Linc said against Holly's lips.

"But—"

"No," he said, filling her mouth again, making it impossible for her to speak. "No more arguments about beauty and women."

"But—"

"We should know each other better before we argue," Linc interrupted again.

"How about discussing it?" she muttered.

"I've just found you. Let's not do anything to spoil it."

When Holly didn't answer, Linc nipped her lips lightly.

"Okay?" he asked.

"But—"

His mouth closed over hers, stilling her words and drawing out her breath in a single powerful kiss.

"Promise me," he said finally, urgently. "Having you back is a dream come true. Just a few days. Just a few days and then we can rant and rave and slang at each other like old marrieds."

Unhappily Holly looked at Linc.

His eyes laughed down at hers.

"I'm not a fool," Linc said dryly. "I know we'll fight. You always were a stubborn wench. But just for a few days . . . ?"

"How many?"

A rueful smile spread beneath his mustache.

"Like I said, a stubborn wench," Linc muttered.

Holly waited silently.

Stubbornly.

"Two?" Linc asked. "That will get us past the Arabian Nights party at the ranch. Then if you want to go fifty rounds, so be it."

She wavered, tempted. Then she shook her head.

"You'd be furious at me when you found out," she said.

"Found out?"

Linc stiffened. His fingers dug almost painfully into her arms.

"Found out what?" he asked harshly. "Are you married?"

Too shocked to answer, Holly simply stared at Linc.

"Are you?" he demanded.

"Do you think I'd have touched you if I was married?" she shot back.

"Other women have," he said dryly.

"Not this one." Then Holly added in biting tones, "Aren't you going to ask about fiancés, boyfriends, and lovers?"

Linc's face changed, becoming a mask once more.

"Are there many?" he asked neutrally.

"Not a single one!" Holly exploded, words tumbling out of her recklessly in her anger. "In fact, I'm a—"

Abruptly she got control of her temper and her tongue. She looked away from Linc, embarrassed by what she had almost revealed.

His expression shifted subtly, alive again.

"You're a what?" Linc coaxed.

Holly's chin lifted in a defiant gesture. She put her hands on her hips, unconsciously echoing the moment yesterday when she had faced Linc's contempt as Shannon.

"I'm not very experienced with men," Holly said bluntly. "But that shouldn't surprise you. As you pointed out, I'm so damned plain."

With that, she turned away from him and stalked back toward camp.

He caught up in three long strides, put one arm across Holly's back and the other beneath her knees, and lifted her across his chest.

She gave him a cool, shuttered look.

"Like I said," Linc muttered, "we should declare a truce for two days while we get to know each other. Then we'll get engaged."

Holly's breath caught.

The look on her face made Linc's pulse kick hard.

"Three days after that," he said huskily, "we'll get married. And then the word 'no' will vanish from my vocabulary."

Tears of joy and hope and something very near pain burned behind Holly's eyes. She wanted to say yes instantly, to bind him to her before he found out about her alter ego, Shannon.

The thought of Linc's contempt for beautiful models frightened Holly.

Linc's saw neither the tears nor her fear.

His lips were moving over her throat, her hairline, her ear.

"Holly," he breathed into her ear. "Is my request for a two-day truce so unreasonable? Surely you can keep your temper that long?"

"But—"

"Damn it, woman," Linc interrupted, "what does it take to convince you?"

"I just don't want you to hate me later."

"I could never hate you, *niña*. Don't you know that?"

"Linc, you don't know me. Not all of me."

He glanced upward in exasperation.

"That's the idea of the truce, remember?" Linc asked the sky. "We stop arguing about silly things and talk about rings and weddings and babies."

Holly trembled and hugged Linc hard. The kiss she gave him was almost desperate.

"You do want babies, don't you?" he asked finally.

"I want your babies," she whispered. "I always have."

Linc lifted his head and looked down to the golden-eyed woman in his arms.

"Then please trust me," he said in a low voice. "I'll be very gentle with you. I'd given up hope of ever holding you and I'm afraid of losing you all over again before I even have a chance . . ."

Linc couldn't finish. He didn't have the words to describe his yearning for the warmth and happiness that he once had felt with Holly.

So instead of speaking, he simply kissed her with all the longing he had felt through the years they had been apart.

Holly didn't resist the kiss that stole her breath, replacing it with Linc's, or the tongue that touched every part of her mouth in mute pleading.

When he finally lifted his head, she sighed and smoothed her cheek against his warm neck.

"Truce?" he asked huskily.

"Truce."

"Good."

Linc set off toward the tent with a purposeful stride, still carrying Holly in his arms.

"Where are we going?" she asked.

"The tent."

"The tent?"

Linc looked down at Holly, surprised by the hint of nervousness in her voice.

"I thought I'd put my clothes out to dry," he said, smiling slightly.

Holly tensed, but said nothing.

Linc stopped walking.

"You told me you haven't had much experience with men," he began.

She nodded.

"Are you a virgin?" Linc asked.

"You make it sound like terminal acne."

"Are you or aren't you?"

"Does it matter?" Holly retorted. "This is the modern world, you know."

"I know. That's why I'm asking. You look as

innocent as an angel," Linc said, "but you didn't act like a virgin this morning."

"Sorry about that," Holly said in clipped voice. "Chalk it up to false advertising. I'm as virgin as they come."

Linc stared at her angry face in frank surprise.

"My God," he said after a moment. "Don't they have any men in New York?"

"Crawling with them."

"Well?"

She hesitated, then shrugged.

"They weren't you, Linc," she said simply.

Holly felt a tremor move through the man holding her. His lips brushed over her eyes, her mouth, her forehead.

The kisses were so gentle Holly couldn't stop the upwelling of emotion that transformed her eyelashes into black nets glimmering with captive tears.

"I don't deserve you," Linc said huskily.

Holly's lips trembled into a smile.

"You're stuck with me," she whispered.

For a long moment he simply held her. His eyes closed as he let her words and her presence sink into him like water into dry land.

Then he eased her down his body until her feet touched the ground once more. Slowly he released her.

"I'll get Sand Dancer," Linc said. "You get properly dressed. The way that jacket keeps flopping open would test the self-restraint of a saint, and God knows I'm not one of them."

"Aren't we going to—to—dry your clothes?"

Holly sensed a flush creeping up her face and wanted to curse. She felt like she should be digging a bare toe in the dirt, chewing on the end of her braid and saying brilliant things like "Aw, shucks."

Linc had a way of cutting through the sophisticated shell she had built around herself that was as maddening as it was . . . reassuring.

Slowly Linc's thumb traced the high, slanting line of Holly's cheekbone and smoothed the silky arch of her eyebrow.

"Get dressed, *niña*," he whispered, "before my good intentions go up in flames."

Holly studied Linc for the space of several breaths.

"Just because I'm a virgin?" she asked.

"Yes."

"It's a curable condition," she pointed out reasonably.

"No arguments, remember?"

Her eyes darkened even as they narrowed.

"I wouldn't dream of arguing with you," she said sweetly. "We'll *discuss* it over breakfast."

Giving Linc her best Shannon smile, Holly turned and walked back to the tent, letting her hips swing just that extra bit every step of the way.

Eight

The interior of the tent was warm. It was filled with golden light that seeped through tiny pores in the canvas.

It was also a mess. Clothes were strewn everywhere. So were other things. The duffel had been all but emptied out in Holly's earlier frantic search for aspirin.

But when she looked around the tent, all she really saw was memories of Linc. Heat zigzagged from her breastbone to her knees as she relived the instant the sleeping bag had fallen away from his lean hips.

She had stared at him. She had liked every bit of him that she had seen.

And she had seen it all.

Even worse, she had wanted to go back to him, to kneel by his side, to run her hands all over his sleek body . . .

Is that why Linc said I didn't react like a virgin? she wondered silently.

What does he expect a virgin to do when she sees the man she loves naked? Scream? Faint?

With a wry twist to her full lips, Holly unzipped her pants and kicked them aside. She
wore nothing underneath the jeans because she
had been too cold to worry about underwear
last night.

*I wonder what Linc would have done if he had
discovered that?* she asked herself. *Screamed and
fainted?*

Softly she laughed aloud at the thought of
anything making Linc scream or faint.

Laughter faded as Holly tried to undress.
The jacket zipper was as stubborn as ever. She
peered down at it.

A single look told her that the zipper was
hopelessly off track. With a shrug, she slipped
the jacket down over her hips and stuffed it
into the bottom of the duffel.

For a few moments she stood naked in the
warm tent, remembering how Linc had looked
in the light pouring through the open canvas
flap.

*Would he think I was as beautiful naked as I
thought he was?*

The memory of Linc's very male body
caused a stirring in Holly that was becoming
familiar. Fine wires of sensation tightened,
teasing her with their promise of pleasures she
had not yet felt.

And, according to Linc, I'm not going to feel.

She muttered something that wasn't a normal part of her vocabulary as she pulled underwear out of the duffel.

The bra and matching briefs were made of

indigo lace. Their blue-black color made Holly's skin glow like dark honey, but she was in no temper to appreciate the sensual contrast between lace and skin.

Impatiently she yanked on her jeans again. She buttoned the rumpled blue chambray blouse all the way up, which was how she usually wore it.

Then, deliberately, she undid a few buttons. The result was just enough cloth to cover the indigo lace of her bra.

Some of the time.

If Linc wants a virgin, she thought, *I'll give him a virgin. On a blue chambray platter, hot and steaming, garnished with sage!*

The image made Holly smile, then laugh at herself. She fastened one more button, brushed her hair, braided it quickly, and put on her shoes.

When she was finished dressing, she straightened the clutter inside the tent with the efficient motions of an experienced camper. On the way out, she grabbed a canteen and the firewood she had stored in the tent to keep the wood dry.

Holly started a campfire inside a ring of stones as easily as she had made order out of the tent's chaos. When the flames had eaten solidly into the wood, she balanced a metal grate on the stones.

She filled a bright new coffee pot with water she had hauled last night from the springs. Then she set the coffee pot on the grate and watched it darken with the sooty caress of woodsmoke.

After a moment she poured water into the mess kit's biggest pot and put it next to the coffee on the grate. Finally she picked up the latrine shovel and set off into the brush.

"The tent is ready when you are," she called over her shoulder.

Although she couldn't see Linc, she knew he would be nearby, probably giving Sand Dancer a rough grooming with a handful of sage.

Linc's answering shout came from the direction of the springs, telling Holly she had guessed correctly.

She returned to camp carrying an armload of wood balanced on top of the ice chest Linc had retrieved from the Jeep. One of the tarps Holly had packed kept the interior of the vehicle reasonably dry during the storm.

A second trip to the Jeep took care of the rest of the camp equipment she needed. She dipped out enough water to wash her hands and went to work on breakfast.

With quick motions she draped bacon in a small skillet and put it on the grate to cook. After adding a few more sticks to the fire, she turned away and hung wet clothes on the ropes that supported the tent.

Soon the twin smells of coffee and bacon were tormenting Holly, making her stomach grumble insistently. She looped the last of her wet underwear over a rope and hurried back to the fire.

While she was turning the bacon, Linc strode into camp. He carried a saddle over his right shoulder and a saddle blanket in his left hand. He flipped the blanket onto a tent rope to air out.

The force of the blanket landing sent a piece of Holly's wet underwear fluttering down like an exotic bird.

Linc caught the bit of scarlet lace on his fingertip, smiled slowly, and looked over his shoulder at Holly.

"Yours?" he asked.

"Couldn't be," she said, turning the last piece of bacon. "I'm a virgin. Must be yours."

He laughed aloud, enjoying her quick mind.

With unconscious hunger, Holly watched Linc slip the saddle off his shoulder onto a boulder. She loved the masculine play of muscle and tendon, the easy grace of his movements, his casual acceptance of his physical strength.

"Bacon is burning," Linc said without turning around, knowing that she was watching him.

Holly gave the bacon a startled look. It wasn't even crisp yet.

"No, it isn't," she said.

"Funny," Linc said, hanging she's lacy briefs over the tent rope with elaborate care, "I could have sworn I smelled something burning. Do virgins burn, *niña?*"

His voice was low, as sensual as his fingers

smoothing the scarlet lace of her bikini briefs.

A liquid heat spread through Holly at the thought of being touched in the same way.

When she looked away from Linc's fingers, he was studying her, waiting for her answer.

"Yes," she said.

"Good," Linc said softly. "But I'm going to wait until you're as hungry as I am."

"One, two, three." Holly snapped her fingers. "That's it. I'm as hungry as you are."

She came to her feet in one graceful motion and started for the tent.

Laughing, Linc vanished inside the tent before Holly reached it. He held the flap shut behind him.

"Bacon's burning," he said.

"I like it that way," she retorted, tugging at the flap.

As she wrestled unsuccessfully with the tent opening, bacon grease spattered noisily.

She looked over her shoulder. Flames were licking over the edge of the frying pan.

"Damn," Holly muttered.

She threw a last, frustrated look at the tent before she ran back to the fire and rescued the bacon from certain incineration. A few deft pokes with a stick knocked down the fire.

After another look at the tent, Holly gave up and concentrated on breakfast instead of Linc. She opened a loaf of bread and put five slices to toast on the grate. The cooked bacon went into one of the two tin plates that had come with the mess kit. The coffee perked companionably, almost ready to drink.

"How many eggs and what way?" she called without looking up.

"Three. Over easy."

Linc's voice was unexpectedly close.

An instant later Holly sensed movement behind her. Linc's long, masculine fingers traced the line of her chin and teased the curve of her ear.

Turning, Holly rubbed her lips over his palm. Then she bit the pad of flesh at the base of his thumb with just enough force to be felt through the callus.

Linc drew in a swift breath. When he spoke, his voice was as smoky as his eyes.

"You keep that up," he said, "and I'll trip you and beat you to the ground."

"Promises, promises," she retorted.

Her tongue flicked out to the sensitive skin between Linc's fingers, then moved more slowly.

"Mmmm," Holly said. "You taste better than bacon."

"Holly," Linc said thickly, "you promised not to argue."

"Who's arguing?"

He took her hand and held it to his lips. His tongue retraced every pathway hers had taken.

Her fingers were trembling when he released them.

"The toast is burning," Linc said.

With a groan Holly turned back to the flames that seemed cooler than his touch.

As she turned the bread with quick motions, she wondered what Linc had been doing in the tent. He was still wearing his wet jeans.

She glanced quickly at the tent ropes. A pair of men's briefs hung next to her bright bra.

"Butter in the ice chest," Holly said. "Honey, too."

She broke eggs into the bacon pan, poured two cups of coffee, and laid most of the crisp bacon on Linc's plate. She flipped the eggs deftly, counted to ten, and slid them onto his plate. Three of the five pieces of toast went on top.

"Come and get it while it's hot," she said. "And no smart remarks or I'll eat it all myself."

Laughing, Linc took his plate of food and began to eat.

Holly cooked two more eggs, reached for her toast, and saw that Linc had already prepared it for her. A rich sheen of butter and honey swirled over the bread and dripped over the crust to make tiny golden beads on her plate.

Though Holly ate quickly, Linc finished far ahead of her. He poured another cup of coffee and sat on his heels next to the rock she had chosen for a chair.

"You're amazing, *niña*," he said, sipping the coffee.

"Yeah. Right," she said, licking honey off her fingers. "Not too many geriatric virgins these days."

Linc chuckled.

"That's not what I meant," he said.

"Huh."

He shook his head, denying her skepticism.

"First you drag me to shelter and take care of me," he said. "After that you go back out and risk your neck in a thunderstorm taking care of my crazy horse."

Whatever Holly might have said was lost in the big bite of toast she took.

"Then I wake up in the morning," Linc said slowly, "and I think I'm still dreaming because there's the taste of you on my lips. Then . . ."

His words died as memories of the early morning blazed in his hazel eyes.

After a moment Linc let out a long breath and sipped gingerly at the coffee. He looked at everything around the camp except Holly. He knew if he kept thinking about this morning in the hushed intimacy of the tent, he wouldn't be able to keep his hands off her.

"Later," Linc said, "I'm gone for fifteen minutes rubbing down my horse and I come back to find the tent organized, a fire going, breakfast waiting and sexy lingerie hanging next to my wet socks."

He took Holly's hand and rubbed his mustache against it. With a gentle squeeze, he released her fingers.

"You have no idea," he said, "what a shining pleasure it is not to be saddled with a gorgeous, useless woman."

Holly winced. "Not all gorgeous women are useless."

"I don't remember my mother ever cooking up anything but goo for facials," Linc said, contempt in every word.

Unhappily Holly chewed on her toast.

"My stepmother was even worse," he added. "She wouldn't have been able to set up a tent, much less know how to trench around it in case of rain. Neither one of them would have gone out in a storm to take care of a horse."

Without a word Holly ate the last few bites of her breakfast. Linc was right about those two particular women, and the whole valley knew it. His father had unfailingly been drawn to beautiful, completely self-absorbed women.

Even worse, Linc's father had never seen that his marital problems couldn't be laid at the feet of the children who needed the love of at least one parent. Alcohol had been Martin McKenzie's solace and retreat when his marriages went bad.

Then Linc and his much younger half-sister had only each other when the world went cold and harsh around them.

"Hell," Linc said, his voice icy, "neither one of those females would have gone out in a drizzle to save their own children. But they'd crawl naked through cactus to a cheap motel room."

Narrow-eyed, he stared out over the fire, seeing only the cruel past.

Holly set down her empty plate. She put her

hand on his bare shoulder, blending her warmth with his.

"I'm sorry they hurt you," she said.

The beard stubble on Linc's cheek rasped lightly over the back of Holly's skin.

"It's over and done with," he said.

"Is it? You still hate beautiful women for no better reason than their beauty."

Abruptly his cheek lifted away from her hand. Displeasure showed clearly in the flat line of his mouth. It was a subject he was not willing to discuss.

But for Holly, the subject was far too important to ignore in the hope that it would never come up again.

It would.

The longer she waited, the worse it would be when Linc found out that Holly was also Shannon.

"Would your mother's and stepmother's selfishness have been any easier to bear if they had been ugly?" Holly asked quietly.

"If they had been ugly, they wouldn't have been selfish."

His voice was smooth and cold, leaving no opening for disagreement. It was as though he had just said that the sun set in the west.

A fact, indisputable.

Holly started to speak, then thought better of it.

Linc had been hurt by actions, not words. It would take actions, not words, to convince him that not all beautiful women were selfish and cruel.

I made a small start just by being myself, she consoled herself as she stared silently into her coffee cup. *I helped him and cared for his horse.*

Holly hadn't done any of it to impress Linc. It was simply the way she was. She could no more hide her basic nature than she could step out of her own skin.

Linc had no trouble believing that she was generous and kind. The rest of her truth was going to be hard for Linc to accept.

Under certain conditions, Holly could be very beautiful, yet she was never cruel.

In time, Linc had to see that.

Linc is right, she admitted to herself. *We need a truce, a time to know each other better.*

She prayed that two days would be enough.

Nine

Holly rubbed the skillet with sand, wrapped it in newspaper, and stacked it in the supply carton. She carried the box to the Jeep along with the tarp that had covered Sand Dancer.

Though it was not yet ten o'clock, the sun cut through her thin blouse like a laser. The sky was blue-white and brilliant with water vapor. Even now the first clouds were forming against the highest peaks. By evening, summer thunder would come again to the dry land, bringing the gift of water.

From habit Holly moved quietly, enjoying the desert sounds. Quail chuckled beneath the chaparral. Brush rubbed over itself with a soft, leathery sound. Bees hummed endlessly, frantic with their efforts to take advantage of the brief bloom that followed midsummer rains.

The thundershower had unsettled the desert inhabitants. Many of them lived underground, letting the land itself insulate them from the sun's killing heat. The hard rain of last night had filled underground holes and burrows with water, driving everything living up to the surface.

There the animals would stay until the water sank beneath the level of their homes. In the winter rainy season the land softened and allowed water to drain quickly out of the burrows. In the summer it took longer, for the land had been baked by the sun like clay in a kiln.

At the Jeep, Holly shifted the gas can aside to make room for the carton. Metal clanged noisily against metal.

In the silence that followed, the dry buzz of a rattlesnake sounded like thunder.

Holly froze.

For an instant she was thirteen again, taking a shortcut through her backyard to the corral. She hadn't heard the rattlesnake that bit her, but she had seen it strike, sinking its fangs into her leg just above her cowboy boots.

Her jeans had protected her somewhat, but not enough to prevent some of the poison from entering her blood. The venom had been like molten metal burning through her.

At the time Holly had screamed in agony because she couldn't help herself.

She was screaming now, remembering.

"Holly!"

Finally she realized that Linc was holding her, calling her name again and again, his eyes made dark by fear.

With a convulsive shudder, she returned to the present.

"I'm all right," she said hoarsely.

"What happened?"

"Rattlesnake."

Instantly Linc's glance raked the nearby desert. He saw nothing threatening.

Holly gave a shaky laugh.

"It's gone now," she said. "It probably was as scared by my scream as I was by its rattle."

Without a word Linc knelt and yanked up her pant legs, looking for puncture wounds left by fangs.

"The snake wasn't close enough to get me," she said.

"You're shaking like it did."

"I know, but it didn't."

As Link stood up, Holly took a deep breath and tried to still the trembling of her body.

"Sorry," she said. "I feel like such a fool. There are always snakes around the springs. I shouldn't have been so surprised."

He looked at her white lips and at the sweat that stood out on her skin. Gently he gathered her in his arms again. One of his hands made slow, soothing sweeps down her back.

"It's all right," Linc said. "Even if the snake had bitten you. I always have antivenin in my saddlebags."

Silently Holly shook her head.

"No good," she said.

"What do you mean?"

"I was bitten when I was thirteen. I'm allergic to the venom. I'm even more allergic to the antivenin. Dad barely got me to the hospital in time."

When what she was saying sank in, Linc's face went almost as pale as hers. He stepped back abruptly and looked at her.

"When I came to the next day," Holly said, "the doctor told me that unless I happened to be in an emergency ward the next time a rattler nailed me, I would die."

"Then why in the name of God did you come to Hidden Springs?" Linc demanded in a voice made harsh by fear for her.

Though her lips were still pale, she smiled up at him.

"Lots of people have the same problem with bee stings," she said, "but they don't stay shut up in their houses. I used have an adrenaline kit with me, but once I went back east I stopped carrying one."

Linc looked grim.

"It's okay," Holly said. "I just have to remember where I am, and then I won't panic if I see another rattler."

Briefly Linc closed his eyes and said something beneath his breath that he hoped she didn't hear.

"At least," Holly added with a catch in her voice, "I hope I won't panic."

"New rules."

She stared at Linc, surprised by the cool steel in his voice.

"What does that mean?" she asked warily.

"You get a new adrenaline kit and you carry it with you at all times."

She nodded.

"You don't walk or ride anywhere in the desert alone," Linc added flatly. "When you do go out, you go second, not first. Let somebody else find the snakes."

Holly's first impulse was to argue.

Her second was to agree with his common-sense approach to the problem. He wasn't telling her that she had to stay locked in a house. He was simply trying to work out a safe way for her to enjoy the desert she loved.

Smiling, Holly bowed and waved toward camp.

"After you, *monsieur*," she murmured.

Surprise showed on Linc's hard face.

"Agreeable, aren't you?" he asked, not quite believing her.

"Uh-huh. Docile, loyal, and obedient, too." She grinned. "Want to scratch my ears?"

Linc laughed, taken off-guard again.

"You're full of surprises," he said. "There was a time when you would have raised hell if I told you to do something sensible."

"I'm not sixteen anymore."

Suddenly serious, Holly looked up at him with eyes that were almost gold.

"Six years, Linc," she whispered. "I've changed in a lot of ways. I can be very beautiful. Will you still want me when you realize that?"

His eyes narrowed.

"Do you think I don't know how—" he began angrily.

Abruptly Linc took a deep breath, shutting off his irritation.

Truce, he told himself sardonically. *Remember?*

"You're a warm, capable, stubborn woman," Linc said after a moment. "Very warm. Very woman. And very damn stubborn."

As he spoke, his hazel glance lingered almost unwillingly over the opening in Holly's blouse. The gentle swelling of her breasts was visible, tantalizing.

"You noticed," she said, smiling.

It was a different kind of smile, a remembering kind.

A sexy kind.

"Linc—" she began.

"No," he interrupted promptly. "I've got a headache."

"Isn't that supposed to be my line?" Holly retorted, recalling what he had said to her that morning.

Linc shook his head in rueful amusement.

"I'm glad you aren't sixteen any more, *niña,*" he said. "I'm having a hell of a time with my conscience as it is."

"Why?"

"You're a virgin," he said simply.

"You make me wish I wasn't. If I were experienced, I would know how to touch you so that you would want me so much you—"

"Truce," he interrupted, groaning.

"—wouldn't be able to stop yourself."

Without warning Linc bent and put his mouth over Holly's. His tongue parted her lips with deep, slow strokes that brought a low sound from the back of her throat. Her body melted against his with hungry ease and breathtaking thoroughness.

A bolt of raw desire lanced through him, shaking his powerful body like thunder shaking the land. When he finally lifted his mouth, his eyes were glittering with desire.

"You don't need to know one damn thing about turning me on," Linc said harshly. "Just kissing you is more exciting than sleeping with another woman."

At first she smiled. Then the image of Cyn's voluptuous, experienced body flashed before Holly's eyes. She stiffened, remembering Cyn and Linc in Palm Springs.

He felt the change in Holly, saw it in her suddenly wary eyes.

"What's wrong?" he asked.

"Another woman," she said, trying to make her voice light. "How can I compete with Cyn, being a plain virgin and all? And you so damned handsome and experienced."

Holly looked away, unable to bear the narrowed intensity of Linc's eyes.

"Cyn." His voice was curt. "Who told you about her?"

Silence and a shrug was Holly's only answer.

"Look at me," he said.

Reluctantly, she turned her head. His expression was gentle and intent. His eyes searched hers.

"I've always been very careful in my affairs," Linc said quietly. "Do you understand?"

"That you're not a virgin? Sure."

He smiled wryly. "That's not quite what I meant."

"What did you mean, then?"

"I've always used condoms. Always. You won't have to worry about catching anything from me."

Holly knew she was blushing, but she didn't care.

"I wasn't thinking about that," she admitted.

"You should have been. As for Cyn—" He shrugged. "We had an arrangement that was mutually convenient."

Holly remembered Cyn's full breasts and hips pressed against Linc's body. His arm had been close around her, and his eyes were amused and indulgent as he looked at the little blond.

And those same hazel eyes had been so scornful of the woman called Shannon.

"Had?" Holly whispered. "It's over with Cyn?"

"It's history. You're all I want, Holly. You're more than I dreamed I'd ever have."

"Then why won't you make love to me?"

Linc smiled crookedly.

"I have," he said.

"You know what I mean."

"Is being a virgin so terrible?" he teased.

"Not terrible. Painful. I ache, Linc."

He drew in his breath sharply. His eyes narrowed to smoldering lines. Passion burned behind his thick lashes.

"You're getting there," he said huskily.

"Getting where?"

"To the point where you're as hungry as I am."

Holly groaned. "You mean it gets worse?"

"Much worse. And then it gets much, much better."

"Worse? That isn't possible."

"Want to bet?"

Even as Linc spoke, his long, lean fingers slowly unbuttoned her blouse. When the soft blue folds parted, he smoothed the fabric off her shoulders.

For a long moment he simply looked at Holly, from the startled beauty of her eyes to the gentle fullness of her breasts rising beneath dark blue lace.

Her heart turned over in answer to the desire that leaped in his eyes. Heat spread beneath her skin, making it glow. Under the bra her nipples tightened visibly, aroused simply by his look.

His fingertips stroked her throat, cherishing the pulse that raced in answer to his caress.

"I've never wanted a woman more than I want you now," Linc said huskily.

Holly tried to speak but couldn't force out anything more than a throaty sound that was his name.

In hushed silence she watched Linc's face, watched his eyes grow intent, his lips part in a sensuous smile, his tongue move between his teeth to claim her mouth.

At the first warm touch of his tongue, wires tightened and sang all through her.

"What an odd sound," he said. "Are you frightened?"

Holly shook her head.

"Want me?" Linc asked softly.

She nodded.

"You're shivering with passion," he said, "and I've done nothing more than look at you and touch the life beating in your throat. You tempt me, *niña*. My God, how you tempt me, and you don't even know. . . ."

He slid the blouse down her arms and over her hands. He left tiny, biting kisses on her fingertips as they emerged from the blue sleeves.

With a husky sigh, Holly closed her eyes, caught in the sensuality that radiated from Linc like heat from the sun. He took her mouth in a kiss that was as deep as it was quick.

"Look at my hands," he whispered against her lips.

Her dense black eyelashes lifted. She looked down and saw his hands on her body. They were brown and strong and very male against the delicate lace of her bra.

And she changed beneath his hands, rising

to meet his caresses. When his nails raked lightly over her nipples, her breath stopped, then started again, much more raggedly.

Holly kept watching Linc's hands despite the wires of sensation tightening throughout her body, making her burn. She was fascinated by the beauty of his fingers, held by his lightest touch more surely than if she had been chained.

With dreamlike slowness, one of his hands curved around her breast. He caught her nipple between his thumb and finger, rubbing lightly. She arched against his hand, tormented by a touch that was too light and too knowing. He bent and took the nipple tenderly between his teeth, making her gasp with pleasure.

Linc lifted his head almost immediately. His fingers moved over the front fastening of her bra. Even after it came undone, indigo lace still clung to the fullness of her breasts.

One of his long fingers slipped beneath the lace, peeling it slowly away from first one breast, then the other, watching her with eyes that were nearly green with the intensity of his passion.

Holly saw Linc's lips close over her breast. Her nipple hardened even more as his tongue and lips tugged at her in a loving caress that made her moan. She held his head between her hands and succumbed to the heat that twisted through her, melting her.

His teeth closed over her again, less gently this time, knowing she was too aroused to feel a light touch any longer. She made a fierce sound of pleasure and buried her fingers in his hair.

For a time Linc held Holly hard against his body, taking as much pleasure from the desire that shook her as she did. Then his mouth gentled again, nibbling between her breasts, ignoring her sensitive nipples. He blew on her hot skin, teasing her until her nails dug into his arm in frustration.

"Linc?"

"Nope."

"You're right," she said huskily. "It's worse. Love me, Linc."

He laughed softly despite the talons of need that had raked his body into full arousal.

"I said *much* worse," he reminded her.

Before she could protest, he took her mouth in a kiss that consumed her. She gave it back just as fiercely, needing to feel the power of his body against her naked breasts.

With quick, almost fierce movements, Linc undid her jeans. He pushed the faded fabric down over her hips, then her thighs, then all the way to her ankles. When he was finished, only a wisp of indigo lace covered her.

Holly trembled but made no protest. She wanted him with a force that was shaking her.

His hands roamed over her smooth skin, savoring her heat and the tremors of desire that quivered through her. His right hand moved over her lacy briefs, then slid beneath the elastic. Fingers rubbed lightly over her hidden softness.

When Linc found that Holly was moist with desire, he had to clench his teeth against losing control.

He hadn't known he could want a woman so much and not take her.

Slowly, gently he stroked the soft folds he had discovered. His fingers slid easily over her, for he was slick with her helpless response. With tender care he searched out the hardening bud of her passion and caressed it.

Holly gasped and shuddered convulsively, gripped by intense, wild pleasure. Her fingers dug heedlessly into Linc's naked back.

He smiled narrowly, fighting his own need.

"What are you doing to me?" she asked shakily.

"Not a tenth what I'd like to," he said, his voice thick. "The passion in you makes my head spin."

His palm cupped between her thighs, pressing against her, sharing her heat. With a groan he knelt to kiss her shadowed softness.

"*Linc—!*"

Shock and desire were mingled equally in Holly's voice.

With a shudder he turned his head away and rested his cheek on her stomach. For a time he was rigid, fighting to control himself.

Then Linc stood up fast and hard. He pulled her jeans into place with swift motions.

"Sorry," he said. "I didn't realize that your virginity isn't just a technicality. No man has ever really touched you."

Linc picked up her bra and blouse and handed them to her.

"Put these on," he said tersely. "I don't trust myself. I want you too much. Too damned much!"

He turned away and began loading the Jeep with quick, fierce motions.

"Linc—"

"No more, Holly," he interrupted in a raw voice. "I can't take it right now."

She hesitated, then looked down at her own hands. They were shaking.

If it's this bad for me, she realized, *how much worse must it be for him?*

Silently she turned away and began putting her clothes back on.

Ten

Holly dressed quickly. She was too shaken by her own headlong passion to argue with Linc that they could end the ache of unfulfilled hunger by making love.

Yet as soon as her surprise at her own reaction to his touch passed, she wanted nothing more than to feel like that again, weak and strong, burning and melting, aching and ecstasy all wound together.

A glance at Linc's strained features kept her from saying anything about how she felt. He looked like a man at the end of his rope.

Without a word Holly helped him finish loading the Jeep and tie the last tarp in place. By the time the work was done, he was looking much less forbidding. He was even smiling when he came around the Jeep to her side.

"Record time," Linc said. "We make quite a team."

Relieved that the fierce tension had left his face and body, Holly returned his smile. Impulsively she ran her finger over the edges of his mustache.

"Took you long enough to figure it out," she said softly.

Linc's eyes changed as he remembered just how well they did some things together. He reached for her, then stopped himself with a muttered word.

"We'll never get home that way," he said.

"Depends on what you mean by 'home.' "

"A bed with you in it," he said bluntly.

"We just packed it in the Jeep."

"Damn straight. I made sure the bed went in first. Just thinking about this morning . . ."

He shook his head, baffled by his urgent, nearly overwhelming need for Holly.

"Linc? What's wrong?"

"I don't have any self-control with you," he said after a moment. "When the time comes, I'll do my best not to go too fast. If I lose it, I'll make it up to you. Okay?"

She wasn't quite sure what he was talking about, but she agreed anyway.

"Okay," she said. "Anytime you want to, er, lose it, just let me know."

Linc gave a bark of laughter and shook his head, bemused by Holly's acceptance of a situation that he didn't understand himself.

And thinking about it just aroused him all over again.

With a silent curse, he turned away from her. He gave the sky a measuring look.

"Antelope Wash looks like a bad risk," he said after a moment.

Holly looked up. There was a blue-black

density to the margin between cloud and land that told of mountain storms at the higher altitudes. He was right. Antelope Wash was out, which meant she had to stay at Hidden Springs.

She groaned.

"Now I'll have to set up camp all over again," Holly said.

"No. We'll both ride Sand Dancer out. I'll send some men to pick up your stuff tomorrow."

"I can pick it up after the shoot on Monday."

The instant the words were out of her mouth she regretted reminding Linc about her job as a model.

"Them!" His voice was scornful. "The tame Viking and his black-haired whore."

When Linc saw Holly's stricken expression, he controlled his tongue with an effort.

"Sorry," he said. "I forgot. You're with them. Of all the mismatches—"

Abruptly he cut off his words. He simply shook his head and forced a smile.

Tears and anger and fear twisted Holly's throat, squeezing her voice until it was barely recognizable.

"Royce models are just that," she said. "Models. I'm one of them."

Linc heard her distress more than her words. He hugged her gently.

"I'd make a terrible diplomat," he said against her black hair, "breaking my own truces and saying all the wrong things."

Holly made a muffled sound.

"The last thing I want to do is hurt you," Linc said, kissing her forehead. "Truce? Again?"

"You're wrong about Roger's models," she insisted.

"I'm wrong about Roger's models," Linc repeated dutifully. "Truce?"

She knew that he hadn't changed his mind. Words alone weren't enough to take away the cruel lessons of his childhood.

"Truce," she agreed. "But someday I'm really going to have to rearrange your prejudices."

Linc smiled thinly. "It took a lifetime to arrange them."

"And all I have is two days."

"You have a lifetime, *niña*, if you want it."

"Do I?"

He sensed her despair, although he didn't understand its cause. He held her in a fierce grip, trying to banish the fear he saw in her golden eyes.

She leaned against him, glorying in the rasp of beard stubble against her cheek. First, her hands slid around his back, then her arms. She held him with a woman's surprising strength.

Holly and Linc stood pressed tightly together, each storing up the other's presence like land drinking water after a long drought. There was nothing sexual in their embrace, simply an elemental need to comfort one another.

The long ride to his ranch in Garner

Valley was the same for Linc and Holly, a time
of simple closeness, of comfort given in silence
and accepted the same way. She rested her
cheek against the warmth of his naked back
and gave herself to the remembered rhythms
of being on horseback.

Feeling at peace despite the uncertainty of
her future with Linc, Holly let the familiar
landscape of desert slide by around them.

All too soon Sand Dancer climbed over the
ridge that separated the lush Garner Valley
from the desert. The valley lay between two
ridges of the San Jacinto Mountains. The contrast between the sand and rock of the high desert and the pine and grass of the valley was
startling.

"It hasn't changed," Holly said dreamily.

"What hasn't?"

"The Mountains of Sunrise. The ranch is
even more beautiful than I remembered."

Linc smiled, pleased that she still liked his
home. Part of him had feared that the ranch
would look less appealing after six years in
Manhattan's sophisticated concrete and neon
wilderness.

"The ranch takes a lot of time and money to
keep up," Linc said.

"It's worth every minute, every penny."

The white fences around the house, show
rings, and paddocks were as clean as the clouds
gathering against the mountains. The irrigated
pastures were green. The grazing Arabians

were sleek, elegant, lively, obviously bursting with health.

On either side of the Mountains of Sunrise were other horse ranches—Garner Valley was famous for its carefully bred, expensive horses.

A big yellow dog came trotting out from the barn and stood near Sand Dancer. The dog looked up, waving a thick tail in greeting. Linc lifted his right leg over the horse's neck, slid down to the ground, and scratched the dog's ears affectionately.

"Hello, Freedom," he said, looking around. "Did you lose Beth?"

Holly landed lightly beside Linc. She got a big lick from Freedom as soon as her feet hit the ground.

Linc was still looking around for his younger sister.

"Beth will be glad to see you," he said. "She missed you almost as much as I did."

"I missed her too. Of all the kids I baby-sat for, she was the only one I wanted to keep."

Linc smiled rather grimly.

"Good thing you didn't let on," he said. "Dad and my dear stepmother always made Beth feel like they would give her away to the first adult who came in the door."

"You wouldn't have let her go."

"I still won't, even though she's driving me nuts."

"Beth?" Holly asked, surprised.

"Beth," Linc said.

He sighed heavily, gave the dog a final pat, and turned to face her.

"Beth is at the age when all her friends stay in town," he explained. "She'd rather be at our Palm Springs house than at the ranch."

"It must be lonely for her here."

"Don't you start in on me," he said in curt tones.

Warily Holly looked at Linc.

He grimaced.

"Sorry," he muttered. "Beth and Mrs. Malley keep harping on how much nicer it is in Palm Springs."

"Um," Holly said. "If you say so."

"I don't. They do."

"So send them off for a few weeks."

"Mrs. Malley can't keep Beth on a short enough leash," Linc said bluntly, "and I can't afford to be away from the ranch for weeks on end."

"Beth used to love the ranch."

"That was before she discovered boys. Now all she can think about is painting her face and buying flashy clothes."

Holly touched Linc's arm.

"Hey," she said, smiling gently. "It's normal at fifteen."

"You weren't like that."

She shrugged and made a dismissing gesture with her hand.

"I was an awful tomboy," she said.

Smiling, he didn't disagree.

"Is Beth doing well at school?" Holly asked.

"She's a straight-A student."

"Are her friends wild?"

"Her girlfriends wear too much paint," he said, "but they're nice kids underneath all the crud."

"Then you're worrying over nothing."

"I sure as hell hope so."

Linc rubbed his hand through his hair in a gesture of frustration that was becoming familiar to Holly. Then his mouth flattened into an unyielding line.

"Some days Beth reminds me so much of her mother it scares the hell out of me," he admitted. "But Beth won't end up like that if I have to lock her in her room and eat the key."

Holly winced. Before she could say anything, the back door of the house slammed and a girl nearly as tall as Holly came running toward them. She recognized Beth by the long, honey-colored braids that bounced behind her.

"Holly! Is it really you?" Beth asked.

"It really is."

Beth threw herself into Holly's arms and held on almost as fiercely as Linc had.

"I always told my brother you'd come back," Beth said. "Where did you come from? How did Linc find you? Why were you riding double? Are you back to stay? Did—"

Laughing, Linc put his hand over Beth's mouth.

"Slow down, Button," he said.

"*Button!*" Beth muttered hotly beneath her brother's palm. "I'm nearly *sixteen!*"

Holly looked at Beth's clean, shining face and felt like an ancient lump of mud.

"I'll flip you for the bathtub," she said to Linc.

"We could share," he said, only half-joking.

Holly threw a startled glance at Beth.

The younger girl looked surprised, then smug.

"You can use my bubble bath," Beth offered.

Smiling, Holly shook her head.

"Spoilsport," Linc said.

"Me?" Holly asked, despite the red staining her cheeks. "I seem to remember a certain male of my acquaintance who couldn't stop saying no when I—"

"Use the master bath," Linc interrupted quickly. "Beth and I will take care of Sand Dancer."

"Huh?" Beth said. "But I want to talk to Holly."

"Later," he said. "Right now you can tell me all about the latest dress you want to buy for the Arabian Nights party."

"Which one?"

"The one that's years too old for you to wear."

"How did you—" Beth began.

"Psychic," Linc interrupted dryly.

Without looking over his shoulder, he began leading Sand Dancer toward the barn.

"Go get him, tiger," Holly muttered to Beth. "I know where the bathtub is."

Beth's eyes gleamed. She started after her

brother with a determined stride. As soon as she caught up with him, her clear voice floated back to Holly.

Dresses weren't the topic.

"Okay, big brother," Beth said. "Yesterday you rode out of here alone with a shirt and a saddle. Today you show up shirtless and bare-back with Holly. Give."

Smiling to herself, Holly headed for the house.

Linc's home was just as she had remembered. The rooms were spacious, clean, cool, and decorated in the same earth tones of the old Navaho rugs that Linc's father had collected.

Holly had never been in the wing of the house that held the master bedroom, but she knew where it was. The size of the bathroom that adjoined the bedroom startled her.

"My God," she said aloud. "This is as big as my whole apartment in Manhattan."

The sunken bathtub—with Jacuzzi—was nearly big enough to do laps in. And like a swimming pool, the tub was kept full of hot water beneath a transparent plastic lid.

Holly looked at the tub longingly, but could not bring herself to waste all that water just to clean one body.

A quick search of the bathroom turned up soap and shampoo. She took off her clothes and stepped into the oversized shower. With a sigh of sheer pleasure, she let hot water pour over her, washing away the dust of the long ride up and over the ridge to the ranch.

Finally she got out, pulled a towel off a nearby hook, and was nearly buried in an avalanche of soft cloth. Obviously the towel had been made for Linc. It was longer than she was and twice as wide.

Smiling, she rubbed herself dry, then took the unused half of the towel and went to work on her hair.

When she was finished, she deftly French-braided the sides and crown, blending the shorter hair around her face into a sleek cap and leaving the longer hair to dry in gentle waves down her back.

A quick look in the mirror made her frown, goaded by the memory of Cyn's lush, soft beauty. Holly coaxed a few tendrils of hair loose around her face, hoping to soften the slanting lines of her eyes and cheekbones.

A few little curls weren't enough to change the result. She still looked too young and too plain to attract a man like Linc.

Muttering unhappy words, Holly wrapped the big towel several times around herself and gathered up her clothes. Dirty laundry in hand, she headed out of the bathroom to look for a washing machine.

The master bedroom door opened and Linc walked in.

"Just in time," she said.

"Looks more like too late to me."

His hazel eyes took in the towel that covered Holly from collarbones to feet.

"I was going to offer to scrub your back, among other things," he said.

She hesitated. As much as she wanted to lose herself to Linc's passionate lovemaking, they weren't alone anymore.

Not the way they had been at Hidden Springs, alone but for Sand Dancer and the desert storm.

"What about Beth?" Holly asked.

"I don't think she wants to scrub you nearly as badly as I do," he said, deliberately misunderstanding.

"Linc—"

"Don't worry about Beth," he interrupted softly. "She'd move heaven and earth to get you in my bed."

Holly couldn't hide her shock.

The smile that he gave her was real, if a bit thin.

"You can hardly be surprised that Beth knows about men, women, and beds," he said. "She grew up fast. With a mother like hers, she had to."

"It's not that," Holly said evenly. "I'm shocked that you would bring your . . . playmates . . . to your home."

Linc's eyebrows shot up.

"No matter how mature you think Beth is," Holly said, "I doubt that she likes having breakfast with your most recent amour."

"If I'm sleeping double, I sleep somewhere else," he said bluntly.

"Oh."

"You'll be the first in my bed at home, *niña.* And the last."

His fingers wound in her long black hair. Gently he pulled her toward him and tilted her face to receive his lips.

Just as his mouth touched hers he whispered, "Marry me today. We could be in Mexico in less than an hour."

Before Holly could answer, Linc pulled her against him, kissing her so thoroughly she couldn't breathe. She returned his kiss with a passionate abandon that made both of them tremble.

When he finally ended the kiss, he watched her with eyes that were clear and certain.

"I won't hear anything except yes," he said. "So if you want to argue, you'll just have to wait until after the party. Truce, remember?"

Holly wanted to say yes more than she had ever wanted to do anything in her life. She had always known that she loved Linc. Now she was learning just how much.

But until he knew that Holly was also Shannon, she couldn't accept promises he might not want to keep.

"I'll wait until our truce ends to say yes," she said. "Then we can go to Mexico or the moon or anywhere, so long as we're together."

Linc's face became very still.

"Why wait if it's yes?" he asked.

"When the truce ends, you may want to withdraw the offer."

"You think we'll have a horrible fight right away?" he asked, smiling crookedly.

"I know we will," she said, unsmiling. "But if you want me afterward, you've got me."

Linc slid his fingers between the towel and Holly's breasts.

"Do I have to wait that long?" he asked, caressing gently.

She drew in a quick breath.

"Only for the marriage," she said huskily. "The woman you could have had anytime since dawn."

Beth's voice came down the hallway.

"Linc?" she called. "Are you in the shower yet?"

Slowly he withdrew his hand, but otherwise made no move to separate himself from Holly.

"In here," Linc called.

Beth breezed into the room, saw Linc with his arms around Holly, and grinned with open delight.

"Does this mean that after six years I'm finally going to have Holly as a sister?" Beth asked.

"I'm working on it," he said. "She's damn near as stubborn as I am."

"Try one of your famous truces," retorted Beth.

"I did. Midnight tomorrow, she says yes."

Beth whooped and threw her arms around both Holly and Linc. They each put an arm around her and hugged her in return.

"Midnight, huh?" Beth asked, laughing. "Cool. Just like Cinderella!"

Linc laughed aloud, but Holly's answering smile was a little forced.

Midnight hadn't been Cinderella's finest hour.

Eleven

"Holly?" Beth called. "Can I come in?"

Holly glanced toward the bedroom door. She had chosen to stay in the guest bedroom across the hall from the master bedroom, rather than in the master bedroom itself.

It was one thing to be engaged to Linc.

It was quite another to have Linc keep his little sister on a "tight leash" and then leave the leash off himself entirely.

"Come on in," Holly said.

The door flew open. Beth came in with a rush.

"Linc told me to tell you he'll be in the barn for a while," Beth said. "One of his best horses needs him."

"A while, hmm?" Holly said. She smiled slightly. "I remember Linc and his prize Arabians. Could be five minutes or five hours, right?"

"It's the mare's first foal," Beth explained. "She can't decide whether to lie down and have it or stand around and look surprised. It could be all night."

Holly sighed and buttoned her freshly washed blouse.

"Then we'd better think about getting some food out to Linc," Holly said. "Breakfast was a long time ago."

Beth grinned. "I already took him three sandwiches and a quart of coffee."

"He's lucky to have a sister like you."

"That's what I keep telling him."

Smiling, Holly tested her hair.

"Finally," she muttered. "Dry enough to braid."

Her fingers flew, deftly weaving long strands of hair into an intricate pattern.

"You make that look so easy," Beth said after a minute.

"What?"

"Your braid. It looks so smart. But mine— ugh."

Beth held up one of her own long braids as though it was a dead snake.

"You have pretty hair," Holly said.

"Ha," Beth said succinctly. "Pigtails or po- nytails. Yuck."

"There are other things you can do with long hair if you don't want to cut it."

"I want to cut it, but Linc won't let me."

Holly's eyebrows rose in black arches.

"No makeup," Beth said in a rush, "no cool clothes and the same hairdo I had six years ago."

"Linc again?"

The younger girl's full mouth twisted into a grimace.

"Linc," Beth agreed. "I didn't mind for a while, but now . . ."

Her voice faded. An expression of wistful yearning came over her face.

"A boy?" Holly asked, already knowing the answer.

Beth smiled shyly and nodded her head.

"Who is he?" Holly asked.

"Jack. My best friend's older brother."

"How much older?"

"You sound just like Linc!"

Holly smiled. "That's because we both love you."

"Jack just turned eighteen and I'll be sixteen in a few months so there's really only two years. He's not too old for me!"

"Of course not."

Beth smiled with relief.

"I'm glad you feel that way," she said. "Linc doesn't. And the way he makes me dress just makes me look like I'm in kindergarten."

"If Jack is worth your time," Holly said, "he won't care about your clothes or hair."

Beth's mouth flattened into a stubborn line that reminded Holly of Linc.

"That's what my brother says," Beth muttered.

"He's right."

"Maybe. But why do *I* have to be the one to test *Linc's* theories? Besides," Beth added bitterly, "when he goes out with a woman, he sure doesn't pick the plain ones."

Remembering Cyn, Holly could hardly disagree.

"You aren't plain," Holly said.

The younger girl turned and looked at Holly with level eyes.

"I'm as plain as a post," Beth countered.

The tone of her voice and her stance told Holly that Beth believed every word of what she was saying.

"You're not plain at all," Holly said firmly.

Beth gave her a sidelong glance and said nothing.

"Your smile alone is beautiful enough to turn heads," Holly added.

"Oh, my teeth are straight," the younger girl said grudgingly, "and my skin is clear. Other than that, I'm . . . plain."

Holly measured Beth as though seeing her for the first time.

The younger girl's eyes were the glowing, pale turquoise of a rain-washed desert sky. Her lips were full, ready to smile or pout or laugh. Her skin was smooth, lightly tanned, and glowing with health. At fifteen, she had a lovely, lithe, feminine figure.

With a discreet amount of makeup, the right clothes, and another hairstyle . . . Holly thought. *Yes, she would be a knockout.*

Is that what Linc is afraid of?

"Holly?" Beth waved her hand in front of Holly's face. "Anybody home?"

"Come on," Holly said, holding out her hand.

Beth took it instantly.

"Where are we going?" she asked.

"Palm Springs."

"Huh? Why?"

"If we hurry, we'll have an hour or two before the shops close."

"Shops?"

"Clothes," Holly said succinctly.

"Oh, yeah. You look about my age in that get-up, except for your hair."

Holly glanced in the mirror. Rumpled blue shirt and ragged jeans. Clodhopper shoes, no makeup, and her hair pulled back from her face.

She's right, Holly thought. *I barely look old enough to drive.*

Ruefully, she shook her head and patted her pockets to make sure her credit cards were in place.

"If Roger sees me like this," Holly said under her breath, "he'll disown me."

"Who's Roger?" Beth asked instantly.

"My boss."

"Oh. What kind of work do you do?"

"I'm a model."

Beth took a quick breath. Dismay showed clearly on her young features.

"Does Linc know?" she whispered.

"Yes," Holly said, "but he doesn't really believe it."

"Holly—" Beth's voice broke.

"I know."

"Do you?" she asked in a strained voice. "Linc *hates* models. His mother and mine were both models."

"Uh-huh. I know."

Beth made a distressed sound.

Holly smiled at Linc's sister with a cheerfulness that was pure bravado.

"Let's go shopping," Holly said. "Are you coming to the Arabian Nights party?"

"Wouldn't miss it."

"Knowing Linc, I'll bet you need something special to wear for the party."

Glumly Beth nodded. "But he won't let me buy anything unless he's along."

"You wouldn't turn down a gift from me, would you?"

"A gift?"

"Party clothes."

The younger girl brightened.

"Oh," Beth said. "Would you really?"

"Watch me. Does Linc still keep his car keys in the dish by the back door?"

"Uh-huh."

Holly drove one of Linc's cars, a bronze BMW coupe that was built for twisting mountain roads. The air was sultry. Vague hints of thunder muttered among the clouds and mountaintops.

As soon as Holly reached Palm Springs, she turned to Beth.

"Where to?" Holly asked.

"Oh, there are lots of places."

"Sure, but where's the best one?"

"For you?" Beth asked.

"For both of us."

The younger girl grinned.

"Turn left at the next light," she said eagerly.

Beth's choice was Chez Elegance. The small, exclusive boutique featured clothes that were suitable for teenagers as well as women over twenty.

Discreetly Holly checked the styles and fabrics at random. She was relieved to see that even the most avant-garde designs depended on quality rather than shock alone for their impact.

Beth went from rack to rack with an innocent greed that made Holly smile.

"See something you like?" Holly asked.

"Everything," she said, sighing. "This is the coolest store, but Linc never lets me buy anything here."

"Too expensive?"

"Too 'advanced,'" Beth said sarcastically.

"Trust me," Holly said. "When I'm through, you won't look like any more than you already are. Or any less."

An hour later they emerged from the shop with a loose, off-white silk blouse and a floor-length silk skirt of the same pale turquoise as Beth's eyes. There were thin, matching turquoise ribbons to braid into her hair. Delicate silver sandals with modest heels completed the outfit.

Beth was ecstatic. As soon as they were out

on the sidewalk, she clutched the packages to her body and whirled around and around, crowing her delight.

"What a wonderful homecoming present, Holly! I can't wait for the party! Jack's coming with his parents! Wait until he sees me! He'll—"

Beth's exuberant words stopped abruptly when she bumped into someone.

"Watch those big feet of yours," Cyn snapped.

Holly and Beth turned around as one.

"Sorry," mumbled Beth.

"There's nothing wrong with her feet," Holly said coolly. "She handles them better than you do your tongue."

Cyn's narrowed eyes took in Holly's blouse and jeans and shoes.

"A new ranch hand?" Cyn asked, turning to Beth.

The younger girl smiled with pure malice.

"Didn't Linc tell you this morning when he called from the barn?" Beth asked innocently. "Holly is going to be Mrs. Lincoln McKenzie."

Cyn's face changed, older now. And much harder.

"Listening in on the extension again?" she asked.

For a moment Beth looked uncomfortable.

"I'm not surprised," Cyn said. "Plain girls like you have to be sly. They have nothing else going for them."

Beth tried to hide how much Cyn's words

hurt, but couldn't. She simply wasn't old enough to match insults with someone like Cyn.

"If you take out those dark-blue contact lenses you always wear," Holly said distinctly, "you would see that Beth is beautiful."

Cyn's laughter was as light and delicate as her perfume.

"You've got to be kidding," Cyn said. "She's almost as plain as you are. Haven't you heard? Men like their women soft, petite, and round in all the right places."

"Especially the heels?" Holly suggested.

Cyn turned on her like a cat.

"Just because you saved Linc's life doesn't mean he wants you," Cyn said in a voice that cracked with anger. "He'll get tired of your Plain Jane innocence fast enough. He's all man. And face it, sweetie. You have all the sex appeal of a concrete slab."

"Concrete slab?" murmured Holly.

Her eyes were narrowed and every bit as hard as Cyn's.

"Come to the Arabian Nights ball," Holly invited. "Watch men stand in line to talk to me. And then I'll watch you wish you'd never been so blind and bitchy as to call Beth plain. Got that, *sweetie?*"

Cyn stared at Holly in disbelief.

"You couldn't get your mirror to look at you, much less a man," Cyn said.

Holly just smiled. The smile was as cold as her eyes.

"I'm coming to the ball," Cyn said, "but the men will be looking at me, not you. See you there. But you won't see me. I'll be buried in men."

The sound of Cyn's laughter drifted on the air even after she was halfway down the block.

"I hate her," Beth said in a strained voice. "I don't know what Linc sees in her."

Holly grimaced. She knew exactly what Linc saw in Cyn.

"He's accustomed to her, uh, face," Holly muttered.

Beth touched Holly's arm in silent sympathy.

"I'm sorry," Beth said in a small voice. "You didn't have to crawl out on a limb to defend me. I know I'm plain."

"You are not plain," Holly said, emphasizing each word.

A wan smile was Beth's only answer.

Guessing the source of her concern, Holly gave her a wink.

"Come on," Holly said. "Let's go to the hotel and pick up my stuff. You're going to be almost as surprised as Cyn when I do my caterpillar-to-butterfly act."

But nobody, Holly thought, *is going to be as surprised as Linc when Shannon rather than Holly shows up at the ball.*

It wasn't a happy thought.

Thunder burst overhead just as a gust of hot, humid wind washed over the land. The wind smelled of sand and dust and rain.

As one Beth and Holly hurried to the car.

They just beat the storm home. When Holly pulled into the driveway of the Mountains of Sunrise, lightning was stitching through the clouds overhead.

"Linc?" called Holly, as she walked into the kitchen.

No one answered.

"Still in the foaling barn, I'll bet," Beth said.

Holly nodded and sighed. She had decided on the drive back from Palm Springs to talk with Linc. Somehow she had to prepare him for the transformation of Holly into Shannon.

If I can just find the words. And the courage, Holly admitted to herself.

Surely he'll give me a chance to explain, to prove to him that not all models are heartless bitches.

Won't he?

"Holly? Are you okay? You look kind of odd."

"Just a little tired."

"You sure?"

Holly nodded.

Beth hesitated, then headed for her own bedroom, packages in hand. She stopped in the hall and looked over her shoulder.

"Are you sure you won't let me pay you back?" Beth asked. "Daddy left me money in my own name, even though Linc controls it until I'm eighteen."

"That outfit is my homecoming present for you."

"It's an awfully expensive present."

"Don't worry, honey," Holly said, smiling. "Every penny of it is going to come out of Sandra's hide."

"Yeah, Linc told me about that. What a bi— er, witch. She even kept my letters from you."

Holly's smile vanished. Without it, she looked remote, unapproachable, every inch the fighter life had forced her to be.

"You wrote to me, too?" Holly asked softly.

"Sure. Except for Linc, you were the only one who ever loved me."

Holly crossed the kitchen and hugged Beth hard, packages and all.

"I still love you," Holly said fiercely. "And I wrote to you."

Beth's eyes were bright with emotion.

"I love you, too," she said. "I wish Sandra had never come. Linc would have been happier and so would I."

"So would I," Holly said, releasing Beth.

Smiling, Beth looked at her.

"You know," Beth said, "if it hadn't been for Sandra, I bet I'd have been an aunt by now."

And Shannon would never have been born, Holly thought immediately.

Strangely, the idea disturbed her.

From the first, the glamorous Shannon mask had made Holly uneasy. That was why she had chosen to work under a name other than her own.

But the name itself was part of Holly—her middle name, her mother's maiden name.

Shannon.

From the beginning, Shannon had grown out of Holly's own needs, whether she admitted it at the time or not. Whatever Holly wasn't, Shannon was.

Shannon had never been orphaned at sixteen. Shannon had never wept to be beautiful so that the man she loved would notice her. Shannon had never been awkward or too tall. Shannon had never been lonely.

The list of their differences was endless.

Or is it? Holly asked herself for the first time.

Shannon didn't fall in bed or in love with the men who pursued her. Neither did Holly.

Shannon didn't want to be purchased and worn like a life-size charm on a rich man's bracelet. Neither did Holly.

Shannon dreamed of Linc, felt his skin beneath her palms, tasted him on her lips. So did Holly.

Shannon was intelligent, hard-working, and responsible. She wanted to be the best, and she was. She was the Royce Reflection.

And so am I, Holly thought.

Slowly, imperceptibly, the two expressions of her personality had grown together.

Or maybe it's just that I grew up, she thought. *I'm finally able to accept all of myself. I'm plain Holly and fancy Shannon—and so is every woman.*

But the essential inner person was the same no matter what the outside trappings, plain or fancy. The woman beneath the changing exterior was herself unchanging.

And that woman loved and wanted to be loved by only one man.

Lincoln McKenzie.

"Is the idea of having babies so boggling?" Beth asked.

Holly blinked, called out of her own thoughts. She smiled.

"Not at all," she said. "I'll just have to get Roger to design a line of maternity clothes."

"Your boss designs clothes?"

"No more questions about my boss or my work until midnight tomorrow," Holly said quickly.

"Ask you no questions and you'll tell me no lies?" Beth said, smiling, yet somehow tentative.

"I wouldn't lie to you. I haven't lied to Linc."

"Thank God," Beth said. "He hates that most of all."

Holly sighed.

"Well, I haven't told Linc all of the truth, either," she admitted. "But then, if your dear brother had twenty-twenty vision instead of blind prejudices, I wouldn't have to!"

Beth looked shocked, then laughed aloud.

"You're going to be good for him," Beth said. "He's too used to being the boss all the time."

Still laughing, Beth hurried off to her own room to hang up her prized new clothes.

"Come to my bedroom when you're finished," Holly called after her. "I have something to show you."

Holly took her own luggage and makeup

case to the guest room. Beth came in moments later. She poked through the makeup case while Holly unpacked.

By the time she was finished hanging up her clothes, Beth was elbow deep in makeup. When she looked up and saw Holly watching her, the expression on Beth's face was a combination of apology and sheer stubbornness.

Instead of saying anything, Holly sat down next to Beth on the bed.

"Well?" the younger girl asked defiantly.

"Well what?"

Beth looked at herself in the makeup case's mirrored lid.

"I like it," Beth said firmly.

Privately, Holly thought Beth looked wretched. Black eyebrows, black lashes, scarlet lips and cheeks, powder everywhere, burying her skin's normal healthy glow.

The makeup had been applied without thought to age, natural coloring or to the individual lines of Beth's face.

But Holly said nothing aloud. She had learned that using makeup correctly, like cooking or painting, was a learned skill. No one was born with it.

"Let me try something," Holly said in a mild voice.

She turned the mirror aside so that Beth couldn't watch what was happening. Then Holly removed makeup from half of Beth's face, sorted through the available cosmetics, and chose different colors.

"In class," Holly said, "we were told to put our normal makeup on half our face. Then the teacher came around and made up the other half."

As Holly talked, she worked quickly, her years of practice showing in each deft stroke.

"Makeup is as individual as the person wearing it," she said. "What I'm using on you now would look odd on you at twenty-five, ridiculous at thirty-five, and pathetic at forty-five."

Beth continued to look stubborn.

She and Linc are a real pair, Holly thought dryly. *But then, I'm no fragile little flower, either.*

"Each age has its own unique needs and beauty," Holly said. "But what I'm using now would look terrible on me at any age, including fifteen."

"Why?"

"The same reason most of the colors I wear would look terrible on you."

"What do you mean?" Beth asked.

"I'm dark," Holly said matter-of-factly. "You're blond. I have light brown eyes. You have light blue. My nose is off-center. Yours is perfect. You have lovely full lips. I don't. My cheekbones and eyes are too slanted—"

"Too slanted!" Beth interrupted in disbelief. "There's no such thing."

Holly just smiled.

"My face is triangular," she continued. "Yours is oval. In short, we need different makeup to bring out our special qualities."

"I don't have any 'special qualities' to bring out," Beth muttered gloomily.

"Sure you do. But you won't see them if they're buried under piles of makeup."

Holly worked in silence for a few more moments, concentrating on the mascara. She added a touch more blush to bring out Beth's cheekbones, examined the results, and nodded.

"Can I look now?" Beth asked.

"Sure."

Beth grabbed the makeup case and lifted the lid. For a long time she studied the two halves of her face.

"Boy," she said finally. "You know a lot more about makeup than I do."

With that the younger girl grabbed tissue and cold cream and wiped off the makeup that Holly hadn't applied. Then Beth studied her face again. Carefully she compared the right side, which had makeup, to the left side, which had none.

While Beth looked in the mirror, Holly undid the girl's right braid, leaving the left braid untouched. She brushed the freed half of Beth's shining, waist-length hair until it was smooth. Then Holly pulled the hair back from Beth's face and began styling it in different ways.

Finally Holly made loose French braids on the side and crown to keep the hair from overwhelming Beth's face. The remainder of the hair on the right side of her head was left free to fall in honey waves down the center of her back. The result was a simple yet sophisticated style that brought out the oval perfection of Beth's face.

"A shampoo and some hot rollers will take out the kinks from wearing pigtails," Holly said. "I have some earrings that will be perfect with your new skirt."

Belatedly she realized that Beth wasn't listening.

"Beth?"

"Huh?"

Then Beth blinked as though waking up and tore her glance away from the makeup mirror.

"Is that really me?" she whispered to Holly. "My eyes look so blue. And big. And my hair—I even like my hair! What did you do to my cheekbones? I don't look like a kid anymore. How did you do it?"

"Yes," said Linc's cold voice from the doorway. "Do tell me how you turned a sweet young kid into a tart."

Twelve

Beth froze, looking guilty and defiant at the same time.

Holly kept her back to the door and spoke as though Linc wasn't there.

"Hold the mirror so that you can watch," she said to Beth. "I'll show you what I did."

She put her fingers under Beth's chin and turned the pigtailed, plain side of her face toward Linc.

He drew in a swift, hard breath as he measured the difference in the two halves of his sister's face.

A closed, savage look settled over Linc's face. His whole stance changed. He was a stranger again, staring scornfully at a woman whose beauty offended him.

Holly's stomach turned to ice.

My God, she thought. *Linc knows Beth! He knows that she isn't selfish or cruel, yet he's looking at her like he hates her.*

It's the way he looked at Shannon.

It's the way he'll look at me when he finds out.

Only the helpless pleading in Beth's eyes kept Holly from losing her temper or crying out of despair.

Willing her hands not to tremble, she began applying a sheer foundation to the left side of Beth's face.

"No," Linc snarled. "You'll make her look like a two-dollar slut!"

The sound Beth made stopped him abruptly. Swearing beneath his breath, he fought for self-control.

It had never been harder for him to find it.

Without pigtails and a scrubbed face, Beth was the image of her beautiful, adulterous mother.

As though nothing had happened, Holly continued applying makeup with sure strokes.

"No more," Linc said curtly.

Holly didn't even pause. Nor did she look up from Beth's face.

"Holly, damn it!" he said.

"Are you calling off our truce?" she asked.

"If anyone is calling it off, you are," Linc retorted with cold fury.

In silence she compared the foundation she had just applied to what was already in place on the rest of Beth's face. The match was good. Holly picked up the pale brown eyebrow pencil.

"I'm not arguing," she said evenly. "You are. I haven't even raised my voice."

It took every bit of her professional poise to appear casual as she set aside the eyebrow pencil, picked up pale turquoise eye shadow, and turned back to Beth.

"A two-dollar floozy," Holly continued in a neutral voice, "wears brassy makeup and puts it on with a trowel."

"My point exactly," Linc shot back.

"This makeup," she said, "is chosen for subtlety and there isn't a trowel in sight."

His face became completely expressionless. He crossed his arms and leaned against the door. He looked unreasonably big, filling the opening.

"Beauty is as beauty does," he said flatly.

"No argument there," she said.

She reached for a pale, warm-toned eye shadow to blend with the turquoise.

"But you've done your best to keep Beth as plain as possible, haven't you?" Holly pointed out.

"You can bet on it."

"Why?" Holly asked softly. "Don't you trust her?"

"What the hell is that supposed to mean?"

Beth stirred at the whiplash of her brother's voice.

Holly pressed a hand over the younger girl's arm, silently urging her to stay where she was.

"I mean," Holly said, "that you've chosen Beth's clothes and hairstyle with an unerring eye—"

"Thank you," Linc interrupted sarcastically.

"—toward hiding the natural beauty that is

coming to Beth as she grows older," Holly finished.

His expression became even harder.

"She looked fine the way she was," he said coldly.

"To you, obviously. Beth wanted a different look."

"She isn't old enough to know what's good for her."

"And beauty can't be good?" Holly asked softly. "Is that what you're saying?"

Linc's mouth flattened into a line that was as thin and unyielding as a steel blade.

"Can't you see that even though the outside of Beth changes, the inside is still worthy of love?" Holly asked quietly.

Silence was his only answer.

"My God, Linc," Holly said, appalled. "You raised Beth. She's like your own daughter!"

"She is also her mother's daughter," he said savagely, "and her mother was a worthless slut."

"I hate you!" cried Beth.

She leaped up and ran out the door, tears streaming down her face.

Saying nothing, Linc and Holly listened to Beth race down the hallway to her bedroom. A door slammed shut. Hard.

With shaking hands, Holly packed up the case containing her cosmetics.

"Do you really think Beth is a slut?" she asked, her voice vibrant with rage.

"Of course not!"

"Then when you both cool off, I suggest you tell her that."

Holly snapped the makeup case shut. Then she stood and confronted Linc, holding the case protectively against her body. Her face was drawn into lines as unyielding as his.

"And what about me?" she asked.

"What do you mean?"

"When I get out of my childish clothes and hairstyles, when I put something more than soap on my face, will I become magically degraded in your eyes?"

"Holly—"

"Will a stylish dress," she continued relentlessly, "and a few strokes of an eyebrow pencil turn me into a worthless, lying, cheating slut?"

"Holly—"

"Will it?" she asked, her voice rising.

"Don't be ridiculous."

"Beauty is as beauty does, right?"

"Always," Linc said.

"Except," Holly said, "when beauty interferes with your prejudices. Then no matter what beauty does, beauty is a beast."

"I thought we had a truce," he said coldly.

"I'll gamble my own future on a truce," Holly shot back, "but I'm damned if I'll gamble Beth's!"

"What is that supposed to mean?"

"The way you're hounding Beth, you'll push her into tight clothes and back seats before the year is out."

"That's crap!"

"It's the truth," Holly cut in. "Beth is becoming a woman."

"Jesus, do you think I haven't noticed?"

"Then stop trying to turn back the clock."

"She's only fifteen!" Linc snarled.

"Nearly sixteen. Just how old did you say I was when you first noticed me as something other than a child? Fourteen?"

"That has nothing to do with Beth."

"It has everything to do with her. Girls mature more quickly than boys. Beth wants to be as beautiful as she can be for her young man."

"I want her to be Beth, that's all," Linc said. "Just Beth. That's good enough for any man."

"We're not talking about men," Holly said. "We're talking about Beth. Her desire to catch Jack's eye is as simple and natural as breathing. If you try to make Beth hold her breath, you'll get a backlash that could ruin her life."

"That's exactly what I'm trying to avoid and you know it."

"Yes. But you're going about it in the wrong way. Beth is a good, bright, loving, very stubborn person. Show her how to be the kind of woman a man can trust with his love."

"I'm trying to," he said evenly.

"By keeping her in pigtails?"

"By keeping her from turning out like her mother."

"Haven't you been listening? *Beth is not like her mother.*"

"Then why are you trying to make her look like she is?" retorted Linc. "Any man worth the name can look past Beth's outside."

"Assuming that he sees Beth in the first place."

"What?"

"How many good, kind, *plain* women have you given a second look to?" Holly asked sweetly. "Besides me, of course."

He said nothing. There was nothing he could say, and both of them knew it.

She laughed without humor.

"Then there's Cyn," Holly said. "She wears enough paint for a barn. Why is it all right for her to be beautiful and all wrong for Beth or me?"

"Cyn can wear paint and tight clothes and rub all over men because she's a . . . toy. No grown man will fall in love with a toy, no matter how perfectly it's wrapped. So," Linc said, smiling narrowly, "why not enjoy the wrappings?"

"I see your point," Holly murmured. "Having a plain wife would be so boring a man would need to unwrap some fancy toys from time to time."

"That's not what I meant at all!"

Linc crossed the room and put his hands on Holly's arms as though he was afraid that she, too, would run away from him.

"You aren't plain, Holly."

"I know that," she said calmly. "But do you? Do you really believe that I'm as beautifully wrapped as Cyn?"

"You don't have to be," he said roughly.

"Wives have enough power over their husbands without that."

Linc put his hand on her abdomen in a gesture that was both possessive and gentle.

"What do you think it does to a man to know that someday his baby will grow inside his woman?" he asked.

Holly shivered and breathed his name.

"What do you think it does to a man when a woman cares enough to risk her neck dragging him out of a lightning storm?" Linc asked. "What do you think it does to a man when he goes to sleep with her taste in his mouth and wakes up to her sleepy smile? My God, Holly. Next to those things, beauty is just a cruel joke."

"Physical beauty has nothing to do with those things," she said desperately. "Beauty doesn't make them happen and beauty doesn't prevent them from happening."

"You're wrong," he said flatly. "I know a lot more about beautiful bitches than you do."

"The words *beautiful* and *bitch* don't mean the same thing!"

Linc let go of Holly and strode to the dresser. He yanked open a drawer, pulled out a framed photo, and walked back to her.

"Here," he said, shoving the photo into her hands. "My mother."

Holly looked down.

The woman in the photograph was extraordinary.

She had radiant skin pulled taut over bone

structure that would give her face elegance until the day she died. Her hair was thick, long,
framing her perfect features in a chestnut cas-
cade. Her eyes were large, set well apart and
jade green. Her mouth was wide, invitingly
curved, poised on the brink of a smile or a kiss.

Yet there was more than that. There was a
quality to the woman's appeal that was
uniquely female, hinting at the kind of sexual-
ity that set men's imagination on fire.

"She is . . . the most stunning woman I've
ever seen," Holly said finally.

"Yeah." His mouth twisted bitterly. "Mother
had me five months after she and Dad were
married. At the time, he was a big agent in Hollywood. She was a model who wanted to be a
star."

"I can see why. The camera loves her."

Linc's lips thinned into a grim smile.

"There wasn't much call for pregnant star-
lets," he said, "so it's obvious I was an accident. I was five weeks old when Dad's father
died and left the ranch to him."

Holly looked up at Linc. It was like seeing
an intensely masculine version of the picture in
her hands. He had the same charisma, the same
quality of drawing eyes no matter where he
was or what he was wearing.

"Dad was happy to come here," Linc said.
"He hadn't liked being an agent, but he and
Grandfather had never gotten along."

"And your mother?"

"She didn't want to come here. My earliest

memories are of them yelling about Garner Valley versus Hollywood."

Linc ran his hand through his dark hair, so like that of his mother, thick and chestnut and lustrous. Even his eyes looked like hers now, green with leashed emotion.

"By the time I was three," he said, "Mother was back to modeling. At least, that's what she called it. I suppose she even wore clothes from time to time. Dad didn't buy them, though."

Holly's eyelids flickered at the pain in Linc's voice.

"Paying off inheritance taxes almost broke him," he said. "He kept the ranch, but nothing else. And he worked. My God, how he worked. Dawn to dark and then some."

"It must have been hard for them," Holly said hesitantly.

"Not for her. Not that one. She went to Palm Springs. There wasn't any money for baby-sitters so she'd take me along on her 'modeling assignments.' "

Holly forced herself to breathe. The scorn in his voice would have etched metal.

"I don't know how old I was when I realized my mother wasn't modeling clothes in those motel rooms," Linc said. "After that, I spent a lot of hours locked in cars in motel parking lots."

Tears burned against Holly's eyes, but she said nothing. She sensed that if she interrupted him now he would never speak about it again.

"I was seven when she locked me in the last time," he said.

His eyes looked through Holly, focused on a past that was too painful to remember and too savage to forget.

"It was hot in the car," he said. "God, it was hot. I waited and waited for her to come back. I finally fell asleep. When I woke up, it was dark and cold and I was shivering."

Seven, Holly thought in horror. *He was only seven, locked in a car in the desert. He could have died.*

"I waited," Linc said. "No one came. I wanted to get out of that car, but I knew my beautiful mother would raise welts on me if I did."

Holly bit her lips against the words she wanted to speak and the fear welling up in her soul as she realized just how deep his hatred of beauty went.

And how harshly learned it was.

"It's hard to believe how scared a kid can get," Linc said, his voice neutral. "By the time my dad found me the next morning, I was a mess."

Holly wanted to stop Linc from speaking, because knowing what had happened to him wounded her in ways she couldn't describe.

Tears welled up and fell silently down Holly's cheeks, but she made no move toward Linc. She said nothing, did nothing. She simply listened with a grief that equalled his.

He had kept the words and the hatred inside

for too many years, poisoning his own possibilities for love because his father had married the wrong women.

Beautiful women.

"I never saw my mother again," Linc said. "Seems she ran off with one of her men. I don't even know if she's still alive. Not that it matters. She never wanted me and I learned to live without her."

He shrugged, but his eyes were still focused on the past.

"Dad didn't learn much at all," Linc said bluntly. "Three years later he married Jan. I don't have a picture of Beth's mother. I don't need one. Honey blond, slim yet fully female, turquoise eyes, eighteen when they married. Beautiful? Hell yes, she was beautiful."

Holly forced herself to breathe through the pain clenching her heart. Linc spoke the word beauty as though it inevitably meant cold, selfish, immoral.

Cruel.

"I was fifteen when Beth was born," he continued. "Jan had been a model in some of the better Palm Springs stores before she got pregnant. When Beth was two months old, Jan went back to modeling."

Numbly, Holly waited, listening. Enduring.

"Jan liked the money that the ranch was finally bringing in," he said, "but she didn't like the ranch itself. She ignored Beth. She didn't even like Dad to hold his daughter. All I can figure is that Jan was jealous of her own kid."

Holly looked down at her hands. They ached from being clenched together to keep from touching Linc. She wanted to hold him, to comfort him, to love him. She wanted to wave a magic wand and make the ugly past vanish so that it couldn't throw grotesque shadows over the future.

Her future.

Their future.

But it was too late for that. It had been too late before Holly was even born.

"I pretty much raised Beth," Linc said. "Jan was too obsessed with her looks to see anything or anyone else, and Dad—"

Linc stopped talking abruptly. Then he shrugged again. The movement was tight, as though he was shifting a load he had carried so long he no longer noticed its weight.

"Dad drank a lot by then," he said. "I took over more and more of the ranch. Jan spent more and more time in front of the mirror, looking for the first wrinkle, and Dad found the bottom of a lot of bottles."

Holly swallowed against the tears that were choking her.

And the fear.

"Somewhere along in there," Linc said, "Jan started having men on the side. Dad didn't admire her enough, I guess. I sure as hell didn't admire her as much as she wanted, even when she walked into my room dead naked late one night."

Holly made a small sound, but he didn't

hear. His face was utterly cold, rigid with contempt.

"Jan was a real bitch," he said coolly. "When she couldn't get Dad and me to fight over her, she started bragging about her men to us, giving us all the details. And I mean all of them."

Holly made a ragged sound that was Linc's name.

He didn't hear. He was lost to her, caught in the past.

"One night Jan picked up the wrong man," Linc said. "He slapped her around, she called Dad, and he went to get her. On the way back home Dad lost control of the car on a bad curve."

For the first time Linc's eyes focused on Holly.

"Your parents were killed because my stepmother was a slut all the way to her corrupt soul. If she hadn't died in that crash, I'd have killed her myself. She wasn't worth one tear on your face, *niña*. Not then, not now."

"I'm not crying for her," whispered Holly.

Blindly she went to Linc, buried her face against his chest, and held on with a strength that surprised both of them.

"Tomorrow," she said in a choked voice, "tomorrow please don't hold those women against me."

"You aren't like them."

"Remember that. And you aren't like your father. You're strong. He wasn't."

"Holly—"

"No," she interrupted desperately. "You have to listen to me. I'm not like your mother or stepmother. You must believe that. Even when you see me tomorrow, *you must believe that.*"

Linc's mouth moved gently over Holly's, tasting her tears.

"Of course I'll believe it," he said.

"Will you?" she asked in a despairing voice, feeling empty and afraid. "Oh, Linc, you don't know how beautiful I can be."

Before he could answer, the phone rang in his office just off the master bedroom.

"It must be Shadow Dancer again," he said. "That particular phone is connected to the barn."

Holly nodded and let go of him.

Slowly he released her in turn and went to answer the phone. His voice carried easily to her, for the office was connected to the master bedroom just across the hall from her.

"What's that?" he said. "Shadow Dancer is down again? What about the foal? Okay. I'm on my way."

He hung up and started for the door. Once in the hall, he hesitated.

"It's all right," Holly said. "Go see to your mare."

"I'd ask you to come with me, but it could be . . . difficult."

"Go," she said softly. "I understand."

Linc gave her a searching look, nodded, and moved swiftly away from her.

For a long time Holly stood motionless but for the tears running down her face, sensing midnight coming at her like a runaway train.

There was nothing she could do but wait for it to hit.

Time only ran one way, and it was running out.

Thirteen

"Holly, are you awake?"

Beth's voice brought Holly out of a restless sleep. She rolled over in the huge bed and kicked off the comforter she didn't remember pulling over herself.

"I'm awake," Holly said.

"Can I come in?"

"Sure."

Holly rubbed her neck, trying to take out the tension that knotted her tendons.

She felt awful. Her clothes were wrinkled and awry. She had fallen asleep while waiting for Linc to come back from the barn. She had been determined to tell him that Holly was also a model called Shannon.

But Linc hadn't come back.

Beth walked in, carrying a cordless phone. She took one look at Holly and stopped.

"Are you awake enough to talk to your boss?" Beth asked doubtfully.

Holly stretched, then rolled her head, trying to relieve the tension in her neck muscles.

"Sure, why not?" she said wearily.

She reached for the phone.

Beth put it on the bed and turned to leave.

"Stick around," Holly said. "I may need first aid when he's finished with me."

She smiled, but her voice was serious. She knew that Roger wouldn't be happy when he found out where she was staying.

Camping alone was one thing.

Living with a man was something else entirely.

Yesterday she had left a message at the hotel telling Roger that she could be reached at the home of Lincoln McKenzie. She had also instructed that, until further notice, Roger was to call her Holly. Period.

If anyone told Linc about Shannon, she didn't want it to be the "tame Viking."

"Are you supposed to be working?" Beth asked. "Is that why your boss will be mad?"

"No. It's just that Roger won't be happy to know I'm with Linc."

"Is Roger your boyfriend?"

Holly shook her head.

"He thought he wanted to be," she explained. "He really doesn't, but I sometimes have a hard time convincing him."

"Will he fire you over Linc?" Beth asked, wide-eyed.

Smiling again, Holly reached for the phone.

"I doubt it," she said. "I'm too good at what I do. Roger will just be prickly for a while."

She flipped the switch that activated the receiver and the speaker. Beth would be able to hear Roger as clearly as Holly could.

"Hi, Roger," she said. "You're up early."

"It's ten o'clock in Manhattan. I've been on the phone with Sandra since six," Roger said. "How was the camping trip?"

"Wet, stormy, and thoroughly wonderful."

There was a distinct pause.

"Is the name Lincoln McKenzie familiar to me?" Roger asked.

"He manages Hidden Springs," she said, yawning. "Remember?"

"I remember you said that there was nothing between you and that hard-eyed cowboy."

Beth smothered a giggle behind her hand, guessing that Linc was the hard-eyed cowboy in question.

Holly winked at her.

"I didn't think there was," she said.

"And there is now?"

"Yes."

There was a long silence.

Then, softly Roger asked, "Is he good for you?"

Sudden tears tightened her throat. Roger was worried about her rather than angry with her. He might want her as a lover, but he was also her friend.

"I've loved Linc since I was nine," Holly said simply. "We were separated when my parents died and Sandra brought me to New York."

"First love. Bloody hell." Roger laughed curtly. "Who can compete with that?"

"There's no question of competition," she said. "There never was. Ever."

"Are you sure? Frankly, he looked like a pretty hard piece of business to me."

"I'm sure."

"Well," Roger said unhappily, "as long as you still model for me, I'll try to be a good sport."

"Roger, I'd model for you even if I didn't have a contract. Not only do I like you, but you also create the most incredible clothes in the world. It's exciting just to be around them."

"Thank God. It's too late to replace you, Shan—er, Holly."

"I'd kill the model who tried."

Roger laughed, obviously pleased.

And relieved.

"When you get tired of living with the devil," he said, "there's a fair-haired angel who will be glad to lick your wounds."

"Linc isn't a devil."

"From what I saw a few days ago, he'll do until Old Nick comes along," Roger said dryly.

"Roger," she began.

"But I didn't call to argue about McKenzie's devilish looks," Roger interrupted.

Holly let out a soundless breath of relief.

"Okay," she said. "What's up?"

"I'm putting off the Hidden Springs shoot for now."

"Why?"

"Weather," he said succinctly.

Holly frowned.

"We're going to Cabo San Lucas instead," Roger said. "The satellite forecast and the local weather shaman assure me it's hot, dry, and sandy there."

"As opposed to hot, *wet*, and sandy here?" she asked with a lightness she didn't feel.

"Right."

Holly twisted the corner of her blouse between her fingers and wondered what to do. She loved her work, but she didn't want to leave Linc.

Especially not now, with so much unresolved between them.

"How much time before we leave and how long are we staying?" she asked finally.

"We'll leave sometime in the next week," Roger said. "I can't be more specific, because I'm having trouble choosing the male model."

"What happened to the last pretty face? He had wonderful gray eyes."

"He broke his wrist climbing rocks for a cigarette ad."

Holly just shook her head.

"I'm going to look at a few more models today," Roger said. "If I don't see anything I like, I'll try something new."

She grimaced. She remembered the last time he had tried "something new."

"No more dumb jocks, please," Holly said. "Smart ones, yes."

"Where's your sense of adventure? That

piece of beefcake you're referring to sold a lot of jogging clothes."

"He also kept tackling me," she said acidly.

"So his eyesight was better than his IQ."

"Have you thought of using Linc?" Holly asked, only half joking.

"Love must be blind."

"Excuse me?"

"Lincoln McKenzie looks like your desert mountains," Roger said bluntly. "Big, hard, and definitely not for the uninitiated. I like to think my products are a bit more civilized."

Beth was caught between indignation and laughter. Laughter won. She buried her face in a pillow.

"What's that?" he asked. "Sounds like you're choking on a bite of toast."

Holly laughed softly.

"That is Linc's younger sister," she explained.

"Oops," Roger said. "Sorry about that, love."

"No problem. Beth thinks Linc can look pretty rough, too, but that's only when he's mad. The rest of the time he is a pussycat."

"*Felis leo*, no doubt," Roger said dryly. "I've seen his kind on safari in Africa. Or behind bars. Safer that way."

Holly groaned and gave up.

"At least come to the party we're having tonight," she said.

"Sorry, love," he said, meaning it. "I don't think I can. Mrs. L'Acara—remember her, the Queen of Diamonds?—called and invited four models plus yours truly to come to a rodeo or some such thing.''

Holly blinked. ''Rodeo? Are you certain?''

''A horse auction, barbecue, and black-tie ball is how she described it. Naturally I accepted. It sounded so terribly improbable and utterly American.''

''It also sounds like I'll be seeing you in a few hours,'' Holly said, looking toward Beth.

Beth nodded and whispered, ''Mrs. L'Acara called yesterday and made arrangements for five more.''

''What's that?'' Roger asked.

''Mrs. L'Acara is bringing you to the McKenzies' Arabian Nights gala,'' Holly explained.

''Speak of the devil,'' murmured Roger. ''Well, I'll polish my best set of horns and give the old boy his due.''

''Roger—'' she began.

''All right, love. That's my limit on sour grapes.''

''I hope so.''

''Save a dance for me, beautiful lady.''

Roger hung up before Holly could answer.

''Your boss really likes you, doesn't he?'' Beth asked.

''He's a friend. No more.'' She smiled. ''And no less. You'll like him, Beth. And I know he'll like you.''

''Why?''

''Roger always likes beautiful women.''

She yawned again. "What's on the agenda for the morning?"

"Linc's still with the mare. She keeps starting labor and then stopping."

"Poor Linc."

"Poor everyone. He'll be in a lousy mood for the party."

"He never was much for parties anyway, if I remember correctly," Holly said.

"That's not the worst of it," Beth said.

"What could be worse than Linc in a snit?"

"Mrs. Malley called last night," Beth said. "Her sister is in intensive care. I told her to stay in Palm Springs."

Holly gave the girl a sidelong look.

"That's all right, isn't it?" Beth asked anxiously. "We can handle the party without the housekeeper, can't we?"

"Looks like we get the chance to try," Holly said, smiling. "I'll meet you in the kitchen in ten minutes."

"Out back," Beth corrected. "I'll bring you some coffee and a bag of granola for breakfast. No time for anything more."

"That bad, huh?"

"That bad," Beth said ruefully.

Ten minutes later, freshly showered and dressed, Holly met Beth out back. Silently the girl handed over the promised breakfast.

Munching granola and sipping coffee, Holly watched workmen. At the moment they were swarming over the ballroom-sized platform that had been erected in the McKenzies' huge backyard. They were setting up an enormous black, red, and silver tent.

Holly looked at Beth.

"Rain expected?" she asked.

"Yeah. What a pain."

Out beyond the pool's extensive decks and plantings, two barbecue pits had been dug. A side of beef and a whole pig were cooking slowly. The bartender had set up his station on the side patio amid tubs of fragrant flowers.

Although the auction didn't begin until one o'clock, people had been arriving since nine. For the most part they stayed in the sales barn, checking out the horses.

Inevitably, some people were more interested in visiting than in buying horses.

Holly wasn't even halfway through her first cup of coffee before workmen began trotting up to ask questions. Guests wandered up, interrupting with other questions.

Beth handled most of the guests. Holly handled most of the rest.

By noon Holly was frustrated and impatient. She had soothed caterers, chatted with unwanted guests, acted as lifeguard at the pool for two children whose mother couldn't say no, told another couple that their five poodles couldn't run free among the Arabians, and generally tried to put out brushfires as they flared up.

She had done everything but see Linc, her own personal brushfire.

Each time she started for the foaling barn, a

workman grabbed her and started asking where to put this and what to do with that. She had to bite down hard on her first, irritated responses about where to put everything.

By three o'clock, Holly was determined to get to the barn no matter who tried to stop her.

She wasn't even out of the backyard when a hand grabbed her arm. She turned like a cat, not bothering to hide the anger she felt.

"Can't it wait?" she snapped.

Then she saw Beth's dismayed look.

"Sorry," Holly said. "I didn't know it was you. I've been trying to see Linc since nine and people keep grabbing my arm."

"That's why I'm here," Beth said. "He called from the barn. Shadow Dancer finally came through."

"A live foal?" she asked hopefully.

"A filly. Mother and daughter are doing fine."

"Thank God. Sometimes with such a long birth, the foal doesn't make it." Holly rubbed her neck, working on knots. "How did Linc sound?"

"Tired," Beth said. "He apologized for losing his temper last night. I apologized, too. But . . ."

"But?"

"It doesn't change how either one of us feels, does it? I mean, I still want to look older than ten and he still wants me to look like a kid. It just isn't fair."

"Not much is," Holly said wearily. "Give Linc time, honey. He needs to learn that beauty isn't beastly."

Beth looked stubborn.

"Does that mean you won't do my hair or makeup for the dance tonight?" she asked.

"Of course not. Eight o'clock, as agreed."

Beth held out her hand. "It's a deal."

Holly took the girl's hand firmly.

"Partners in crime," Holly said in a wry tone.

"What crime is that?" asked a deep voice behind her. "Stealing candy?"

She turned around and smiled rather warily at Linc.

"Don't ask unless you want to suspend the truce again," she warned.

"I didn't want to suspend it last night. I'm sure as hell not up to a battle now."

Yawning, Linc rubbed his hand through his hair.

The weariness in his face tugged at Holly's heart. She stood on tiptoe and kissed him gently on the lips.

"Truce, then," Holly said. "I'm not feeling very feisty myself."

He pulled her closer.

"Bad night's sleep?" he asked.

"Uh-huh."

"That's what happens when you sleep alone," he said too softly for Beth to overhear.

The caterer called out to Holly from across the yard.

She ignored him.

The man crossed the lawn toward her with quick, determined strides.

She groaned. "Damn that creature. He clings like lint."

"I'll take care of it," Beth said, heading for the man.

"He's probably complaining about the kitchen again," Holly said. "Only one microwave."

"If he needed two microwaves, he should have brought one of his own."

"That's what I told him."

"Then he'll get to hear it all over again. From a McKenzie!"

With a poise and determination far beyond her years, Beth confronted the caterer.

Linc grabbed Holly's hand and pulled her toward the house. Together they tiptoed through the kitchen and up the stairs, avoiding guests and workmen alike.

When they reached his bedroom, Linc put the cordless phone out in the hall and shut the door. Then he stretched long and hard, flexing his back and arms.

Slowly he began to unbutton his shirt. He winced as he shrugged out of the long sleeves.

Holly remembered the storm, the lightning, Linc kicking free of a falling horse and landing against stone.

"Are you still sore?" she asked.

"Just stiff. Shadow Dancer was going to have that foal standing up or know the reason why."

"Too bad you speak English instead of equine. You could have told her the score."

Smiling wryly, Linc flexed his back again.

"She had it lying down, finally," he said. "After a while, she got the hang of it and I could let go of her head."

Holly measured the weariness lining his face.

This isn't the time to bring up Shannon, she thought unhappily. *Linc is too tired to be rational about the subject of beautiful models.*

And he had to be rational if there was any hope for their future together.

"What you need is a rubdown," Holly said.

"Just like a horse, huh?"

"Fortunately, you're somewhat smaller. Barely."

Linc smiled. "I'm a lot bigger than the newest horse on the place."

Laughing, she walked past him toward the bathroom. She came back with the bottle of scented oil she had used after her own shower.

"You'll have to wash off afterward," she said, "but for now you can just hold your nose."

Linc inhaled as Holly came close.

"Smells fresh, clean," he said. "Like you."

With a muffled sigh, he lay facedown in the middle of a big bed. The only way she could reach him was to get on the bed and put a knee on either side of his hips, straddling him like a horse.

She moved into place unselfconsciously,

warmed some oil in her hands, and went to work. She started with the long, resilient muscles of his back, kneading from the waist upward.

She leaned hard into the massage, for his muscles were as strong as they were tight.

Linc groaned.

"Too hard?" Holly asked.

"Too wonderful. Who taught you how to do this?"

"My ballet teacher. We were always pulling muscles or straining something, so he taught us how to rub out the kinks."

She worked in silence for a few minutes, admiring the lines of Linc's back. His spine was a valley just wide and deep enough to accept her fingertip. On either side rose ridges of muscle that were well defined without being bulky.

He was built like a professional swimmer, with long, smooth muscles that were both supple and powerful.

Carefully Holly placed one elbow over a particularly knotted part of Linc's back. She leaned down, applying a steadily increasing pressure to the knot with her elbow.

He groaned again, but it wasn't a complaint.

She warmed more oil and eased forward to knead his shoulders and arms and hands right down to his fingertips. The sighs and murmurs of appreciation he gave made her smile.

As the minutes went by, Holly worked over Linc until her hands and wrists ached, but she didn't really notice. There was a purely sensual

pleasure in touching him that was almost hypnotic.

Until Linc, she had never thought of a man
as beautiful. Handsome, yes. Pretty, all too often, especially in the modeling business. But
never beautiful.

Yet there was no other way she could describe Linc except in terms of beauty, a potent
masculine beauty that enthralled her the same
way deserts and mountains and storms did.

Long after his muscles had relaxed beneath
her hands, she continued stroking him. Finally
she sighed, flexed her fingers, and began working on his legs.

After a few moments Holly made an exasperated sound. The thick fabric of the jeans not
only felt unpleasant to her, it prevented her
from following the line of Linc's muscles to
work out the knots.

"Are you asleep?" she whispered.

His back shook with silent laughter.

"Not likely, *niña*."

"Anytime your back is that tight, so are your
hips and legs."

"So?"

Holly slid off his legs and stood up.

"So the jeans have to go," she said.

Linc rolled onto his side. He propped his
head on his fist and looked at her with smoky
hazel eyes.

"If I take off my pants," he said, "it won't be
to get my legs rubbed."

"Sure it will." Holly smiled. "Trust me."

He rolled onto his back and stretched, watching her out of half-open eyes. Without warning his arms shot out.

Before she realized what was happening, she was lifted off her feet and pulled over his body like a blanket. His legs wrapped around her ankles, imprisoning her.

She felt the heat and unmistakable hardness of his arousal pressing against her.

"It's me I don't trust," Linc said bluntly. "You make me lose my head."

Fourteen

Holly opened her mouth to answer Linc, but it was impossible. He had pulled her lips down against his and was giving her the kind of kiss that made her whole body tighten with pleasure.

She didn't fight the heady embrace. She gave herself to his passion as freely as rain gives itself to the desert.

Slowly his tongue searched her mouth. With intense concentration he traced the delicate serrations of her teeth and probed the soft interior of her lips.

Then he made a sound deep in his throat. Reluctantly he pulled his mouth away.

"I want you more each time I look at you," Linc said huskily. "If it was anyone else but you, what I feel would scare the hell out of me."

The ache that had never left Holly changed suddenly into a lightning stroke of desire. As she shuddered, her hips moved over his hard body in an instinctive, sensuous caress.

"It's the same for me," Holly said. "It always has been. I dream of you, Linc."

She lowered her mouth to his, tasting him with slow, thorough strokes. His hands slid beneath her blouse until the tips of her breasts were caught between his fingers. She twisted against him, crying out with need and pleasure.

Abruptly his hands moved, stroking down her back, fitting her over him. His long, powerful fingers cupped her hips hard against his own, rocking her, turning all of her body into one long caress over his aroused flesh.

Hunger and pleasure burst through Holly. The explosion of sensations just made the ache worse. She dug her nails into his arms out of sheer frustration.

"I want your hands to touch me everywhere," she said. "I want to touch you the same way. I want your mouth to know all of me. I want mine to know all of you."

"Holly," Linc said raggedly. "My God."

"I want your body to be part of mine," she said, her voice shaking.

The kiss he gave her then was like nothing she had ever experienced before. Hard, urgent, almost violent.

Holly didn't object. She wanted Linc in the same way. She wanted to sink into him like a rainstorm into the desert, joining them until there was no Linc, no Holly, only a net of lightning and ecstasy surrounding them like thunder.

When he suddenly rolled aside, she could

have wept in frustration. For a moment there was only the harsh sound of their breathing.

His eyes were closed, his muscles rigid along his jaws, his hands clenched into fists.

"Don't you want me, Linc?" Holly asked raggedly, her voice caught between tears and desire.

With a swift, savage motion, he took her hand and pressed it hard against his abdomen.

Beneath her palm, the reality of his desire was heavy, blunt, rigid.

"What do you think?" he asked through his clenched teeth.

"Then why did you stop?"

When Linc's eyes opened they were more green than hazel, burning with barely contained passion. He was shocked by his lack of control with Holly.

She's a virgin, he reminded himself savagely. *Somehow I'll have to keep a better leash on my own hunger, or I'll end up hurting her instead of giving her pleasure.*

"I want your first time to be perfect," Linc said.

"From what I hear, that's not likely."

He didn't argue. He was afraid she was right.

"But I'm told the second and third and the fourth times make up for it," Holly said, smiling slowly. "Not to mention all the others."

Linc drew a long, uneven breath. Holly's smile was like paradise shimmering just beyond his reach, promising sweet, wild oblivion.

"I don't want to make love to you with one

ear on the door, waiting for some fool guest to barge in," he said.

"I'll lock it."

"I don't want to love you just once and then have to get out of bed and be host to hundreds of people."

"Half a loaf—" she began.

"And I for damn sure don't want to smell like the bottom of the barn while I'm loving you," he interrupted.

Holly nuzzled Linc's chest.

"You smell like Romance to me," she countered.

He lifted one eyebrow in silent query.

She smiled and pointed to the bottle of scented oil on the bedside table.

"Romance," she said.

With a swift, powerful motion, he rolled out of bed, beyond the reach of temptation.

Of her.

"Only the top half of me smells good," Linc said. "The jeans could stand up and walk without me."

"Have you heard of that modern convenience called a shower?" she asked.

She got up and walked to the door that connected the master bedroom with the office. She slid the bolt home. Without looking at him, she walked to the hall door. The bolt clicked into place.

Then Holly turned with all of her model's

grace and walked toward Linc. With each step her fingers undid another button of her blouse.

"Now, about that shower ... ." she said.

For an instant Holly thought Linc was going to agree.

And so did he.

Then he swore, stepped into the bathroom, and quickly locked the door behind him.

Holly leaned against the door, letting the cool wood soothe her flushed body.

"Linc?" she whispered, knowing he couldn't hear unless he, too, was leaning against the door.

He was.

"I have to show horses on the auction block in ten minutes," he said. "If that's enough time for you"—the lock clicked open—"then come in."

"You're the expert," she said. "Is that enough time?"

"For some women, it's nine minutes more than I'd care to spend. For you, I'd want at least a lifetime."

"Starting when?" Holly groaned. "Damn it, Linc, you're not being fair!"

He laughed softly.

"You're not the only one who's hurting, *niña*. I'll make it up to you tonight. To both of us. Truce?"

Holly set her teeth and pushed away from the door.

"Truce," she muttered. "Damn it!"

She buttoned her blouse and went to find the caterer.

If the man still wanted to argue about microwaves, she was ready to oblige.

Beth fidgeted, unable to contain her excitement.

"Can I look yet?" she asked.

Smiling, Holly unwrapped a long strand of blond hair from a fat roller.

"Not quite yet," she said.

"What are you doing?"

"Brushing the hair that I didn't braid."

"I'm so excited," Beth whispered.

"Really?" teased Holly. "I'd never guessed it."

"You're as bad as Linc."

"Sit still or it will take twice as long."

Beth grimaced and tried to sit still. It wasn't possible.

"Jack's here already," she said. "Isn't he wonderful?"

Holly tried to remember one special face out of the group of teenagers who had arrived just in time for the barbecue.

"I must have missed him," she admitted. "Which one is he?"

"The good-looking one."

"They all looked pretty good to me."

Beth giggled.

"He was standing next to the little redhead," she said. "She's my best friend."

"Oh, *that* good-looking one."

Holly untied the cloth she had used to protect Beth's clothes while makeup was applied.

"Okay," Holly said. "Stand up and be counted."

With a subdued squeal, Beth leaped up and hurried toward the mirrored sliding doors that covered the guest room closet.

"Oh. . . ." She sighed.

It was all she could say. Her eyes widened as she looked at her own image in disbelief.

Hair the color of late-afternoon sunlight fanned over the silk of her blouse and curled over the gentle swell of her breasts. The turquoise skirt fell in graceful folds from her slim waist to the tips of her silver sandals. Tiny drop earrings glowed like an echo of her turquoise eyes.

"I can't believe it," she said. "I'm actually pretty!"

Smiling, Holly smoothed a last lock of blond hair into place.

"You're more than that," she said. "You're beautiful, Beth."

A shadow passed over the younger girl's face.

"I look like my mother," she said, her voice suddenly empty.

Holly ached at the pain that darkened Beth's eyes.

"Was she . . ." Beth hesitated, then finished in a rush, as though if she spoke quickly it wouldn't hurt so much. "Was she really a bad woman?"

Holly couldn't lie and didn't want to tell the truth.

"Your mother was a very unhappy woman," she said finally. "Unhappy people do unhappy things."

For a moment Beth looked much older than her fifteen years.

"And I look like her," she said starkly.

"That's just the outside. You're a good person, Beth. Whatever your mother was or wasn't has nothing to do with what you are today."

"Linc doesn't believe that."

"Two beautiful women hurt him very badly."

"Yes," Beth whispered.

"So I guess it will take two other beautiful women to teach Linc that beauty and cruelty don't mean the same thing."

Holly tipped Beth's face up and studied the girl's clear eyes.

"Will you help me teach him?" Holly asked.

Slowly Beth nodded.

"Good," Holly said. "Now it's time for me to do my caterpillar-to-butterfly act. Wait for me?"

Beth looked surprised, but agreed immediately.

"Sure," she said. "Can I help?"

"Nope. I want to surprise you, too."

Beth laughed, but she went and turned on the bedroom's small TV without arguing.

Holly closed the bathroom door behind her. She had showered and set her hair earlier. All that remained was to put on her dress and makeup, and comb out her hair.

Moving quickly, she took her favorite outfit out of its opaque traveling bag. As always, the long black dress delighted her. Its lines were simple and elegant. The neckline was a wide, shallow curve that stretched from shoulder to shoulder. The bodice fitted her like a shadow of her own beauty.

There was no back, simply a black fall of silk from waist to ankle. The skirt swung enticingly with each movement of her body.

Inset at the bottom of each short sleeve was an inverted V strung with loops of unbelievably fine gold chain. The chains were repeated in a diamond shape between Holly's breasts.

The gold warmed against her skin, shifting and gleaming with each breath she took. Although very little of her skin was revealed through the closely spaced chains, they hung in loops that tempted a man's finger into searching beneath the sensual glow of eighteen-carat gold.

Holly smoothed the dress into place before she put on a wrap that went from chin to ankles. She opened her cosmetic case. Smiling, she went to work.

The foundation she applied was so sheer it was all but invisible. Blusher heightened the slanting line of her cheekbones. A touch of scented oil smoothed into each black eyebrow made them glisten.

Eye shadow heightened the tawny color of

her eyes. She applied liner artfully, all but hidden just above her eyelashes. The liner transformed tilted eyes into cat eyes, unblinking and luminous gold.

Mascara brought out the thickness and unusual length of her eyelashes. A smooth, tawny-rose lip liner and gloss emphasized the sensuality of her mouth.

The result was breathtaking, but not to Holly. To her, it was simply her public face, a kind of armor she wore against the world at large, protecting the vulnerable Holly within.

With practiced motions she stripped the rollers out of her long hair. She brushed with deep strokes that made her hair crackle and shift as though it were alive, restless, wild to be free.

She caught up some of the hair at the sides, making silky wings that covered half of her ears. She clipped the hair in place at the back of her head.

The clip was a twist of gold capped by a long tassel of chains that matched those on her dress. Except for that single restraint, Holly allowed her hair to fall down her bare back until black hair and black silk were indistinguishable.

She stepped into high-heeled gold sandals, removed the wrap that had protected her dress, and examined herself critically in the mirror.

Ice formed in the pit of her stomach.

Never had her transformation been so startling, so complete. The sensual awakening that Linc had begun showed in the heat of her skin, the luminous gold of her eyes, the bruised impatience of her mouth.

With a mixture of pride and fear, Holly realized that she had never looked more alluring.

When she opened the bathroom door and walked out, Beth didn't hear. She was standing in front of the television, staring at the screen with a peculiarly intent look.

Holly heard the words before she saw the picture.

". . . Royce, made to be worn over nothing more than a woman's perfumed skin."

It was a commercial Holly had made last year, featuring a line of lingerie that had since sold very well.

"Beth?"

"I've seen that commercial a hundred times," Beth said without turning around. "Shannon has to be the most gorgeous woman in the world."

"Thank you."

Startled, Beth turned and saw her for the first time.

"Holly . . . ?" she asked weakly.

"The same."

Stunned, Beth simply stared.

"Well, almost the same," Holly amended. "A Royce does wonders for any woman, and Roger designed this dress especially for me."

"I—I—" Beth swallowed and tried again. "I can't believe it. Why didn't you tell us?"

"I said I was a model. I am."

Beth shook her head, speechless.

"What was I supposed to say?" Holly asked dryly. " 'Hi, I'm Shannon, the internationally famous model.' If you're famous, you don't have to mention it, do you?"

Beth blinked. Then she started laughing.

"Wait until Cyn sees you!" she said. "Oh, I want to be there. I want to be right *there!*"

"Thought you might," Holly said. "That's why I asked you to wait for me."

"And Linc. Oh boy, when Linc sees—"

Beth stopped abruptly, realizing that her brother was not going to be delighted.

Far from it. Linc would be furious.

"God. Linc's going to have a cow."

"Yeah," Holly said, trying to smile. "That's the other reason I wanted you to wait. I don't think he'll kill me in front of his kid sister."

Beth didn't look all that certain.

Holly took a deep breath, settled her Shannon armor firmly into place, and held out her hand.

"First things first," Holly said.

"What's first?"

"Seeing how far Cyn's jaw can drop."

Fifteen

It was very dark by the time Holly and Beth stepped outside. Wind-driven clouds hid all but occasional pale flashes of moon.

Music rippled through the night, strains of a waltz that was centuries old. Countless strings of tiny white lights wove through trees and over fences, guiding people to the dance pavilion. The pavilion was just beginning to fill, drawing laughter and beautifully dressed couples into its billowing interior.

Some guests had attended the auction and barbecue and then gone to their nearby homes to change into evening clothes. Others had brought their formal clothes and changed in one of the McKenzies' six guest rooms. Still others had simply attended the auction looking as princely as the Arabians they had come to admire and buy.

The mixture of fashion and elegant, silk-tasseled horses gave Holly the feeling of being transported to a fairy-tale world where gleaming Arabians pranced amid a diamond glitter of wealth.

Bemused by the transformation of Linc's ranch, she looked across the yard to where the auction was taking place. The platform was like a large stage, darkened but for a spotlight.

Inside the cone of light, a dark stallion pranced with muscular grace, held by no more than a delicate, braided-silk show halter. With each movement of the stallion's body, elaborate silk tassels on the halter rippled, weaving light into shimmering patterns.

"What a stunning animal," Holly said.

Beth followed her glance.

"That's Night Dancer," Beth said. "He's Shadow Dancer's sire. That's why Linc was so worried about the foal."

"Surely you aren't auctioning off that stallion!"

Beth laughed at the thought.

"Nope," she said proudly. "We're just showing off the best Arabian stud this side of anywhere. Linc does it at the end of every auction we have at the Mountains of Sunrise."

Holly waited for a few moments more, watching the spotlighted platform. But her eyes no longer followed the horse's movements. She sought the tall man in the shadows who held the stallion's silken lead.

From this distance she could not see the man's face. Only the potent grace of his movements as he controlled Night Dancer identified the man as Linc.

"He's quite an animal, isn't he?" Beth asked.

"Yes." She smiled and added dryly, "Both of them."

Giggling, Beth picked up her long skirt and began walking toward the pavilion. Holly followed, holding folds of smooth midnight silk in her hands to keep the hem clear of the grass.

Linc didn't see Holly or his sister walking toward the dance pavilion. He was already heading back to the barn, leading the ranch's most valuable asset.

Holly and Beth joined the glittering guests inside the pavilion. The bandstand was at one end of the enclosure, a bar and buffet at the other, with groupings of tables and chairs in between.

Suddenly Beth took Holly's arm and tried to drag her off to the left side of the vast tent.

She threw Linc's sister a startled look.

"Hurry," Beth explained. "I just spotted Cyanide."

"Cyanide?"

"Over there."

Holly stopped long enough to glance beyond Beth.

Across the room, flanked by several men, stood a petite blond. She was wearing a long, tight, red sheath. It was cut low in front, slit to mid-thigh at one side, and covered completely in scarlet sequins.

"Oh," Holly said. "You mean Cyn. Cyanide, huh?"

"Can you think of a better name?"

"Several, but you're too young to hear them."

Beth smiled with pure malice.

"Bet I've thought of them," Linc's sister said.

Wisely, Holly said not one word.

"Let's go," Beth said, tugging impatiently at Holly's arm. "I can't wait to see her reaction."

"Give Cyn a minute or two. No need to spoil her evening right off."

"Why not? She's spoiled enough of mine."

Holly just smiled.

"Slow down, honey," she said to Beth. "Let me do it my way."

"What's that?"

"In cold blood."

Beth drew in her breath, tried to see Holly's face, but couldn't. She had already turned aside to look at the rest of the people gathered beneath the pavilion's colorful ceiling.

"Okay," Beth said. "I'll wait."

But she still gave a bitter glance to the spot where Cyn stood in sequin-studded splendor. The woman was radiating the kind of sexual signals guaranteed to bring every male within sight to attention.

Just looking at her made Beth feel awkward, young, and plain.

"What now?" she asked, sighing.

"Stay with me. Introduce me to everyone you know."

Beth sighed again, more loudly. Obviously she wasn't impressed by Holly's strategy for revenge on Cyn.

"There's more to attracting men—and keeping them attracted—than a flashy red dress," Holly explained.

"Tell that to Cyn."

"Oh, she'll get the message," Holly said, turning back to Beth. "In spades."

"Cool," Beth said with pure malice. "After I've introduced you to people, what then?"

"Then I'll cut off Cyn's claws and make a bracelet for you."

Beth's breath caught. She looked closely, seeing beyond the beautiful exterior to the core of steel beneath.

For the first time, Beth realized that Holly could be as formidable as Linc himself.

"You know," Beth said, "I hope you don't ever get mad at me."

"I only get mad at people who are cruel. Like Cyn."

Then Holly smiled, softening her expression.

"Come on, Beth. I've got a roomful of people to meet."

"Everyone? Not just the men?"

"Everyone."

Beth groaned, looking at the people in the pavilion.

"There are zillions of them," she said.

Holly laughed at Beth's impatience.

"Not quite," Holly said.

"Where do we start?" she asked glumly.

"Do you know the gray-haired gentleman and the woman in the lavender dress?"

"Sure. But he's old."

Holly's lips quirked.

"No man who is still breathing is *that* old," she said.

Beth gave her a I-hope-you-know-what-you're-doing look, took her hand, and led her to the couple.

"Hi, George, Mary," Beth said. "This is Holly North, Linc's—"

"I'm a friend of the family," she cut in quickly, before Beth could say "fiancée."

After tonight, she wasn't sure that Linc would want to see her again, much less marry her.

But I won't think about that now, she told herself firmly. *Right now all that matters is showing Beth how to handle herself with malicious creatures like Cyn.*

After tonight, a lot of women like Cyn could be strolling through Beth's life again.

And Linc's.

Despite Holly's bleak thoughts, she smiled and held out her hand to Mary and then to George. It was hardly the first time Holly had hidden fear or sorrow behind a breathtaking smile.

"I'm delighted to meet you, Mr. and Mrs.—?" Holly said.

"Johnston," said the man, taking her hand. "But call me George."

"Only if you call me Holly."

Holly squeezed the man's hand firmly, released it, and turned toward his wife.

"That's a lovely color on you, Mrs. Johnston.

I envy you. If I wear lavender, I look like I have terminal flu."

The compliment was genuine, for Holly disliked even the social lies that she had learned were sometimes necessary.

The women's shrewd blue eyes weighed Holly, then forgave her for being too beautiful.

"Please, call me Mary," she said, smiling. Then she laughed. "The idea of you being jealous of me is ridiculous."

"Not to me," Holly said ruefully. "I love purples and can't wear any of them."

"George and Mary own a ranch about three miles up the valley," Beth said. "George raises quarter horses."

Holly gave him a sideways look.

"You'll be disowned if you're caught at an Arabian auction," Holly whispered. "I'll never give you away. Cross my heart and hope to die."

George and Mary both laughed.

"Actually," he admitted, "my favorite riding horse is half Arab."

Holly began a spirited, knowledgeable discussion of various equine breeds and cross-breeds. George and Mary leaped into the conversation. Their lives, like those of many people in Garner Valley, revolved around horses.

Soon other people joined the group, drawn by the laughter and the charming, beautiful woman who was at its center.

When Holly was introduced to the new people, she memorized names and faces. Often she complimented the women on some aspect of their appearance. Always she guided the conversation so that no one was left out.

When the group became too large for easy conversation, Holly signaled Beth with a glance and withdrew without leaving a ripple behind.

Eagerly Beth whispered to Holly.

"Cyn's over there near the cheesecake," she said.

"Hope she doesn't curdle it."

Beth snickered. "C'mon, let's go see her."

"Not yet. There are a lot more people to meet."

Beth groaned.

"Don't look so disappointed," Holly said. "I like meeting people."

"I don't see how meeting old married couples is going to make Cyn eat her words," Beth said bluntly.

"Watch."

"Like I have a choice?" Beth muttered.

Holly looked around. She saw a young couple standing alone and rather uncertainly at the edge of the dance floor.

"Do you know them?" Holly asked.

Beth sighed. "I know everyone."

"Introduce me."

Dutifully Beth led Holly over to the couple.

It didn't take long before other young couples were drawn like bright leaves into a whirlpool. Then several men and women who were alone also joined in.

The conversation ranged from horses to politics to the intricacies of downhill skiing and mountain trail bikes. Again, Holly became the center of an animated, laughing group. Again, it was her real interest in people rather than her beauty alone that held everyone's attention.

Again, Holly withdrew quietly when the crowd reached the point that it no longer needed a center.

As Beth led Holly toward another area of the room, the younger girl smiled like a cat licking cream.

"I'm catching on," Beth said.

"Are you?"

"At least two of those men left Cyn to join our group."

Holly made a noncommittal sound and looked around the room.

Linc still wasn't there.

She had hoped he would come to the pavilion, see her making friends, and perhaps not be so angry with her Shannon appearance.

But no matter where Holly looked, she didn't see a man who carried himself like Linc.

With my luck, she thought unhappily, *he won't get here until we start peeling the handsome single males off Cyn.*

Holly grimaced. She enjoyed meeting people. She did not enjoy being a siren.

Yet in her job as the Royce Reflection, she had learned to do both quite well.

I'll stall a little longer, she told herself. *Then I'll do what has to be done.*

By the time Holly had gathered and faded out of two more groups, Linc still hadn't arrived. Worse, it became impossible to find new people to meet.

Holly couldn't move ten feet without being asked to dance. Her campaign to charm the people who lived nearby and worked with Linc was an unqualified success, one that she enjoyed as much as the people who warmed themselves in her presence.

But Linc had seen none of it.

"Well," she said to Beth, "let's get it over with."

"Cyn?"

"Cyn."

"Cool. She's still by the cheesecake."

Together they walked toward Cyn. It took ten minutes to go fifty feet because Holly was graciously refusing offers of food or dance or conversation at every step.

"Okay," Holly said. "I want you to distract her. I'll come in from the back."

"Distract her? How?"

Holly smiled gently. "Remember the mirror, honey?"

Beth nodded.

"Two of the men don't look much older than you," Holly pointed out.

Beth looked startled.

"Don't you know them?" asked Holly.

"Yes, but—"

Holly waited.

"What do you want me to do?" Beth asked.

"Do you like any of the men?"

"Oh, sure. Jim's a lot of fun, and even though he's only nineteen, he's the best trainer in the valley, next to Linc."

"Then tell him."

Beth blinked and nibbled on her lower lip.

"Go ahead," Holly encouraged. "Nobody will bite you for being honest. Except Cyn, of course. Don't be honest with her. Ignore her completely."

Holly watched while Beth walked slowly toward Cyn. When the girl was only a few feet away, her chin came up and her posture straightened.

As Holly moved to circle around, she saw Cyn's look of surprise when she saw Beth.

"Well, well," Cyn said, "since when does Linc let you play dress up?"

Holly held her breath and hoped that Beth would hold her tongue.

Ignoring Cyn, Beth turned and smiled at the young man next to the alluring blond.

Holly couldn't hear what was said, but it was clear that the young man's attention was no longer on Cyn.

"Where's your chum?" Cyn asked. "The plain one, little miss what's-her-name."

Beth looked up and smiled. "Right behind you, Cyanide."

Cyn turned and looked past Holly, not recognizing her.

Then Cyn looked again. Her mouth opened, closed, and opened once more.

"Hello, Cyn," Holly said casually.

Then she turned her brightest smile on the stranger who had his right hand possessively on Cyn's arm.

"I'm sure I would have remembered if we had been introduced," murmured Holly, holding out her hand. "I'm Holly."

The man gave her the kind of up-and-down look that she found offensive. She kept her smile in place even when he took her hand in both of his and drew her closer.

"My name is Stan," he said. "Where on earth did you come from? Or was it heaven?"

"Manhattan."

She hoped that no one would notice that her smile was as thin as her patience with Stan's sort of man.

She turned to the older man who was standing on Cyn's other side. Deliberately, Holly gave him a flirtatious look from beneath long black lashes. As her right hand was securely held by Stan, she offered her left.

"And you are . . . ?" she asked.

"Gary," he said dryly, taking her hand. "I'm just along for the ride."

She looked at the man more closely, then gave him a genuine smile.

"Aren't we all?" she answered, her voice as dry as his.

He reassessed Holly in a single glance, smiled and nodded. He tucked her hand under his arm.

"You look thirsty," he said, and began to lead her away.

Stan refused to let go of Holly's other hand.

"Not so fast, buddy," he protested.

Holly glanced over her shoulder just in time to see Beth quietly leading Jim and the other young man toward the buffet.

Cyn didn't notice. She was still staring in total disbelief. Holly smiled gently at her before turning to Stan.

"I'm sure there's more than one glass of champagne at the bar," she said. "Why don't you join us?"

He didn't have to be asked twice.

Less than three minutes after Holly had said hello, Cyn was left standing alone.

By the time Holly disengaged from the disappointed men, Roger, Jerry, and three of Roger's models had arrived.

Roger's immaculate good looks attracted as many women's glances as Holly attracted men's. When they danced together, people stared. The combination of light and dark was arresting.

As always, Holly enjoyed Roger's easy wit and conversation, but her eyes kept searching the pavilion for Linc.

"Missing someone?" Roger asked, his tone playful and his blue eyes intent.

"Mmm," she said absently.

She noticed that Cyn had collected another group of men.

"Excuse me," Holly said. "I have some claws to trim."

"Will you be long?" he asked.

Her lips curved in an icy smile.

"Five minutes," she said. "Ten at most."

"I'm devastated."

"Uh-huh," she said, unimpressed. "Why don't you make some women happy and dance with them?"

Before he could answer, she had turned away and was heading quickly toward Cyn. A few minutes later Holly walked away from Cyn, followed by several men, leaving the petite blond alone.

The scene repeated itself, with variations in the cast of men, several more times in the next hour and a half. Only two things didn't change—Roger's presence and Holly's anxiety about Linc's absence.

Roger watched with increasing perplexity and amusement while Holly repeatedly stripped Cyn of admirers, herded them to the other end of the pavilion, and went back to looking for Linc.

It was futile. He was nowhere to be found.

Holly was certain that she sensed Linc's presence. But each time she looked, she couldn't find him.

Roger appeared at her elbow as soon as she shed the latest admirers she had stripped from Cyn.

"Why do I get the feeling you have something against the little blond with the big . . .

sequins?" he asked, laughter rippling beneath his words.

Holly smiled with some bitterness.

"Yes," she said, "I suppose you could say that."

"Competition for the cowboy?" he asked lightly.

Before answering, Holly looked around the pavilion once more. A certainty of Linc's presence kept shivering across her nerves, telling her that he was nearby. Yet she couldn't find him in the brightly lit tent.

Holly looked over her shoulder. There was only darkness outside. No one was on the lighted walkway leading to the pavilion.

Sighing, she turned back to Roger.

"It's a long story," she said.

One corner of his mouth turned up.

"Smashing," he said. "It will be ten or fifteen minutes before Cyn collects enough men to make it worth the walk."

"I'll wait."

Roger glanced over Holly's shoulder and smiled cynically.

"Could be a long wait," he said. "Guess she finally figured it out."

Holly turned and saw Cyn leaving the pavilion on Jerry's arm. The photographer's smile was practiced and predatory.

"Want to make a last foray?" Roger asked.

"Wouldn't dream of it," she said, smiling. "They deserve each other."

"What could Cyn have done to deserve Jerry?" Roger asked.

Holly's smile widened. Of all the people she knew, Roger was the most likely to enjoy the story of Cyn's discomfort. Overdressed women irritated the designer's sense of proportion.

"Cyn and Beth—that's Linc's younger sister—don't like each other," Holly said. "Cyn and I were out shopping. She called Beth a plain little thing."

"Beth? Which one is she?"

"The young lady in the turquoise skirt and glorious golden hair standing next to the tall redhead."

"Oh, that one. She's ravishing, like an unopened rose."

"Beth thought she was plain."

Roger looked at Holly in disbelief.

"When I told Beth she wasn't plain, Cyn asked what I could know about it, since I was as plain as a concrete slab."

Roger's eyes widened.

"I'm speechless," he said.

And meant it.

"The upshot of it was," Holly said, "that I bet Cyn I could have men standing in line to talk to me at this dance."

Roger laughed and laughed.

"She called you plain?" he asked incredulously. "I suspected she wasn't very smart, but I didn't know she was blind."

Holly's smile was as brilliant as her eyes.

"I do look a bit different when I'm not dressed up," she said demurely.

"That," Linc's cold voice said behind her, "is the understatement of the century."

Sixteen

Roger looked from Holly's stricken face to Linc's narrow-eyed fury.

Holly simply looked at the man she loved.

Despite his obvious anger, Linc was handsome enough to break her heart. His evening clothes had been tailored to fit the long, lean lines of his body. Every time he moved, the material outlined another aspect of his masculine grace and power.

Roger looked at the two of them, so consumed by each other that no one else existed. Yet Roger knew that Linc's anger was as real and potentially dangerous as lightning.

With a soft curse, Roger put a finger under Holly's chin, turning her head until she was looking at him rather than Linc.

"I don't know why he's mad," Roger said, "but instinct tells me that his bite is worse than any bark I've ever heard. If you need first aid, you know my room number."

She said nothing.

"Are you listening, Shannon?" he asked softly.

She nodded.

He gave Linc an unreadable look.

"If she comes to me," Roger said coolly, "you're a bloody idiot. I'll wrap her in silk bandages and you'll never see her again."

Roger stared back into Holly's eyes. They were tarnished gold, mysterious, sad. Wary.

"Some men are as dangerous as they look," Roger said. "Be careful, love."

He kissed her lips lightly, brushed past Linc, and disappeared into the darkness beyond the pavilion.

Linc made a harsh sound.

"It's a wonder that the tame Viking isn't immune to beautiful models by now," he said.

As he spoke, he looked Holly over with a thoroughness that made her weak. His eyes lingered on the fine chains that dipped and quivered between her breasts with each breath she took.

"Before I even got out of the house," he said, "people were coming up to me and telling me what a charmer Beth's friend Holly North was. Not just the men, but the women, too. They all fell in love with you."

Breath held, Holly waited, hoping against hope.

"So I hurried out here to enjoy you," he said. "I couldn't find you. I found someone else, though. What's that name again? Shannon?"

"Yes," she said in a low voice. Then, more clearly, "Yes. Shannon. My mother's maiden name. My middle name. Shannon. No secret, Linc. You knew the name six years ago."

He muttered a single, vicious word.

"No secret?" he snarled. "Christ, what kind of a fool do you think I am?"

He heard his own words and laughed with a bitterness that made her flinch. Then he looked at her with cold, hungry eyes, the eyes of a predator.

"Scratch that question," he said savagely. "You already know what kind of fool I am. I'm the fool who thought you were a virgin."

"I am."

"Yeah. Right."

Holly started to speak, but could only gasp as his fingers shot out and clenched around her wrists.

"No," Linc said coldly. "Not one more lying word. See you at midnight, *Shannon*."

He dropped her wrists and strode into the crowd without a backward look.

The rest of the dance moved by in a haze of misery for Holly. Even Beth's transparent glee at Cyn's rout brought only a small smile to Holly's lips. She kept up the facade of charm and pleasure as best she could, but her heart was counting the minutes to midnight.

Linc was like the music, present everywhere.

No matter how often she turned around, he was there, watching her the way a cat watches a butterfly gliding just beyond its reach.

She could only hope that by midnight he

would have cooled off enough to listen to her.

When I explain that I was dancing and flirting only to win a bet for Beth, she told herself, *Linc will understand.*

When I tell him that it was the truce he insisted on that kept me silent about the details of my modeling career, he'll get over his anger.

When I tell him how much I love him—

Her thoughts scattered as a hand closed on her arm just below the gleaming gold chains.

"It's midnight," Linc said.

His voice, like his expression, was remote.

He pulled her toward the dance floor with a strength that was just short of bruising. When they were in the center of the floor, he turned Holly to face him.

"Smile, Shannon," he said. "You've smiled at every other damn man tonight, why not at me?"

Her lips trembled.

"You matter too much to me for easy smiles," she whispered.

Linc's lips formed a cynical curve.

"Very good, Shannon," he said. "I'll have to compliment Roger. He's made you a sure winner in the Pleasure Riding class."

The double meaning of his comment went through Holly like a knife.

"Roger has never been my lover!" she said furiously.

"Keep it up, Shannon. Make the kind of scene my stepmother loved to make. I'll give it right back to you in ways you'll never forget."

"You might think of Beth," Holly said in a tight, low voice.

"The one who looks just like her mother tonight?" he asked. "I'd rather not, thanks."

Linc's arm closed around Holly. Moving with him because she had no choice, they began dancing to the lyric strains of the same ancient waltz that had begun the evening.

She moved awkwardly. It was impossible to dance any other way because her head was tilted back and held by the pressure of Linc's arm over her long hair. She stumbled, wincing as her hair jerked against the vise of his arm around her waist.

When she reached back with her left hand to free her hair, he abruptly pulled her closer.

Holly tripped and fell against him. When she tried to protest, his arm closed so ruthlessly around her that she could barely draw a breath.

When she tried to break free, he simply lifted her feet off the ground.

She had always known Linc was strong, but had never thought he would use his strength against her like this. He left her just enough room to breathe, just enough leverage so that her feet didn't dangle, just enough freedom of movement so that her imprisonment wasn't obvious.

She opened her mouth to speak again, only to gasp as he jerked her against his unyielding body in a casual display of power that forced her to fight for breath.

"Don't say a word," Linc said.

He looked down at Holly with eyes that were dark with memories, glittering with reflected light and anger.

"If I hear one more lie out of those pretty lips—" he said.

Abruptly, he said no more.

His arm kept tightening, squeezing the breath out of her. The hand holding hers tightened mercilessly.

Tears magnified Holly's golden eyes. She turned pale, but made no sound. She didn't want to ruin Beth's victory by making a scene. Nor would she lower herself to the level of Linc's memories of his stepmother.

Teeth clenched, Holly waited until she could talk to him alone and tell him what a stupid, stubborn son of a bitch he was.

He saw the change in her eyes and felt the stiffness in the body that had always yielded so deliciously to his. He realized that he was holding her hard, much too hard.

What am I so angry about? he asked himself silently, sardonically. *For days I've been worried about frightening a virgin with my hunger.*

No worries now.

Abruptly, he loosened his hold.

Holly took a deep breath and cautiously moved her head, trying to ease the unnatural angle of her neck.

His arm shifted, freeing her hair.

Then his hand slid underneath her hair, caressing the bare skin of her back. Hidden by the long, silky fall of her hair, his fingers probed beneath the open waist of her dress until he could feel the taut curves of her buttocks.

With a throttled sound Linc forced Holly's hips against his. The message of his desire was unmistakable through the thin silk of her dress, yet his face showed nothing but contempt.

She struggled to put some distance between them. She succeeded only in rubbing over him in a way that both aroused and embarrassed her.

"No, Linc. Please," she said, pushing futilely against his strength.

"You danced with every other man," he said, his fingers probing intimately beneath her dress. "Why not me?"

"I didn't dance like this!"

Air rushed out of her as she was once again yanked against his body.

"I said no more lies, Shannon."

"I'm not—"

"A liar?" he interrupted coldly. "The hell you aren't. All beautiful women are faithless liars."

Anger coursed through Holly like lightning.

"It's your party, Linc," she said in a cold voice. "If you want a floor show, I'll give you one."

"Yeah, I bet you do a sensational striptease."

"You lose," she snarled. "A down-and-out brawl was more what I had in mind, and to hell with spoiling Beth's victory and not bringing back bad memories of your stepmother."

Holly's voice was loud enough that several other couples looked at them curiously.

He smiled blandly at her, but suddenly she was off her feet again.

She didn't bother flailing about or telling Linc he was holding her too hard.

He knew precisely what he was doing.

Deliberately her left hand moved from his shoulder to the place where his head had struck a boulder two days ago. Her nails scraped lightly over the bruised, still tender skin.

Though she did nothing more, the threat was clear.

His eyes widened in surprise. For a moment he studied her determined expression. He returned her feet to the floor and loosened his hold on her a bit.

"Who taught you to fight dirty?" he asked mildly.

"You. Just now."

Oddly, he smiled.

"There are other ways," he said.

Holly wondered what Linc meant, but decided that asking would be inviting an argument. She knew one was coming, but she wanted privacy for it.

Linc loosed his hold on her even more, giving her freedom to dance with him. At first she moved stiffly, too angry and wary to allow herself to blend with him.

He gathered Holly's body against his with a slow, sensual care that mocked her anger.

"You know," he breathed against her hair, "I can't decide which is most silky—your dress, your hair, or your skin."

His fingertips traced her spine with delicate care, sending showers of sensation through her.

Linc felt Holly shiver and laughed softly. He brought his left hand in close, so that her right hand pressed against his chest.

The back of his hand brushed lightly over her breast each time she breathed.

"Not all of you is silky," he murmured. "Some of you gets delightfully hard."

Holly's breath caught as Linc's knuckle gently circled the tip of her breast. Strands of pleasure spread through her, bringing a subtle tension to her whole body.

It was no longer his hand at her waist that was holding her close to him, but rather her own desire to feel his warmth radiating through the thin silk of her dress.

Linc let go of her fingers and filled his palm with the sweet weight of her breast.

Holly knew she should protest, but could only gasp with surprise and pleasure. She shook her hair until it fell like a dark curtain around her, concealing his hand beneath.

Her soft hair was like a brand against his skin. He groaned, a bare thread of sound against her ear. His fingernails rasped lightly over silk, then closed around her nipple.

"Linc . . ." Holly said in soft protest.

"Shhh. No one can see."

Linc's hand moved toward the warm gold

links that filled the diamond between her breasts. His fingers eased through the chains, seeking her naked warmth.

"I've wanted to do this since I walked in and saw you," he said huskily.

For an instant Holly was shocked into stillness. She could hardly believe that she was in a roomful of people with his fingers stroking her naked breasts.

Whatever protest she might have made was lost in a sunburst of sensations that radiated from the pit of her stomach throughout her body.

Her back arched against his touch in a reflex as old as passion. She felt the tremor that went through his body, the sudden tension in his muscles that she had learned came from heightened desire.

"I want to taste you," Linc said, holding Holly tightly, his voice thick. "I want to slide over you like that damned witch's dress and then I want to—"

Abruptly he withdrew his fingers, stopped dancing, and led her toward the nearest exit.

"What about your guests?" she asked.

"I said my goodbyes before midnight."

"Beth—" Holly began.

"Beth left with her girlfriend an hour ago. She won't be back until tomorrow. Late."

Holly made no further protests. Her body was still shimmering with the hunger Linc aroused in her.

The night was thick with clouds. Thunder

rumbled in the distance. Raindrops from a recent shower reflected the walkway lights like crystal tears.

When Holly stopped to gather the hem of her dress out of the reach of puddles, Linc lifted her into his arms with barely controlled impatience. He walked with long strides toward the house.

A fold of silk escaped her fingers and fell perilously close to the wet path. She tried to gather the cloth up again, but she was being held so tightly that she couldn't move.

"Linc—" she began.

"No more excuses," he interrupted in a harsh voice. "Beth is gone, the guests know their way home, and I'm not going to wait any longer."

Startled by the strain in Linc's voice, she looked his face. Outlined in shadows and white light, it was the face of a stranger who knew neither kindness nor love.

"Don't look at me like that," he said impatiently. "We both know the score. Your game of tease and retreat is over, *Shannon*. Now it's my turn."

Seventeen

Before Linc set Holly on her feet, he shut the door to the master bedroom and shot the bolt. Impatiently he pulled off his tie, tossed it over a chair and unbuttoned his shirt. He pulled a foil packet out of his pants pocket, unzipped his pants, and kicked them aside.

Holly watched with a combination of hunger and confusion.

"What are you waiting for?" Linc asked. "Take off your clothes."

His hands went to the waistband of his underwear. He peeled off his briefs, tossed them aside, and ripped open the foil packet.

Quickly she turned her back. She had seen him without clothes in the camp tent, but that had been different, intimate and warm and exciting.

This was like watching a stranger undress.

Suddenly she felt Linc behind her. His naked strength pressed against her while his fingers closed possessively over the taut curves of her hips.

"Hurry up," he said in a husky voice, "or I'll take you right here, right now. Or is that how you like it?"

Her hands trembled toward the zipper hidden beneath a fold of silk at the back of the dress. Accidentally her fingers touched his rigid, aroused flesh.

She jerked back as though burned.

Linc's breath hissed out. He wanted nothing more than to wrap Holly's fingers around him in a lover's caress.

But she was acting like she had never seen a naked man before, much less touched one.

"Knock it off, Shannon," he said impatiently. "You're no more a shivering virgin than I am."

She spun and faced him.

"I didn't lie to you," she said. Her voice shook with intensity. "I've never made love with anyone but you."

"Uh-huh," he said.

His tone said just the opposite.

Linc's hand found the zipper on Holly's dress and yanked it down. Black silk slid to the floor.

She wore nothing beneath but black lace bikinis.

What control Linc had burned up with the desire that had been devouring him.

Effortlessly he lifted her. His impatient fingers pulled off the band of black lace briefs. His mouth descended, forcing her lips apart. His hands clamped over her hips, lifting her against him with the same careless strength he had used earlier on the dance floor.

The intimate contact surprised Holly. She didn't know how to respond or what he expected from her.

The arousal she had felt earlier gave way to confusion.

"What do you want me to do?" she asked uncertainly.

Linc made a disgusted sound.

"What do you think?" he asked.

"I don't know!"

"Crap."

With that, he carried her across the room and dumped her on the bed. Before she could say a word, she was pinned beneath his weight.

"Linc—" she began.

His mouth closed over hers, shutting off any questions, any protests, anything at all. His hands raked over every bit of her body, demanding a response that she was too inexperienced to give. His weight and intensity overwhelmed her.

After a few minutes Holly didn't move.

He swore and braced himself on his elbows, looking down at her with eyes that had no color, simply darkness.

"It's better if you cooperate," he said.

"I don't know what you want," she said desperately.

"The hell you don't, Shannon. I want exactly what you promised when you held your arms out to me in Palm Springs and begged me to do *this*."

His hips drove against Holly. There was an instant of tearing pain that made her cry out.

A stunned look came over Linc's face. For a long moment he simply stared down at her white face.

With an agonized sound, he withdrew and rolled off her.

"My God, Holly," he said raggedly. "I'm sorry. I thought you were—"

His voice broke. With a choked sound he tried to gather her into his arms.

"*No*," she said wildly.

Holly jerked over onto her side, her back to Linc. Shivering, she huddled around herself like a child.

He lay without touching her, fighting to control the emotions raging through him.

He had been so sure she wasn't a virgin.

And so wrong.

The realization almost destroyed him.

"Holly," he whispered. "I . . ."

When his hand smoothed her hair away from her face, she flinched and retreated.

Very gently he rolled her rigid body over until she faced him once more.

"Holly," he began.

"If you're finished," she interrupted in a clear, childlike voice, "I'd like to take a bath."

Linc would have preferred sarcasm or screams or tears to Holly's simple statement of fact.

He had made her feel unclean.

"Holly . . . don't."

His voice was as ragged as hers had been clear. His hands trembled as he tried to comfort her.

With an inarticulate cry, she shoved him away and ran for the bedroom door. She was too upset to realize that it was still bolted shut. She tugged on the knob with both hands like a child.

Then Holly saw the bolt.

She clawed at it, breaking her nails in her haste as she finally unlocked the door.

Linc's hand shot past her shoulder, slamming the door shut again before she could get out. His other hand flattened against the wall, holding Holly captive between his arms without actually touching her.

His broken breathing stirred her hair like a caress.

She shuddered.

"No more," she said in a raw voice. "I should have told you I was Shannon and you should have believed I was a virgin. But I didn't and you didn't. We're even. Now let me go."

He made a hoarse sound of anguish. His hand shook as he stroked the midnight fall of her hair.

"Holly—"

"My name is Shannon," she interrupted savagely.

Linc made a noise not unlike Holly's as she

had clawed at the bolt, but he didn't let her open the door.

For long moments there was no sound but his broken breathing. When he finally spoke, his voice was so changed it made tears burn behind Holly's eyelids.

"I can't let you go," Linc said raggedly. "You'd never come back."

Holly shuddered again.

"I can't live with that," he said, "with what I did to you, hurting you because I didn't believe you and I'd wanted you for so long. Too long. Too much. I'm so sorry I hurt you. So damned sorry . . ."

He made a choked sound and fought to control his emotions. He wasn't wholly successful.

The feel of a single tear dropping onto her shoulder shocked Holly all the way to her soul.

Slowly she slumped against the bedroom door as though she wished she could sink into its wooden pores and vanish.

"I was told my first time would hurt," she said dully.

"Not as much. Not if I had taken more time to arouse you."

Holly felt the hard, cool wood of the door on her forehead. Only the raggedness of Linc's voice gave her the courage to keep on talking.

"It wouldn't have mattered," she said.

"Like hell it wouldn't."

"Forget it," she said dully. "It's not all your fault. I've been told time and again that I'm frigid. I finally believe it."

"Frigid?"

At first Linc thought Holly was joking.

The defeated line of her body told him she wasn't. He would have laughed if he could, but he was too shocked.

"Holly, you are the most wonderfully sensual woman I've ever known," he said finally.

"Uh-huh."

Her cynical tone was an exact echo of his earlier response when she had told him she was a virgin.

"It's true," Linc said. "I had a hard enough time believing you were a virgin when you were Holly. When you were Shannon . . . my God . . ." He took a swift, broken breath. "Impossible."

"Why do you think I was a virgin whether Holly or Shannon?" she asked bitterly. "I didn't want men."

"You wanted me."

"Not enough."

"Not tonight. I didn't give you a chance."

He lifted her like a child in his arms, ignoring her protest and the stiffness of her body.

"Please, Linc," she said hoarsely. "Please, stop. I can't take any more."

He brushed the top of her head with his lips.

"I won't hurt you," he promised. "It will never be like that again."

"It will never be, period. Don't you understand? I'm frigid!"

Holly couldn't see Linc's smile.

"Put me down," she said.

"Not yet. I won't do anything you don't want me to. I promise. Trust me, Holly."

"I did, once . . ."

Her whisper was more for herself than for him, but he heard.

He froze, finishing the rest of her sentence in his mind even though she said nothing at all.

She trusted me once and then I violated that trust.

Linc took a deep, broken breath.

"I trusted someone called Holly," he said when his voice steadied. "I want to trust her again. It's so easy to trust the first time, but the second . . . ?"

She went still as she understood what he was asking from her now.

Not sex.

Trust.

Again.

Just as she wanted him to trust her.

Again.

Motionless, Linc waited for the longest moments of his life, straining to hear Holly's answer.

It didn't come in words. Slowly she became less stiff in his arms. She didn't rest her cheek on his chest, but neither did she show him only the back of her head.

Letting out a long breath of relief, he carried her past the bed and into the bathroom.

The Jacuzzi steamed quietly, surrounded by lush ferns and wooden containers thick with exotic flowers. Lights hidden amid the greenery glowed like fallen stars.

Slowly Linc set Holly on her feet, supporting her until her legs stopped trembling. Then he opened counter drawers until he found a hairbrush.

Gently he brushed her hair until there were no more tangles in the shining mass. With deft motions, he gathered the strands into a single long braid.

"You're good at that," she said.

Her voice was shaky, almost unrecognizable, but Linc didn't care. He was too relieved that she was willing to speak to him.

"I practiced a lot on Beth," he said.

For a time Holly stood without moving, watching herself and Linc reflected in the mirrored walls. She didn't see her own beauty, the feminine curves of breasts and hips and waist, the tawny rose of nipples against her smooth golden skin, the lush midnight hair below her shadowed navel.

Holly saw only Linc's face, gentle again.

She also saw the strength that coiled beneath his skin with every motion of his body.

He secured the braid on top of her head with the same twist of gold she had worn before. When he was finished, he rested his hands lightly on her shoulders.

His eyes met hers in the mirror for the

space of several heartbeats. Then looked at the rest of her as though he had never seen a woman before.

Holly forgot to breathe, waiting for Linc's hands to follow his eyes.

When his hands stayed on her shoulders, she didn't know whether she was relieved or disappointed.

Both, Holly admitted to herself. *But mostly relieved.*

She was a bit frightened of his strength now.

Linc saw the wariness in Holly's eyes. It hurt, even though he knew he deserved it.

Tenderly his fingers interlaced with hers. As he led her toward the water, he flipped a switch on the wall.

Suddenly jets of water made dazzling silver swirls in the Jacuzzi. Bubbles fizzed and sizzled like a conspiracy of laughter.

Without pausing, Linc walked into the water. He didn't turn toward Holly until he was clothed to the waist in brilliant, opaque bubbles.

Tension eased a bit in her. She hadn't known until this moment that part of her dreaded confronting his nakedness again.

Then she understood that somehow he had known how she felt before she did.

"Watch the first step—" Linc began.

"—it's a lulu," Holly finished, surprising both of them with her wry words.

He smiled, took her hand, and lifted her fingertips to his lips.

"It's also slippery," he said.

When he was certain that she wouldn't lose her balance, he released her hand. He didn't want her to feel restrained in any way by him.

Never again.

The thought of how he had taken her before was like a knife turning in him.

"There are benches built in at two levels," Linc said, sitting down on the lower one. "You're probably tall enough to sit down here without drowning in bubbles."

Holly hesitated, then sat at a midpoint on the lower level. She wasn't next to him. Nor was she as far away from him as she could get.

Linc noted every inch of the difference.

Bubbles frothed up to Holly's chin, hiding her behind their silver dance.

"Too cold?" he asked, seeing her lips tremble.

"Just nerves," she said in a strained voice.

"I won't—"

"I know," she interrupted quickly.

But did she?

He stretched out his long legs beneath the water, bracing himself on the lower bench on the opposite side. He let his head lie back on the padded rim and closed his eyes.

For a time Holly watched him covertly, comparing his face with that of the ruthless stranger who had taken Linc's place when he saw Shannon instead of Holly.

But now Linc's mouth was no longer a thin, sardonic twist. His jaw was relaxed instead of tightened in a grim thrust of male aggression. His unfair strength was concealed beneath a gleaming froth of bubbles that fizzed and shifted each second.

Holly shivered again, a tremor of muscles that were slowly relaxing. With a sigh, she rested her head against the padded rim of the Jacuzzi and let the water's heat claim her.

For several minutes there was no sound but that of the bright water seething over their bodies.

The swirling water was alive with mischief, teasing Holly's legs with a promise of support, then gently floating her toward the center of the Jacuzzi if she gave in.

She braced her arms along the rim. Gooseflesh formed as the cooler air of the room poured over her skin. Her legs floated out and bumped against Linc.

She froze.

His eyes didn't open, nor did his position change. If he had noticed the accidental brushing of skin against skin, he didn't show it.

The third time her feet drifted into his legs, she made a frustrated sound. The Jacuzzi had been built for his six-foot four-inch length. He could brace himself comfortably against the swirling currents, but she couldn't.

"Go ahead and put your feet on my leg,"

Linc offered. "You'll be more comfortable that way."

Startled, Holly glanced at his face.

His eyes were still closed.

After a few moments of hesitation, she let her legs float out again.

Linc's hair tickled slightly as the soles of her feet fitted themselves to the muscular curve of his thigh. She waited, half-expecting the water to carry her off again.

It didn't. His muscular thigh braced her securely.

Linc is right, she thought. *It's much more comfortable this way.*

She sighed and began to relax.

The heat and soothing murmur of the water slowly unraveled Holly's tension. Letting out another long sigh, she rested her head against the padded rim and let her mind drift as aimlessly as a bubble.

After a long time she opened her eyes. Linc was watching her with a gentleness and regret that made her throat ache.

His arm came out of the water, reaching toward her.

She tightened, but didn't move away.

He didn't touch her.

Instead, he leaned past her and took a towel from a stack between two flowering plants. He stood up swiftly, wrapping the towel around his hips as he came out of the water, shielding her again from his nakedness.

When he was on the last step out, he looked back down at her.

"Better?" he asked quietly.

She nodded.

He went to a cupboard and took out one of his huge bath towels.

"Then it's time to get out," he said. "Too much of this will turn your brain to bean dip."

"And your skin into a relief map," Holly said, holding out her wrinkled hands.

Even so, she hesitated before she stepped into the big towel Linc was holding out for her.

He rubbed her dry with impersonal hands. Then he wrapped the towel around her, covering her from collarbone to ankles.

Holly shivered as her body adjusted to being out of the heated Jacuzzi.

Or is it being so close to him that I can count the drops of water on his chest that makes me shiver? she asked herself.

The answer was a startling impulse to lick up each silver drop on Linc with the tip of her tongue.

The thought was as hypnotic as the hot water had been.

"Where did you hide that oil you used on me last night?" he asked.

For a moment Holly didn't realize that he had spoken to her.

"What?" she asked.

She forced herself to look away from the bright rivulets of water that escaped down his flat stomach, only to be caught again in the crisp line of hair that began beneath his navel.

"Oil," Linc repeated patiently.

"Oil. Um."

With an effort, Holly forced herself to glance around the room, but her eyes were too filled with Linc to see anything else.

"I think I left you in there too long," he said.

"What?"

"Your brain has turned to bean dip."

She smiled faintly, echoing the gentle amusement in his voice. Then she spotted an amber container.

"There," she said.

Linc picked up the bottle and walked to the bed. When he turned back to look at Holly, she was still standing in the bathroom.

He waited, saying nothing.

Slowly she walked toward him.

"If you'd rather stay on your feet," he said, "that's fine with me. But you'll get your rub-down either way, or you'll have skin like a horned toad by morning."

Her eyes glanced off his, then settled on her bare toes peeking out of the enfolding towel.

"What about you?" she asked in a small voice.

She didn't see the instant of surprise on his face. He turned away before she looked up at him again.

Without a word Linc pressed the bottle of

oil into Holly's hand and lay facedown on the bed.

"Ready when you are," he said matter-of-factly.

She poured oil into her hands, warmed it, and bent over Linc without getting on the bed next to him.

Silently she rubbed oil onto his back and shoulders. As she did, she tried to ignore the shift and gleam of his muscles and the tingling that began in her palms and radiated up her arms.

When she had massaged her way down to the towel around his hips, she stopped.

Linc bit his tongue against inviting—begging—Holly to keep on going.

I'm lucky she's willing to touch me at all, he told himself bitterly. *And if I want more, tough.*

I had it all, and I blew it.

He started to get up.

"Stay put," she said. "I'm not done yet."

Without a word Linc settled back onto the covers.

Holly went to the foot of the bed and began rubbing oil into his feet and calves. She worked as she had on his back, briskly, avoiding the possibility of sensual pleasure.

The further up his legs she progressed, the more difficult it became for her. She stopped just above his knees.

Linc rolled onto his side.

"Thanks," he said neutrally. "I can get the rest."

Holly watched through half-lowered lids, fascinated by the gleam of oil spreading over his thighs as he finished the job.

"Your turn," Linc said.

He looked at Holly's eyes, waiting for her to decide whether to bolt or to trust him.

Again.

Eighteen

Holly saw nothing but gentleness and regret in Linc's eyes. His tone was neutral rather than intense. His whole posture told her that whatever decision she made, he would accept.

After a moment he looked away from her. He didn't want her to feel pressured in any way. With unnecessary care, he poured a bit of oil into his palm to warm and waited for her decision.

Without saying a word Holly went to the bed and lay on her stomach. Other than her shoulders, arms, and feet, the thick towel covered every bit of her body.

Linc made no move to rearrange the towel so that more of her would be within his reach.

Slowly he smoothed oil into as much of her skin as the towel revealed. He kneaded down each arm to her fingertips, then back up again. He was careful to keep his touch firm and impersonal, a friend's touch rather than a lover's.

Linc massaged up and down Holly's arms

several times. Finally some of the tension left
her body. She relaxed into the mattress, no
longer lying stiffly.

Only then did he sit next to her on the bed.
When she shifted her weight to adjust to his
presence, he gave a soundless sigh of relief. His
hands moved between her shoulder blades,
loosening the towel.

Tension crept into the line of her back.

"Tomorrow," Linc said, "remind me to show
you Shadow Dancer's foal. She's a beauty."

While he spoke, he spread oil over her back
with slow, impersonal movements of his
hands.

The touch reassured and soothed her. She relaxed again into the mattress.

"Shadow Dancer is like a pagan god," Holly
said, her voice slightly muffled.

"When did you see him?"

"Beth and I came outside just as you were
leading him around the auction platform. I
thought you were going to sell him."

Linc laughed. "My prize stud? Not likely."

"That's what Beth said."

With a tiny sigh, Holly relaxed more fully,
reassured by the neutral topic and the fact that
Linc's touch went no lower than her waist.

Linc breathed out another soundless sigh of
relief. Obviously she hadn't sensed the hunger
that was tightening his body with each gliding,
scented movement of skin over skin.

He wanted her to stay relaxed. If she knew
how aroused he was, he was afraid she would

run from him again. Looking at her now, he could scarcely believe she was the exotic seductress known as Shannon.

No, he told himself harshly. *Don't think about Shannon. I can't deal with that right now.*

Grimly he admitted that it was all he could do to deal with Holly's innocence.

And with himself and his desire for her and his hatred of beautiful models.

Thinking about Shannon and tomorrow or the day after or anything but now, right now, will be a disaster, he reminded himself.

Neither Linc nor Holly could survive another such disaster, and he knew it.

Impersonally he continued kneading oil down her back. His hands slid down the muscles on either side of her spine all the way to the swell of her hips.

Holly let out a breath that wasn't quite steady.

Linc's hands retreated instantly.

"No," she said. "It's all right. I don't mind. It feels . . . good."

"It feels good to me, too."

Linc resumed the massage.

Sighing, eyes closed, she let her mind drift as it had in the seething heat of the Jacuzzi. His hands were strong, gentle, and demanded nothing of her.

Yet he was giving her a sensual pleasure that was slowly turning her bones to honey.

Holly made a tiny sound of disappointment

when Linc stopped rubbing oil into her back.

"So soon?" she murmured.

"Just switching ends."

Eyes still closed, she didn't see Linc's hungry, sensual smile. She felt the bed shift as he moved.

"How ticklish are your feet?" he asked.

"Don't you dare," Holly said lazily.

His answer was a laugh that was as gentle as his touch had been.

He took one of her feet between his hands. Rubbing just firmly enough so that he wouldn't tickle her, he massaged her foot. In time his hands worked up her calf, massaging muscles that were resilient rather than hard. She had a woman's strength, different from a man's yet just as enduring.

Holly made a husky sound and flexed her leg with relief. Linc was working knots out of her calf that she hadn't even noticed. But she knew just where they came from.

"I hate high heels," she said in a muffled voice.

"Don't wear them."

"Comes with the territory."

Shannon.

Linc thrust the thought from his mind.

There's only now, he told himself. *Just now.*

When he finished with her calf, he went beneath the towel to the muscles above her knee.

Tension crept back into Holly's body, but she made no objection to Linc's touch.

The towel that had been so tightly wrapped around her loosened with each stroke of his hands. He kneaded her with fingers and palms, surrounding her thigh with warm, gliding pressure.

He was careful not to go too high, too close to the lush softness he knew lay just beyond his reach. He could gauge the point at which he must stop from the subtle tension that came to Holly's body each time he went too far.

Linc worked down to her toes and back up, down and up, his touch impersonal. He made no attempt to turn the scented glide of his palms over her skin into a sensuous prelude to far more intimate touches.

By the time he switched his attention to Holly's other foot, she had stopped tensing every time his hands moved more than halfway up her thighs. Linc had made it clear in his words and in his touch that he wouldn't force any intimacy on her.

I won't do anything you don't want me to. I promise. Trust me, Holly.

Sighing, she shifted her position, loosening the towel still more.

Trusting him.

She drifted again as she had in the water, her mind empty, her body caressed by lovely, warm sensations.

"Time to roll over," Linc said easily.

Even as she started to roll over, Holly murmured tiny complaints at being disturbed.

The movement made her towel come undone. Belatedly she realized what had happened. She made a grab for the cloth, only to find it slipping through her fingers.

"I'll get you a dry one," Linc said.

Turning away as he spoke, he got up from the bed carrying the damp towel. Without so much as a look at the gleaming, naked length of her body, he set off again for the bathroom.

Feeling self-conscious and vulnerable, yet not truly afraid, Holly waited, eyes closed.

Trusting him.

A few moments later Linc returned with another, much smaller towel which he draped over her with a casual motion. Cloth covered her from breasts to thighs.

"That should keep the chill off," he said.

His voice was husky from the relentless hammering of desire through his body. There was nothing he could do about that any more than he could turn back the clock and take back his earlier mix of anger and fear after he had gone looking for Holly and found Shannon instead.

His worst nightmare smiling at him, making his body leap with raw passion.

Is that how it was for Dad? Linc thought. *A hunger that possessed him no matter what his beautiful bitches did to him?*

Thank God Holly is too naive to know the hold she has over me.

But Linc knew it wouldn't always be that way. Inevitably, Holly's innocence would give way to experience.

Then life would become a living hell for him, as it had been for his father.

Savagely Linc shoved his thoughts down. He would deal with the Shannon problem tomorrow or the day after or the day after that. Any time but now.

Now there was only the night and scented oil and Holly lying in his bed.

Trusting him.

The mattress shifted as Linc began massaging Holly again, smoothing away her residual tension and self-consciousness with each stroke. He carefully avoided going any lower than her collarbones.

Soon she forgot that she was lying on her back wearing only a small towel and a fragrant shimmer of oil. She sighed, relaxed, and gave herself over to the pleasure of Linc's touch once more.

"That feels so good," she murmured.

"I'm glad."

"I didn't realize how tight I was," she admitted.

Smiling, Linc touched her cheek. It wasn't quite a caress. More of a reassurance.

She sighed and rubbed her cheek against his fingers.

His heartbeat increased so much that his hand shook. Not trusting himself so close to Holly's sweet breasts, he got up and went to the end of the bed again.

Soon he was rubbing oil into her feet and legs once more. He slid his hands beneath the towel, kneading the smooth curves of her thighs, savoring the silk of her skin.

Holly gave a murmur of pleasure that sent wildfire through Linc's blood.

Slowly he eased his weight onto the bed, straddling her without confining her, never breaking the easy rhythms of the massage.

In a haze of growing pleasure, Holly felt Linc's hands slide up and over her hips, over the flat muscles of her stomach, up to a point just short of her breasts.

Then his hands swept down again, leaving behind a dizzying spiral of sensation that showed as a flush just beneath her golden skin.

The sure, slow pressure of Linc's hands on her body made Holly want to stop time, to float suspended forever while his hands soothed and set her on fire at the same time.

Without realizing it, she sighed his name and shifted her body in the same slow rhythms of his touch.

Linc closed his eyes and tried to still the violent leap of his flesh.

It was impossible. He wanted her more than he ever had, more than he believed he could want a woman.

Even so, he didn't vary the firm, gentle glide of his hands as he skirted the most sensitive areas of her body. Her trust in him was both humbling and more arousing than any experienced lover's caress could have been.

For Holly the tender torment was endless. She was suspended in pure sensation. Linc's hands were advancing, skirting, always retreating just short of intimacy, and the towel slid over her newly sensitive breasts with each breath she took.

Hot wires of sensation began radiating from the pit of her stomach. Her nipples tightened. She moaned without knowing it as Linc's hands slid up the inside of her thighs, only to curve aside at the last instant from the soft nest between her legs.

Restlessly, Holly shifted. She wanted him to touch her as he had at the campsite, tenderness and hunger and heat combined.

"Linc . . ."

Instantly his hands stopped moving. Holly felt the outline of his fingers press briefly against her stomach. Then his weight shifted as he moved to get off the bed.

She sat up in a rush, not caring that the towel slid off, leaving her naked.

"That isn't what I meant," she said.

"What did you mean?"

Linc's voice was neutral. He wasn't looking at her.

Holly took his hands in hers and put them back on her stomach.

"I want more, not less," she whispered, lying down again.

She felt the shudder that went through his powerful body. Only then did she understand that his casual words and gestures had been an act to reassure her.

He wanted her as much as he had earlier.

It should have frightened Holly. Instead, it sent another hot thrill through her body.

"You don't have to," Linc said huskily.

Then he turned and looked straight into her eyes, hiding nothing of his desire.

She shivered as stirrings of that same sweet and violent need went stitching through her like silver lightning.

"Frightened?" he asked.

"Not really," she whispered.

She shivered again.

"I meant what I said earlier," Linc said in a low voice. "I won't touch you at all, if that's what you want."

Holly took a deep, uneven breath.

"I can't guarantee anything," she said honestly. "I don't know what to do."

"You don't have to do anything at all. Let me pleasure you."

Linc bent forward and kissed Holly's eyelids. Then he traced the base of her eyelashes with the tip of his tongue.

The odd, tender caress made her tremble.

"Fear?" he asked huskily.

"No."

Her whisper was soft, shaky, almost a sigh.

"Whenever you want me to stop," he said, "tell me."

"I don't think I'll want you to stop. I . . . ache."

So did Linc, savagely, but he didn't think this was the time to say anything about it.

"Do you?" he asked softly. "I'll make it go away."

Despite Holly's growing hunger, she couldn't help tensing against what she knew was coming next. It had hurt the first time. She was afraid it would hurt the second time as well.

Linc warmed a tiny pool of oil in one palm. The oil sent up a fragrance that was clean and tantalizing. He sensed that for all her brave words, she wasn't ready for intimacy.

So he began seducing her all over again.

He started at her fingertips, but this time he went from her shoulders to her waist.

She gasped when his hands flowed over her breasts and moved on as though he had not noticed the taut rise of her nipples.

His hands kneaded down her stomach toward her thighs.

Holly held her breath, waiting for Linc to find and caress the aching warmth between her legs.

Again he disappointed her. His hands divided and slid around her, caressing down her thighs, setting fire to her skin.

When his hands drifted upward again, fingertips teasing, she unconsciously moved her legs apart, silently asking for his touch.

Linc almost gave in to the temptation. But he had taken too much for granted the first time. He would go slow this time if it killed him.

It probably will, he thought with a mixture of humor and raw need. *Because I won't take her again unless she wants me as much as I wanted her the first time.*

An invisible shudder went through Linc. He didn't know if it was possible for a woman to want a man that much, until there was nothing else that mattered.

But he knew he had to find out.

With Holly.

Nineteen

Deliberately Linc's palms caressed up the length of Holly's thighs.

Her breath caught in her throat, only to be let out in a groan of dismay. He did no more than let his palms glide over her, ruffling the midnight nest of hair.

"Linc?"

"Hmm?"

She opened her eyes and saw the intense pleasure he took simply in watching his hands on her body.

When he sensed her look, he smiled and let his hands move slowly from her navel to her breasts. The nipples hardened even more beneath his fingertips, telling him of her growing arousal.

Linc's breath came out in a rush. Slowly he lowered his face between her breasts, kissing her with great gentleness.

Only then did he admit to himself how much he feared he had lost her.

After a long moment Linc lifted his head and

kissed Holly's lips with an unhurried pleasure that made her tremble. Then he lowered his head to trace her nipples with lazy strokes of his tongue. His teeth closed delicately around her taut flesh, drawing gasps of pleasure from her.

Slowly, deliberately, he caressed the length of her body with his teeth and tongue and lips, pausing to taste each new curve of flesh. And all the while his hands moved in slow, undemanding rhythms over her skin.

When Linc's teeth found the softness of Holly's inner thighs, she twisted slowly against him. Her fingers threaded into his thick hair in a sensual demand she wasn't even aware of making.

She felt an agony of suspense as his mouth hesitated, then moved upward. He nuzzled aside her midnight hair and discovered the scented, melting heat of her response.

Linc whispered her name and her beauty against her softness. Then he began a slow, thorough savoring of all the textures of her desire. He felt the waves of pleasure that claimed her, heard her broken breathing, trembled to hear his own name called with each ragged breath she took.

After a time Linc resumed his languid exploration of Holly's body. His tongue teased her sensitive navel, made her breasts ache with pleasure, and gently tormented her lips.

His hand stroked her from her earlobes to the vulnerable hollow of her throat. He cherished her breasts, her navel, then eased his fingers into the silky hair between her thighs. Tenderly he sought the sleek, incredible softness inside her.

Holly made a sound deep in her throat and moved hungrily against him, asking.

Linc went rigid, gripped in a vise of relief and hunger that almost overwhelmed him. Many women enjoyed love play. Not as many liked having a man inside them. He had been afraid that he had killed that expression of passion in Holly.

"What's wrong?" she whispered.

Her hands slid over Linc's face, tilting his head up to her, looking at his eyes.

"I was afraid you'd never want me inside you again," he said raggedly. "But you do. Your body can't lie."

His fingers stroked intimately.

The rhythm of his caresses stole the breath from Holly's throat in a husky sigh. Her hips moved against his hand with a sinuous demand that shredded his control.

Linc closed his eyes, fighting to master his fierce response to her innocent sensuality.

When he opened his eyes, she was watching him. She held out her arms to him.

"I'm not afraid of your strength anymore," Holly said simply.

Despite her words, Linc gathered her against his body as though she were more fragile than her new trust in him.

Holly's hands slid down his naked back,

pulling him closer, savoring the power of him, a power that he was holding in check for her.

But she no longer wanted him to hold back.

She took his hand and guided it down her body. The intimacy of his fingers was no longer a shock, but rather a revelation of her own sensual possibilities.

With each sleek, probing movement of Linc's hand, the languid weakness that pervaded Holly became a tension that had nothing to do with fear. A fine mist bloomed over her skin and her breath shortened. She moved against him with liquid warmth, melting over him with small moans.

Linc shivered as wild hunger fought self-control.

When her fingers found the towel that was still wrapped around his hips, she tugged it off impatiently.

"Holly—" Linc began.

"I want to feel your skin against mine. All of you."

This time when Holly touched his heavily aroused body, she didn't retreat.

As warm fingers closed around him, Linc couldn't control the groan that shuddered through his chest. Guiding himself to her sleek center, he rubbed gently against her soft, very sensitive flesh.

A sunburst of fire went through Holly. She twisted against him, trying to touch all of him at once, seeking something that would end the beautiful agony gripping her. She whispered his name in a litany of desire, asking him to be part of her.

"Are you sure?" Linc said huskily, fighting his own consuming need to be inside her. "I couldn't live with hurting you again."

She shifted, opening herself to his body with a trust that almost undid him.

Hands trembling, he reached into the bed-side drawer. With swift motions he sheathed himself.

"Linc—?"

"Gently, Holly. Very gently."

He guided her legs around his waist. Then he teased her slick softness with his body until she cried out and melted all over him again.

At that instant Linc began to take her, using the same tender care that he had in seducing her. He advanced by fractions, always giving less of himself than she wanted.

"Linc," she said, trembling. "You said you would make the ache go away. You've made it worse!"

With a husky sound that was Holly's name, Linc let himself sink into her.

Holly's eyes widened with surprise as she felt how deeply they were joined.

"Does this—hurt you?" he managed.

She tried to answer. She couldn't. A sweet heat was melting her very core, spilling over to him.

It was the only answer Linc needed and far more than he had expected. He moved slowly within Holly, deeply, watching her surprise and wonder as her own sensuality consumed her, giving her wholly to him.

Arching, shivering, crying his name again and again, Holly clung to the man who was giving her ecstasy.

Linc kept moving slowly, wanting it to last forever, to spend his life held within the shimmering instant of Holly's consummation. Fiercely he willed himself not to give in.

Then he felt control being stripped from him heartbeat by heartbeat. Each silky contraction of her body was a tongue of fire licking over him.

With a throttled cry he bent down and drank the cries of ecstasy from her lips, letting himself drown in the sweet rain of her release.

The next morning Holly woke up still held closely along Linc's powerful body. Their legs were tangled together, his arms were around her, and the hair on his chest both tickled and delighted her.

With unselfconscious pleasure she burrowed against him. She enjoyed the intimacy of his hard thigh between her legs, his muscular chest warming her breasts, the strong tendons of his neck beneath her palm. She moved even closer to him, savoring the changing pressure of his body on hers.

Memories of their lovemaking sparked through her. Last night had been a time of sleeping and waking in warm darkness to the feel of Linc's mouth loving her. Passion had broken over them like a desert storm, shaking them until they cried out and held each other in an ecstasy as fierce as lightning.

Then Holly had slept again and awakened with a smile because even in total darkness, she knew Linc was near. She could taste him, touch him, drink in his presence with every sense in her body. Then she could pull his male strength around her until he filled her and lightning rained down again.

Heat uncurled in the pit of Holly's stomach as she remembered how it had been. She tried to lie quietly, but finally the temptation of having Linc so near was too great to resist any longer.

She stretched sensually against her sleeping lover, caressing and being caressed by his body in return. Smiling and murmuring softly, her skin so sensitized to his presence that it was almost painful, Holly stretched again.

Even before Linc was fully awake, his arms tightened around her. He pulled her onto his chest and smoothed his hands down her spine to her hips.

Holly shivered with pleasure and sensual anticipation. She smiled down at him.

"Good morning," she said huskily.

Linc looked at Holly for a long time. His hazel eyes were dark with emotions that she couldn't name, but she sensed that all of them weren't as warm and peaceful as hers.

"You're even more beautiful in the morning," he said, thinking about the night before.

Memories of Holly, sweet and wild and abandoned in his arms, responding to him as no other woman ever had.

Memories of himself, responding to her as he never had to any woman.

Then came memories of his father, a shell of a man obsessed by a woman too beautiful to be faithful to just one man.

"My God, what am I going to do . . . ?" Linc asked in a raw tone.

Holly's breath caught at the tension in him, the darkness in his eyes and voice. She knew he was thinking of his mother and stepmother, as cruel as they had been beautiful.

"You're going to trust me," Holly said. "I'm not like them."

Before he could respond, she bent her head and traced his lips with the tip of her tongue.

"I love you, Linc."

He groaned and buried his fingers in her thick, long hair. He held her mouth against his in a passionate kiss.

The phone on the bedside table rang.

He ignored it. The mating of her mouth with his was too good to end.

The phone kept ringing.

Five times. Six.

"I never should have plugged the damned thing in again," Linc said against her lips.

Silently Holly agreed. Silently, because Linc was kissing her again, deeply, telling her with each slow movement of his tongue how much he wanted her.

Ten rings.

Eleven.

Twelve.

With a savage curse, Linc turned aside. His finger raked over a switch, activating the speaker on the phone.

"People usually give up after twelve rings," he snarled.

There was a pause, then Roger's laughter floated up out of the phone.

"Good morning to you, too," Roger said dryly. "Is Shannon still around, or did you have her for a midnight snack?"

Linc raised an eyebrow in Holly's direction. She sighed.

"Good morning, Roger," she said with a total lack of enthusiasm.

She tried to ignore Linc's expression, changing as she watched, stopping just short of the hard-faced stranger who had taken her so casually the first time.

Then she remembered his anguish when he realized what he had done . . . and the single tear that had burned all the way through her skin to her very soul.

Silently Holly prayed for more time with Linc.

He'll learn to trust me, she thought, *if only I have more time before we're torn apart.*

Roger cleared his throat.

Holly realized he must had said something that she hadn't responded to.

"What was that?" she asked.

"Sorry if I caught you at an inappropriate moment," Roger said. "We leave for Cabo San Lucas in an hour."

"That's not enough warning—" she began.

"It's all I have," he interrupted. "Hurricane Giselle is closing in on the cape."

"But—"

"If we're lucky," Roger continued relentlessly, "we'll get five days. If not, only two. Giselle and the fashion seasons wait for no man. I've packed up your stuff here. Meet us at the airport in an hour."

Holly made a sound of frustration.

"Can't I fly down after you have everything in place?" she asked.

"It's already in place. I sent the technicians there when Hidden Springs was rained out."

She muttered something.

So did Roger.

"Really, love, I'm sorry," he said finally. "But we're behind schedule as it is. If we don't get the shots we need, the Romance campaign is in the loo."

"Get another model," Linc said.

His voice was clear and hard enough to make Holly flinch.

Roger's laugh was equally hard.

"You're joking," Roger retorted. "Shannon *is* the Royce Romance campaign."

Linc looked at her.

Waiting.

"I'll be at the airport in an hour," she said tonelessly.

She flipped the switch before Roger could reply.

Linc got out of bed in a single, savage motion. He stood with his back to her. Every muscle in his big body was rigid with tension. When he spoke, his voice showed the effort it took to control himself.

"Why?" Linc asked.

"It's my job."

"Quit."

"I'm under contract."

"Break it."

Holly's breath came in with a rough sound.

Too soon, she thought wildly. *This is all happening too soon.*

"No," she said.

Slowly Linc turned around. His eyes searched hers. She met them squarely.

"Is it so important for you to be wanted by more than one man?" Linc asked.

"What?"

"You heard me."

"That has nothing to do with it!"

"It did for the two 'models' I knew," he said coldly.

"They weren't typical," Holly said. "Women who call themselves models and sell sex on the side don't last long."

"Yeah. Right."

"You bet I'm right," she said in a rising voice. "What those so-called models are peddling is nothing special. It can be found in any town big enough to have an alley."

Linc's disbelief showed in the sardonic curl of his mouth.

Holly got up and walked over to him.

"Listen to me," she said. "Real models work on their feet, not their back, and they work damned hard."

"Doing what? Undressing?"

"Real models hold poses in impossible positions for hours on end and smile convincingly on command," she said flatly.

Linc looked skeptical.

"Real models don't eat when they're hungry," Holly said. "Real models exercise when they'd rather be asleep, work long hours under miserable conditions and then put up with insults from ignorant, bigoted people who think that model is another name for whore."

Linc watched her with eyes that were nearly black, as opaque as stones at the bottom of a twilight river.

She took a deep, shaking breath, caught between anger and a fear that was turning her stomach to ice.

"Models aren't whores," she said. "Fashion is a business. Models are part of it."

"Some business. Showing off overpriced clothes for rich women."

"Wrong again," Holly said. "High fashion is a very small part of the industry."

"Industry?" he asked scornfully.

"Precisely. Everybody who wears clothes is part of it. Even you. Fashion is part of the gross national product just like cars, candy bars, and computers."

With a tight, frustrated gesture, Linc ran his fingers through his hair.

"Fine," he said, his voice grudging. "Fashion is a flaming national asset. Is it more important to you than being with me?"

"Why don't you come to Cabo San Lucas with me?" Holly countered. "Then we'll not only be together, but you'll also see what modeling is—and isn't."

"I have work to do. Real work."

"And just how is raising overpriced horses for rich men more important work than mine?" she challenged.

"Raising horses isn't work, it's my life."

"Yes, I know."

Linc's expression changed, showing more surprise than anger.

"Is that what you're trying to say?" he asked slowly. "Modeling is your *life?*"

"It's part of me."

"More important than what we could have?"

"I'm not making you choose between me and your work," Holly said desperately. "Why are you making me choose?"

He turned away, walked across the room, and began pulling clothes out of his closet.

"I'll drive you to the airport," he said.

She crossed the room quickly and stood behind him. Tentatively her fingers traced the muscled ridges of his back. Her arms slid around his body in a hug.

"I love you," Holly said softly.

She felt him stiffen, then let out his breath in a long sigh.

Gently he unwrapped her arms from around his body and turned to face her.

"Don't love me," he said, his voice rich with anger and sadness.

"But—"

"Loving me will hurt you more than anything I could do to you. And in spite of what I think of models, I don't want you hurt."

"I don't understand," Holly said in a low voice.

Linc gathered her hands and kissed her fingertips tenderly, watching her with eyes that were far too dark.

"Love is a game for masochists, Holly. You can't win, you can't stay even, and you can't get out of the game."

"I don't believe that," she said shakily.

"You will."

Linc released her hands.

"Get dressed," he said, turning away. "You don't want to be late for work."

Twenty

Holly's smile was brilliant. It ignored the hot needles of fatigue that stitched across her shoulders and made her thighs quiver beneath the flowing, sea-green chiffon gown.

Behind her reared the desolate splendor of the rocks that formed Cabo San Lucas. Barren, weathered, shimmering beneath the brutal tropical heat, the heaps of stone endured the sun and sea that would eventually destroy them.

A desultory breeze lifted clinging folds of chiffon from Holly's sticky skin. The fragile cloth rippled and gleamed, echoing the waves swelling toward the brutally hot sand.

The net of diamonds around her throat sparkled like drops of water flung from a breaking wave. Late afternoon light turned her eyes to gold and made even the jagged rocks look velvety, almost inviting.

The director raised his bullhorn.

"Right," he said in a clipped voice.

Holly held her breath and let herself hope that the shoot was finally over.

"Again," the director said. "But get Shannon's hair first."

"Damn," she said under her breath.

She put her fists in the small of her back and knuckled hard on knots of burning muscles. Her body was cramped from hours of bending and turning and posing on the uneven ground.

The motion sequence she was doing now was easier physically, but mentally it was infinitely worse. Walking down to the water and standing ankle-deep in foam was easy.

Stepping into Roger's arms and looking eager for his embrace was not.

It was bad enough to be held by a man who was not Linc. To be kissed was unbearable.

For the hundredth time Holly wished that Roger had chosen a stranger, rather than himself, to be the Royce male model. It would have been easier for her to ignore desire in a stranger's eyes.

With outward patience she stood while the stylist fussed over her long hair.

"Bloody damned nuisance," the stylist muttered. "Whatever I do, the wind will undo before I turn around."

"Tell me about it," Holly said sardonically. "My scalp is raw from all the combing."

With a complete lack of sympathy, the stylist raked the brush through her long hair again.

Holly sighed and stood still, enduring what was necessary for her profession. Roger wanted her hair unbound, rippling and lifting in the wind like a midnight cloud. The effect would be sensuous and romantic.

If it ever worked.

The air moving off the sea was sultry, salty, and uncertain. It turned Holly's hair into tangled strings. The unpredictable breeze also required her to hold poses until her muscles cramped while the photographer waited for the generator-driven fans and nature to stop fighting for control of her long hair.

At least the still photos are almost done, she thought. *For that small blessing I give thanks.*

One more crack from Jerry about icicles and I'll shove his camera down his throat.

After a final brutal sweep with the brush, the stylist trotted off the set, leaving Holly to the elements once more.

"Shannon, are you awake out there?" the director yelled through the bullhorn.

She gritted her teeth and waved.

"Remember," the director continued, "this is supposed to simply ooze sensuality. 'When you meet the man of your dreams, be wearing a Royce.' "

She waved again.

"Remember the theme," the director yelled. "It's the man of your secret dreams walking out of the water, not some stranger!"

"I've read the script," Holly called.

"Then bloody well act like it!"

"Then bloody well get on with it!" she yelled.

There were sidelong looks around the set.

Before this shoot, Holly had had a reputation as the least temperamental of models.

No longer.

The crew had seen—and heard—more of her temper in the last five days at Cabo San Lucas they had in the last five years.

"Action!" yelled the director.

Automatically Holly followed the directions in the script. She waited for a wave to break on the shore. Then she turned languidly and bent over, trailing her fingertips through the water that foamed lightly across her feet.

She tasted the salt on her fingertips with a lingering touch of her tongue. Then, slowly, she arched her back and lifted her long hair into the wind.

She looked sad and wistful and very much alone, a woman longing for her lover.

The expression came easily to Holly's face. She had been aching for Linc since he had left her at the airport five days ago.

She had called him three times.

The housekeeper had answered each time.

Linc had not returned the calls.

"Makeup!" yelled the director.

With an irritated jerk of her head, Holly dropped her arms. Impatiently she waited for the makeup man to come out and repair whatever damage the director had spotted.

Roger was farther out in the water, just behind the place where waves curled over into thunder and foam. Swearing, he dove through the breaking waves and started wading toward her. His path was the incandescent wake of the sun across the face of the sea.

Quickly he came ashore and stood by Holly's side, watching her with a mixture of sympathy and worry. He had worked with enough volatile women to know that the normally unflappable Holly was very close to slipping the leash on her temper.

"Under the eyes," the director instructed through the bullhorn. "Gloss the lips while you're about it."

Roger stood very close, examining her critically.

"You really should try sleeping at night," he said.

"I do try."

"Then try succeeding," he said in a clipped voice.

Holly started to retort, but the makeup artist shut her up by applying gloss with a heavy hand.

The hair stylist rushed forward again, ever alert for the opportunity to brush her hair into a flyaway cloud of black silk.

The makeup man went to work erasing unwanted shadows under her eyes.

"I sleep just fine," Holly said the instant her lips were free.

"Rot," Roger said. "I've heard you pacing your balcony all night, every night."

She compressed her lips and said nothing.

There was nothing she could say. She had slept only a few hours a night since Linc had dropped her at the airport without so much as a goodbye kiss.

"I'll tiptoe from now on," she said tightly. "Sorry to keep you awake."

"I'm more worried about your sleep than mine."

"Don't be."

"Bloody hell," he snarled. "I don't want the Royce Reflection to look like a half-starved, overworked waif."

He made an impatient gesture when Holly started to argue.

"Don't bother denying it," Roger said. "I'm the one who has had to take in your dresses down here. Twice."

"Sorry," Holly said again.

He swore.

"I don't want apologies, I want you happy!" he said.

"Is that in my contract?"

There was a taut silence.

"It's that damned cowboy, isn't it?" Roger asked finally.

Holly's face changed despite her efforts to show nothing. Then she pulled her professional smile over her face like a mask.

"It's the humidity here that's too rough," she said casually. "A regular sauna. Guess I'll never make a tropical princess."

"It can be just as humid in Palm Springs," Roger pointed out.

She just smiled again, a smile as empty as her eyes.

The makeup man finished and left as silently as he had come.

Holly hardly noticed.

Her whole attention was focused down the beach, beyond the roped-off area that kept the curious public away from the set. She thought she had seen a man there, a tall, well-built man, walking toward the water.

The man had moved like Linc.

Holly's heart stopped, then beat frantically. She stared out over the ocean, but could see only a lean, muscular man silhouetted against the incandescent wake of the sun.

He dove into the brilliant colors and vanished.

"What's wrong, love?" Roger asked. "You're shaking."

For a moment she couldn't answer.

He turned away and called to the director.

"Wrap it up," Roger yelled crisply. "Shannon has had enough for today."

"No," Holly said.

The stark refusal stopped him. He looked back at her.

She didn't notice. She was too busy raging at herself that just the shadow of a powerful, easy-moving man could upset her so much that she forgot where she was, who she was, why she was here in sultry Cabo San Lucas.

This has to stop, Holly told herself harshly. *I can't go on like a sleepwalker blundering through a dissolving dream.*

I owe Roger more than the shell of Shannon.

In the past she had pretended that Linc
was nearby when she performed for the
camera.

*I'll just have to pretend again, using new mem-
ories they same way I used old ones.*

New memories that were hot enough to melt
the icy fear that came when she thought of his
words.

Don't love me.

*Love is a game for masochists. You can't win, you
can't stay even and you can't get out of the game.*

Yet she could no more help loving him than
breathing.

"This is the best time," Holly said to Roger.
"The light is like honey."

"There'll be another afternoon tomorrow,"
he said.

"The hurricane won't stall off the coast forever. Tomorrow might be too late."

"But—"

"Ready!" she called out to the director, cutting across Roger's protest.

And this time she was.

She pulled her memories of Linc around her,
wrapping herself in shimmering sensuality.
She remembered the moment when she woke
up in Linc's arms, his warm tongue teasing her
lips, making her smile.

Jerry, who was on the sidelines taking still
photos for the magazine campaign, crowed triumphantly.

"That's it! God, babe, that's fantastic!"

"Quiet!" the director shouted.

Holly heard Jerry and the director as though they were at the end of a long tunnel. Wrapped in memories, she radiated a sensual hunger that was all the more compelling because her face was shadowed with loneliness.

Wind swirled around her. It caressed her skin, lifted her hair, and billowed the countless layers of sea-foam chiffon, revealing the perfect curves of her legs.

Light poured over her like a lover made of molten gold.

Roger, wet with salt water, his hair in artistic disarray, walked out of the breakers toward her. A black mask and snorkel dangled from his left hand. Slanting light picked up the gleam of water trickling down his tanned skin. Black swim briefs clung to his athletic body.

Holly watched him walk forward and mentally fitted Linc's likeness over Roger.

It didn't work.

She closed her eyes and tried again.

The director's frustrated comments bounced off Holly's concentration. She held out her hand and let herself be pulled into Roger's arms.

His head bent slowly toward her. He kissed her with cool lips as he had all afternoon, kisses that were meant to appear sexy but were simply part of the script.

Then his arms tightened and his tongue shot between her teeth, trying to change a stage kiss into something much more intimate.

After an instant of shock, Holly stiffened her

arms against Roger's chest and angrily shoved away from him.

"Cut!" yelled the director.

He strode down the beach, bullhorn in hand.

"Shannon, what in bloody hell is wrong with you?" the director demanded.

"Ask Roger."

The director turned to his boss.

Roger sighed, shrugged, and glanced at Holly.

"Sorry, love," he said to her. "You're such an overwhelming temptation."

"I'm supposed to be," she said coolly. "That's the whole idea of the campaign. Your idea. Remember? An *act*."

Roger smiled charmingly, but there was real masculine hunger beneath his polished surface.

"Women who look like you need more than kissing," he said quietly.

With a hissed word, Holly turned her back on him.

Roger took the director's arm and walked the angry man back up the beach, talking to him in soothing tones.

Holly didn't bother to listen. Her eyes were closed and her whole body was tight. Motionless, she fought her instinctive revulsion at being kissed so intimately by any man but Linc.

Actresses kiss men like that all the time—and hate most of them, if the gossip is true, she reminded herself savagely.

Surely I can be kissed by a good friend without freezing up.

Yet even as Holly lectured herself, she doubted that she could bear another intimate kiss from Roger without going for his eyes like an outraged cat.

Technicians rushed with frantic speed around her, adjusting lights and reflectors, reading light meters, cursing.

She knew why. The lighting of the scene was crucial. Her face had to be illuminated mostly by the setting sun rather than artificial light. Roger's face had to be almost entirely in shadow.

And the sunset behind them had to radiate all the colors of desire.

To achieve the three effects at once was a feat that had the technicians in a frenzy.

"Is Roger in place?" yelled the director.

Holly shaded her eyes and looked into the dazzling reflections left on the surface of the sea by the setting sun. The blaze of light blinded her, but she could make out a tall masculine form walking out of the waves toward her.

She fought the coldness creeping up from her stomach. She didn't want Roger to touch her again.

Not like that.

"We're ready," Holly shouted.

"Action!"

Once again she pulled her memories of Linc around her and went through the motions of a woman watching the man of her dreams emerge from the sea.

Once again she held out her hand to him almost shyly, blinded by the dying sun.

But before the man's fingers touched hers, memories and reality collided.

"Linc!"

He took her hand and pressed her palm against his lips.

Wind swept up Holly's dress and her hair, wrapping Linc in a sensual caress even as he pulled her into his arms.

His lips were firm, sweet and salt, better than her memories, as wild and beautiful as the setting sun.

She flowed against him, fitting herself to him without reservation, abandoning herself to his potent heat. When she felt his tongue caress hers, she thought she would die of the pleasure coursing through her.

"Cut!" the director yelled. "That was perfect, but I believe in insurance. One more time. Hey, out there! Cut!"

Slowly Linc lifted his head. His eyes were hooded, his mouth still hungry.

"They think you're Roger," Holly said breathlessly.

"I know. I've been watching him kiss you all afternoon."

Linc's voice was as hard as his eyes. Before she could answer, his arms closed around her like iron bars. His mouth came down swiftly, expecting resistance.

She responded with a force that equaled his, dragging his head down to her lips, probing his mouth with her hungry tongue. She didn't care about the people on the beach, the expensive dress whipping in the wind, the warm sea creaming around her calves.

She only knew that she was starving for the taste and feel of the man who had walked out of the sun to hold her in his arms.

"Shannon! Who the hell is that out there with you?" Roger called indignantly. "How did he get past the ropes!"

Holly ignored the shout, ignored everything but her overwhelming need to drink Linc's presence into every pore.

When he tried to end the kiss, she held him all the more tightly.

With casual strength, Linc jerked free of her arms and walked back into the incandescent sea.

Shaking, almost wild, Holly held out her hand and called his name again and again.

There was no answer.

Linc dove beneath a wave and vanished into the burning sea.

Twenty-one

"Shannon, are you all right?" Roger shouted.

Holly couldn't answer.

He ran down the beach toward her.

"Shannon? Can you hear me?"

He didn't stop running until he was standing right in front of her, forcing her to acknowledge him.

"I'm fine," she said shakily.

"Who the hell was that?"

"Linc."

Roger's lips turned into a thin, downward-curving line.

"I should have guessed," he said bitterly. "You kissed him like he was a god come to claim you."

Shivering visibly with passion, Holly didn't disagree.

Roger took her face between his hands. His eyes noted every bit of the sensual excitement blazing in her golden eyes and the hunger trembling in her red lips.

"If you had kissed me like that," he said,

"I wouldn't have walked away. Shannon, let me make—"

"Stop it," she interrupted harshly. "Stop it!"

Trembling, she jerked away from him and stared into the sea where Linc had vanished.

She saw nothing but the distorted, blinding reflections of the dying sun.

The director stormed up. He was waving his bullhorn about like a sword.

"This is a zoo, a bloody zoo!" the director yelled. "I get the best shot of my life and Jerry keeps yapping that it's the wrong chap!"

"Couldn't you tell it wasn't me?" Roger asked irritably.

"Hardly," the director said, his voice clipped. "A tall, well-built chap walks out of the surf and kisses Shannon, right? It's been happening all day, right?"

"Right," Roger snapped.

"The only difference," the director said angrily, "is that this last time the light was perfect, the wind was perfect, and the two of them damn near melted the lenses off the bloody cameras."

"You couldn't see his face, the difference in height?" Roger asked.

"You're in silhouette, your face is in shadow," the director shot back. "You have to bend over to kiss Shannon. So did he. Am I supposed to notice that one of you bent down a few centimeters farther than the other?"

"Bloody hell," was all Roger said.

"Too right," the director retorted. "One more time."

With that he turned and stalked back up the beach, yelling through his bullhorn with every step.

Technicians scattered.

One of the light men walked up to the director, pointed to the sun. It was now barely a fingernail above the horizon. Then the technician pointed toward the beach where lighting equipment waited amid an orderly tangle of cables.

The director made an angry gesture at the technician and waved everybody into place.

Holly turned back toward the sea, but saw only Roger's retreating figure heading into the water. She looked up the beach, beyond the ropes where people stared and pointed at her and the cameras.

There was no tall, powerful man among them.

There was no one at all between her and the shimmering expanse of sand and rock leading to the cliff-top hotel.

It was as though she had conjured up Linc out of her own tearing loneliness, but he had been too potent to be held by her spell. He had pulled all the colors of her desire around him.

And vanished.

"Wake up, Shannon!" shouted the director. "I said action!"

Empty, she turned and waited for the wrong man to walk out of the sea to her.

Like a nightmare, the scene repeated itself endlessly.

The dark outline of a man coming out of the scarlet sea.

The meeting of hands.

The kiss.

Each time it was worse. Each time it was harder for Holly not to show the rebellion of her mind, her body, her very soul at having to endure another man's touch.

It was Linc she wanted.

Only Linc.

The nightmare continued. Warmth drained from her body even more quickly than light drained from the sky.

When the director finally decided that there was no point in continuing, the sky held only a faint blush of orange.

Shivering, aching, chilled despite the heat, Holly walked beyond the reach of the luminous waves.

And Roger.

Quickly he caught up with her. He walked very close to her, but was careful not to touch her. His brilliant blue eyes watched her every movement, measuring her strain in the tightness of her body and the bleak lines of her face.

Common sense told Roger that she should have looked less appealing to him now that she was strained, almost haggard.

Yet she didn't.

Holly simply looked withdrawn, mysterious, her beauty heightened by the darkness that moved just beneath her golden surface.

Silently Roger cursed the man who had gotten past Holly's legendary guard, only to cut her to her heart.

When the director would have come over to her, Roger waved him off.

"But we could try it with—" began the director.

"Stuff it," Roger said curtly. "Can't you see that she's dead on her feet?"

Without another word he led her through the bustle of technicians to the tent she used for changing costumes.

Inside the tent hung three more dresses just like the one Holly wore. They were expensive insurance against the random leap of waves. Two of the gowns showed stains of salt and water at the hem, testimony to the unpredictable ocean.

Roger began unfastening Holly's dress with the deft, impersonal fingers of a man who made his living clothing women.

Abruptly she came out of her daze.

"No," she said.

"Don't be ridiculous," he said. "I've undressed you a thousand times—and dressed you, for that matter."

She stepped beyond his reach.

"Not this time," she said flatly.

"I'll wait outside, then."

"You don't have to wait."

"I'm taking you to supper," Roger said.

"No."

"That's an order, Shannon, not an invitation. I'll be damned if I'm going to take in those dresses again."

"But Linc—"

"If Linc wanted to be here, he would be here, wouldn't he?" Roger interrupted.

Holly looked away, unable to meet the anger and compassion in Roger's blue eyes.

"He's probably at the hotel, waiting for me to finish working," she said.

Roger grabbed a cordless phone off a wardrobe trunk and turned his back on her.

"Change your clothes," he said curtly.

After a moment of hesitation, Holly began taking off the clinging dress. She heard Roger talk to the hotel desk and waited with her breath held while Linc's room was rung.

No one answered.

Roger asked for Lincoln McKenzie to be paged in the hotel restaurants and lobby.

No one responded.

"Right," Roger said.

He hung up and put the phone back on the trunk.

Holly didn't say a word.

"Linc must be having supper somewhere else," he said.

His tone said *with someone else.*

Numbly she pulled on the soft, loose cotton float she had worn down to the beach that morning.

"Supper," Roger said firmly.

She went past him, headed toward her

room. All she wanted was a shower and the peace of an empty room.

Not quite all, she admitted. *What I really want is Linc.*

But Linc had disappeared as unexpectedly as he had appeared in the first place.

Roger walked Holly to her room. Along the way he made conversation that she didn't really hear and didn't bother to answer.

Eagerly she unlocked her door. If she couldn't have Linc, she wanted the solitude that waited just inside. But before the door opened more than a few inches, Roger put his hand on her arm to prevent her from slipping past him.

"I'll pick you up in forty-five minutes," he said.

"I'm not hungry."

"How would you know? You haven't tried eating for five days. You might find you're starving."

Holly shrugged.

He looked closely at her. His eyes changed, darker now, the color of twilight.

"If not food, then something else," he said. "Invite me in, Shannon. You'll never be hungry again. I guarantee it. You know how good I am with a woman's smooth body."

"Don't, Roger," she whispered. "Please don't. I—"

The rest of her words were lost in a gasp as the door to her room was jerked open from inside.

·"I'm afraid you'll have to put it on hold," Linc drawled almost lazily.

But his eyes were cold when he looked at Holly. They were even colder when he shifted his glance to Roger.

"Don't worry," he said to Roger. "I can't stay long. You'll understand if I don't invite you in."

Roger grimaced.

Linc gave the handsome designer a sardonic smile.

"But I do appreciate you warming her up," he added smoothly. "Like I said, I don't have much time."

With that, Linc pulled Holly inside and locked the door.

"That wasn't necessary," she said tightly. "I've said no to Roger before without your help."

"Really?" he said, reaching for her. "I didn't hear a damn thing that sounded like no."

"Linc—" She turned her face aside, avoiding his lips.

"What's the matter? Wrong man?"

Linc's expression was harsh. He let go of Holly and reached for the door.

"I'll call Roger back," Linc said.

"That's not it!"

"Oh?"

His voice was still lazy, and his eyes were still like polished stones.

"Then what's the problem?" he asked. "Do you need a camera to perform?"

She stared at him, too shocked to answer.

He shrugged.

"That shouldn't be hard to arrange," he said coolly. "This is Mexico, after all. A bribe gets you anywhere, even into locked hotel rooms. One camera, coming right up. Or do you need more?"

"Why are you doing this?" Holly whispered.

"Doing what? I cut short my trip to Texas—"

"I didn't know you were—" she interrupted.

"You didn't ask about *my* work," Linc interrupted curtly.

"I thought the Mountains of Sunrise—" she began.

Linc talked over her.

"I was looking over some Arabians in Texas," he said, "but I couldn't stop thinking about you, about what you'd said."

"About us?"

His eyes became shuttered.

"About modeling," he corrected. "I realized that maybe I didn't really know what professional models did for their pay. So I chartered a plane to Cabo San Lucas."

Holly let out a long sigh of relief.

"Then you understand what it's like, now," she said.

Linc's lips twisted in a travesty of a smile.

"Yeah," he said. "I sure as hell do."

A chill went down her spine.

"Just what do you think you understand?" she asked.

"Nothing new. I spent the afternoon watching your half-naked boss kiss you and listening to the men around the rope speculate about what you're like in bed. Hell of a way to sell clothes."

"I'm glad it was so exciting for the spectators," Holly said harshly. "For me, it was about as romantic as cleaning fish."

Linc looked startled.

"For me they were stage kisses," she continued in her hard Shannon voice. "All show and no go."

"All of them?" he asked skeptically. "All afternoon?"

"Except once, when you walked out of the sea and kissed me and I felt like I had fallen into the sun."

His expression changed as her words sliced through his anger to the hunger beneath.

It was the same wild hunger he sensed beneath the anger in Holly's words and glittering eyes.

"I doubt that Roger would agree about stage kisses and cleaning fish," Linc said.

"That is Roger's problem," she said, clipping each word.

Linc's hand rubbed through his hair.

"And my problem?" he suggested quietly. "Is Roger my problem, too?"

"Only if you want him to be."

"What does that mean?"

"It means that I want only one man on earth. You."

Linc's breath caught.

"Shocked?" Holly asked. "I don't play games, Linc. I love you too much for that."

"Then why won't you quit modeling?"

Now his voice was neither angry nor hard, simply curious.

"Wrong question," she said.

"Why?"

"What you really want to know is why I won't destroy half of myself to please you," Holly said. "That's not love, Linc. That's hate."

"But—" he began.

She kept on talking.

"If I asked you to kill the part of you that loves the ranch," she said, "what would you call it? Love or hate?"

Linc drew in a sharp breath.

"Love you, love your modeling," he said. "Is that it?"

"Modeling is a part of me just as the ranch is a part of you. If you can't accept that, then you can't accept *me*."

There was a long silence.

"I didn't come here to argue," he said.

"Really? Then why did you come?" she asked.

"You know why. You knew it when you kissed me."

Holly's eyes widened. Shadows moved in their tawny depths as she remembered the wildness and passion Linc drew so effortlessly from her depths.

"Is that all you want from me?" she whispered.

"It's the same thing you want from me. Don't bother to deny it. I've never been kissed like that."

She shivered. "Because I love you."

Linc gathered her close to him. He groaned deep in his throat as his hands felt her naked warmth through the thin cotton dress.

"Kiss me like that again," he said. "Send us both falling into the sun."

"But—"

He pulled her against his thighs, letting her feel his need.

"Tomorrow," he said thickly. "We'll talk tomorrow."

Twenty-two

Holly awoke before her alarm went off.

It was always like that when she was working. She hated the alarm so much that she had developed a mental alarm clock that went off early, just to avoid the mechanical one.

Gently she eased out from under Linc's arm and pushed in the alarm button on the clock. Except for the golden glow of a nightlight across the room, it was dark.

Linc muttered and moved restlessly, seeking Holly even in his sleep. She slipped beneath his arm again. Still sleeping, he gathered her against his body and sighed deeply.

Holly savored the stolen moments of his warmth. She enjoyed the weight of his arm wrapped around her hips. She delighted in the smell and texture of his skin. She loved the taste of him on her lips and the feel of him against her body.

She even liked having her nose tickled by the dark hair on his chest.

The clock ticked its unhappy reminder of

time flying by, when all Holly wanted was for time to be as still as she was. She knew she should get out of bed right now. There was barely time to do her exercises, shower, wash and set her hair, check her nails . . . all the endless, time-consuming things that came with the territory called modeling.

But she had missed Linc too much to leave him easily now.

"I love you," she whispered.

The words were a bare thread of sound in the silence.

They were answered by silence alone.

She hadn't expected anything else. Even if he had been awake, he wouldn't have said what she longed to hear.

I love you.

Uneasiness twisted through Holly, cold fingernails of fear that she couldn't ignore.

During the night Linc had made love to her repeatedly. He had touched her deeply, teaching her to respond to the siren call of his potent body. Each time had been better for her, a sensual progression that finally had consumed them both.

He had given her the most intense pleasure imaginable. And then he had doubled it, showing her the limitations of her own imagination with each sweet movement of his body over hers.

There had been no end to her wanting.

Or his.

Even now Holly wanted Linc with an intensity that frightened her. He had become as necessary to her as her eyes or her hands or her heart.

Yet he could leave so suddenly, so completely, a shadow diving beneath an incandescent sea.

When she thought of it, she felt vulnerable.

No. Face it, she told herself bluntly. *I'm scared.*

It was like being alone in a desert storm with lightning raining down, lightning striking closer to her each time . . .

And the only shelter around was locked and bolted against her.

If Linc loved me, it wouldn't matter that he is sinking into me, becoming a part of me all the way to my soul.

If Linc loved me, he would cherish and protect me from my own vulnerability to him.

If Linc loved me, he would open the door to himself and not lock it again until I was safe inside.

If he loved me . . .

But he didn't.

It wasn't merely the words he didn't say that warned Holly. For all his passionate intensity, for all his consummate skill in touching her, the laughter and gentle caring they had shared with one another at Hidden Springs was gone.

He never called her *niña*. He hadn't since he had learned that she was Shannon.

Holly gave herself to Linc, mind and body and soul. In return he gave her . . . pleasure.

Body without mind or soul.

He hid from her behind a physical fire that grew hotter each time they made love.

They were being consumed, not renewed.

Yet she couldn't stop wanting him. She loved him. She needed to assure him that it was safe to love her. She could never hurt him. He was part of her soul.

Surely he must know that, Holly thought. *Surely he must realize that I couldn't respond to him with such abandon if I didn't love him.*

Surely he couldn't respond to me so completely if he didn't love me.

Just a little.

A beginning, not an end.

The clock ticked, marking off dark minutes. Each tick was a needle pricking her conscience. She really had to get to work.

Slowly Holly lifted Linc's arm from her body and eased out of bed. She pulled on the first piece of clothing she found—his shirt—and began her morning exercises.

Quietly, relentlessly, she stretched, strengthened, and toned muscles. The exercises were for her own satisfaction as well as for the camera's relentlessly critical eye.

She was nearly finished when Linc rolled over, opened his eyes, and looked at her in disbelief.

"Good God, it's not even dawn," he said, groaning. "What in hell are you doing up?"

"Welcome to—the glamorous world—of models," Holly said between sit-ups.

He sat up and turned on the small bedside light. He stared at her damp, flushed face.

"Fifty-four," Holly said aloud. "Fifty-five."

She lay back with a small groan.

"Finished?" Linc asked.

"Don't I—wish," she panted.

With that, she rolled onto her stomach and began doing pushups, counting under her breath.

"All that for a beautiful body?" he asked neutrally.

"A—healthy—body."

For several minutes there was nothing but the sound of Holly counting off pushups.

Linc watched her with increasing astonishment. For the first time he realized that Holly's sleek, resilient body hadn't just come to her along with her bone structure and tilted golden eyes. Her grace of movement was the result of training and hard work.

Boring exercises, to be precise.

Finally she sighed and switched to a cross-legged position. Slowly she bent over her knees until her forehead touched the floor. She repeated the exercise several times, holding the stretched position longer each time.

"Which is worse," Linc asked finally, "the sit-ups, the pushups, or the forehead-on-the-floor?"

"Yes."

For a moment he looked puzzled. Then he laughed aloud as he understood.

Holly stopped and stared at Linc. It was the first genuine laughter she had heard from him since he had found out she was Holly *Shannon* North.

With a smile and a new lightness of heart, she resumed the stretching exercises. She had chosen each one of them so that she would be able to execute and maintain improbable poses for impossible photographers.

While looking effortless and graceful, of course.

With a growing sensual glint to his eyes, Linc watched his shirt ride higher and higher up Holly's thighs as she worked out.

"I can think of more pleasant ways to exercise," he said huskily.

"So can I."

She gave him a sidelong glance and a smile that he returned almost lazily. Yet the look in his eyes was anything but lazy.

"That's why I'm going to take a shower next," Holly added.

"Why?"

"Why do you think?" she retorted. "I'm sweaty."

Linc's smile changed, as hot as the gleam in his eyes.

"You were sweaty last night," he pointed out. "I loved licking every bit of it off your skin. Everywhere."

Her heartbeat quickened. She couldn't control a shiver of desire as she remembered.

"Linc . . ."

"I'm right here."

Naked, he climbed out of the bed and came toward her. With each easy movement he made, muscles shifted and gleamed under his skin. His arousal was obvious.

Once it would have frightened Holly. Now it set her on fire. She knew what kind of ecstasy waited for her in Linc's embrace.

Silently he sat cross-legged on the floor facing her. He was so close that their knees rubbed and her hair fell across his thighs when she bent over to stretch.

Then she looked up at him. His expression made a liquid heat bloom deep within her body. Long masculine fingers began undoing the buttons on the shirt she had borrowed.

"I have to shower, do my hair, and get to the set," Holly said.

Her voice was breathless from more than her exercise.

"When?" Linc asked, unbuttoning as he spoke.

"I should be in the shower right now."

The shirt fell away, revealing the golden curves of her breasts. Her nipples were already hard with desire.

His fingertips touched the taut pink buds as delicately as a kiss. The sound Holly made at his caress sent a shaft of pure fire through him. His hard flesh leaped visibly.

The obvious hunger of his body sent a wave of glittering heat throughout Holly.

He caressed her nipples again, savoring her throaty cries. Finally his palms moved over her waist and hips, hungry for the soft, sleek textures of her very core.

When his fingers glided up her thighs to caress her intimately, her passion spilled over him like liquid fire.

Abruptly Linc's breathing was as ragged as Holly's. His caress slid inside her with an ease that made his whole body go rigid. He moved within her, stroking her with slow rhythms that unraveled her.

The sultry pulses of her response brought him right up to the edge of his control.

"You want me as much as I want you," Linc said roughly.

"You sound surprised."

He didn't answer.

"I'll always want you, Linc. I love you."

"Come sit in my lap."

"But I'm late."

He lifted her legs over his. His thumb rubbed the hard bud of her passion.

She gasped at the wave of pleasure that bit into her.

"Linc—"

"It won't take long," he said. "You're as hot as I am. You can shower afterward."

Holly arched and shivered as he plucked at her most sensitive flesh, his fingers slick with her helpless response.

"We were supposed to talk," she said.

"We will."

Linc lifted her hips. Then he held her so that she just brushed against his heavily aroused flesh. The knowledge of how close they both were to completion made Holly moan.

"When will we talk?" she gasped.

"Tomorrow."

"But—"

"Shhh. You want this as much as I do. And you can feel how much I want you now, can't you?"

Slowly Linc fitted Holly over him like a living glove. Whatever words she might have wanted to speak were lost in a kiss as deep and hot as the joining of their bodies.

With a low moan, she began moving over him, giving herself to him and to the incandescent pleasure they created together.

Tomorrow, Holly promised herself as the first wave of ecstasy hit her, shaking her. *We'll talk tomorrow.*

"All right, that's a wrap!" called the director through his bullhorn.

Then he looked at Roger. The designer was standing nearby, elegant in a sage-colored safari shirt.

"Unless you want to try a few takes for Desert Designs . . . ?" the director asked.

"The Desert Designs campaign isn't due for six weeks. Let's not be greedy."

"Why not? It's going well. At last."

Though neither man said anything, both knew the shoot had been going well for the last four days because Holly's lover was there with her. Whatever passed between them had given her both a radiance and an edge of shadow that had transformed her from a beautiful model to a compelling woman.

Broodingly Roger watched Holly as she sat in the shade of a huge umbrella, rubbing a cold bottle of water against her wrists.

"Just for the rest of the day?" the director asked.

"No."

"But—"

"With the edge of that hurricane finally moving in," Roger interrupted, "the sky doesn't make a very convincing desert backdrop. It will be too hard to match with whatever we shoot later at Hidden Springs."

He turned to his assistant.

"Break out the peppermints," Roger said clearly.

A subdued cheer went up from everyone within hearing.

Holly tried not to show her acute relief. If Roger was passing out mints, the shoot was over. It was a Royce tradition.

She accepted the first mint, smiled at the crew and left the set feeling as though a train had run over her. They had been working for nine straight days. Every muscle in her body ached.

At least Roger hadn't been complaining about the fit of her clothes anymore. Her appetite had returned with Linc and had stayed, as he had stayed.

She looked beyond the roped-off area, seeking Linc.

Almost all the spectators were gone, swept back to their distant homes by hurricane warnings. Linc was not among the few people left beyond the rope.

Fear shot coldly through Holly. She searched for him with a growing sense of panic.

Surely he hasn't left without saying goodbye to me?

When she heard her own thoughts, the depth of her own uncertainty and vulnerability shocked her.

In the last four days Linc had been very much a part of her life. He had been civil to Roger and charming to the rest of the people.

Linc had watched her work, beginning before dawn and not stopping until the last light left the sky. If he didn't understand something about her work, he had asked for explanations later.

And he had listened, really listened, when she answered.

Holly's hope had increased with each question, each answer, each time she looked up and saw Linc watching the intricate dance of director and model, camera and lighting technicians, makeup and hair stylist and seamstresses and all the thousands of details that went into a professional shoot.

She had told herself that he was finally coming to understand how little the reality of modeling had to do with irresponsible, amoral women like his mother and stepmother.

With each day, Holly had told herself that he

was coming to appreciate the amount of talent and training and plain hard work that went into her career. She had allowed herself to believe he was changing his mind, outgrowing the past.

But her panic when she didn't see Linc waiting beyond the ropes told her how fragile her hopes really were. Deep inside she was haunted by the knowledge that each moment with him could be the last.

He doesn't believe I love him, because he still believes beautiful women are too selfish to love anyone but themselves.

Linc doesn't love me . . . yet.

There was a universe of hope in that single word.

Yet.

As long as we're together, she told herself, *I have a chance to make him believe that I love him.*

It wasn't the first time Holly had reassured herself when fear of losing Linc sent shadows over the radiance of being with him.

When he believes in my love, he'll finally be able to let go of the past. He'll be able to love me in return.

Even as she repeated the hopeful thought, she shivered with a chill that never left her unless she was in Linc's arms, their bodies locked together, fused into a single being by ecstasy.

At the very least, she told herself, *he will no longer hate and or distrust women simply because they're beautiful.*

Like me.

Because Linc finally knew just how beautiful Holly was.

She saw it in his eyes if she turned unexpectedly—shadows that matched her own. Questions. Uncertainty.

Fear.

Like me.

Until he trusted her, she would live in fear of losing all that she had given to him.

Heart and body and soul.

It's early, she told herself firmly. *He probably doesn't know we're finished with the shoot yet.*

He's probably back in our room or in the pool or the ocean or . . .

Be here, Linc. Believe in me.

In us.

All but running, Holly went to the dressing tent. She changed with a disregard for the clothes that would have shocked Roger.

Impatiently she went back outside and searched the spectators for Linc's tall form.

He was nowhere in sight.

Fear blossomed like a cold flower within her.

In that moment Holly knew that when she found Linc—if she found him—she would have to force him to talk to her.

The "tomorrow" he kept putting off had finally come.

Twenty-three

"Shannon?"

Holly turned and saw one of the technicians waving at her. With barely concealed irritation she waited for the man to approach.

"What is it?" she asked with unusual sharpness. "I thought we were through with the shoot."

"Uh, Linc said he would be in your room if you got through early, that's all."

Holly flashed the technician a smile that was startling in its radiance. Impulsively she bent and kissed the little man's cheek.

"Thanks," she said breathlessly. "You're a darling."

She turned and ran toward the hotel, leaving behind an entirely bemused technician.

When she unlocked the outer door and went down the short hall to the suite, the light in the room was dim yet oddly luminous. It was the haunting, all-over radiance peculiar to tropical storms just before they broke.

Linc was sitting on the bed, propped up

against the headboard. He was wearing only a towel wrapped around his hips. His hair was still slightly damp from the shower. A faint sheen of moisture made the hair on his chest gleam with each breath he took.

Oh, Linc, Holly asked him silently, *how can you distrust beauty when you're so beautiful yourself?*

Arabian stud books and breeding charts were spread out on the bed around him. He was so intent upon what he was doing that he didn't notice her standing in the doorway, drinking in his presence like desert sand drinking rain.

Drapes swirled fitfully at either side of the open balcony doors. Like Holly, Linc preferred fresh air of almost any temperature to the stale, closed-in "comfort" of hotel air conditioning.

She let out a long sigh.

He glanced up, smiled, and went back to the breeding charts.

"Thought I'd lost you," Holly said lightly.

He made a noncommittal sound and wrote another note along the margin of a chart before looked up.

"You're off early," he said.

"We're finished."

She stretched and laughed aloud with a relief that owed little to having completed a difficult modeling assignment.

"Five glorious days of vacation," she said.

"When?"

"Beginning right now."

Linc looked at his watch.

"Well," Holly admitted, "it's only four days, actually. Today's about gone."

He glanced around the luxurious, obviously expensive suite that Royce Productions had rented for Holly.

"Does that mean we're evicted?" he asked dryly.

She shook her head with enough force to make her hair ripple and gleam like black water.

"Roger told me that we can stay here if we like," she said.

"Civilized of him," Linc said neutrally. "But then, Roger is nothing if not civil."

Restlessly Holly moved toward him. She had no illusions about the "civility" he and Roger shared.

She also had no intention of discussing it. Not now.

There were more important things to talk about than rehashing Roger's futile attraction to his top model.

But how to begin? Holly asked herself.

With a flash of wry insight, she wondered if Linc felt the same way about opening this particular conversation.

Maybe that's why he keeps putting things off, she thought. *Maybe he doesn't know what to say.*

She went and stood beside the bed. The temptation to reach out and comb her fingers through the pelt of hair on Linc's chest was so great that she put her hands behind herself and locked her fingers together.

Not now, she told herself firmly. *This time I won't let him distract me.*

Heat shimmered in the pit of her stomach as she remembered just how deliciously distracting he could be.

"I told Roger you'd probably want to go home," Holly said.

Linc glanced out the window. For a minute he studied the unsettled, slowly seething sky.

"The weather might have other plans," he said.

"Roger checked. Unless the center of the storm comes right through here, none of the flights will be canceled."

"What are the odds of the center missing us?"

"Pretty good, but most of the crew is flying out now. They have families waiting."

Linc turned back to Holly.

"Are you really off the leash?" he asked skeptically.

She hesitated. As the Royce Reflection, she was essentially on call twenty-four hours a day, every day.

At first that had angered Linc. He had made a lot of sharp remarks about how short a leash Roger kept on Holly. Then Linc had noticed that everyone else kept the same hours.

After that, he had simply ignored the subject, accepting her long hours with outward indifference.

"I'm off the leash like you're off the leash at the ranch," she said finally.

"Meaning?"

"I'm free until something goes wrong. Or in my case, right."

Linc raised his eyebrows.

"Such as?" he asked.

"Whenever the ad company finally brings in the perfume campaign Roger wants," Holly said, "I'll have to fly to whatever place they've picked as a suitable backdrop."

"Hasn't Roger heard of studio shots?"

"He loathes them. Says all that control kills the sensual surprise."

Linc grunted and gathered up his papers.

"I didn't mean to interrupt you," she said guiltily. "I know you must be getting behind in your work by staying down here with me."

Saying nothing, he stacked the books and papers on the bedside table. Without warning, he reached out, grabbed her lightly, and pulled her onto the big bed.

Off-balance, she fell across his lap. Before she could recover, his mouth was on hers.

"Mmmm," Linc said. "Peppermint."

He licked Holly's lips appreciatively.

A familiar warmth spread throughout her in shimmering waves.

It would be so easy to let go of all worry about the future, she admitted silently.

It would be so easy to succumb to him, to let herself be like clouds gathered against a mountain's hard planes, filling with sweet violence until the world shattered into lightning and thunder rolled and rain came down, fusing cloud and mountain into a single ecstatic being.

It would be so easy. . . .

And so foolish.

If Linc and I don't talk, really talk, Holly told herself desperately, *one day I'll wake up and find that he's gone, taking my love with him.*

And never believing it. Never believing in my love.

Reluctantly she turned away from his caressing mouth.

"Linc, we have to talk."

"Later," he murmured.

He shifted her in his arms so that she was held against every inch of his body. The long, blunt ridge of his hunger pressed against her belly. She shivered with the desire only Linc had ever discovered and freed within her.

"When?" she asked, her throat tight.

"When what?"

The tip of his tongue teased the curve of her ear. Teeth nibbled sensuously.

"When will we talk?" she asked.

"Tomorrow." Linc's voice was husky. "We'll talk tomorrow."

Holly steeled herself against the fiery pleasure sliding through her veins with each caress.

"You've said that before," she whispered, turning away.

He caught her chin in his hand. Gently he pulled her back to face him.

"What's the hurry?" he asked. "Tomorrow will always be there."

"And we'll always be here, won't we?"

Linc's fingers tightened on her chin until she couldn't move.

"Are you tired of me already?" he asked, his face as neutral as his voice.

For an instant Holly was too shocked to speak. Then she wrapped her arms around him and hugged him fiercely.

"I'll never be tired of you," she said. "I love you!"

She felt him stiffen in rejection.

Fear returned to her in cold waves. Until Linc believed in her love, he would never believe that his own love would be safe with a beautiful woman.

Somehow I have to make him believe that I love him, Holly thought desperately. *Somehow . . .*

They needed to talk about her love and many other things, unhappy things like his childhood and his fear of trust.

Yet the only communication Linc permitted was the wordless language of sensuality.

So be it, Holly told herself. *If that's the only way to get past his defenses, I'll just have to do a better job of it than I have been.*

She slid away from him.

He made no effort to hold her.

Fear closed like a vise around Holly's heart. Slowly she began taking off her clothes. She didn't stop until she was as naked as the clouds gathering beyond the windows, clouds looking for mountains to call down their rain.

"I know you don't believe me," Holly said,

her voice soft, urgent. "You think words are nothing, less than breath."

"Holly—" Linc began impatiently.

"No," she interrupted. "Let me love you."

She looked down at him, her tawny eyes huge with her need to make him understand.

"Listen to my hands, to my body," she said. "Let me show you my love. Then you'll have to believe me. Please, Linc. Listen . . ."

Surprised by the intensity of her plea, he went still.

"I'm listening," he said.

"Lie down."

"Will that help me to hear better?"

"I hope so," Holly said.

With an odd half-smile, Linc stretched out on the bed.

"All right?" he asked.

She nodded.

"Now what?" he asked.

"I don't get to touch you as much as I want," she said.

He looked surprised.

Before he could ask the question Holly saw in his eyes, her fingers slid deeply into Linc's thick chestnut hair.

"Your hair feels cool, like rough silk between my fingers," she said softly. "I like touching it, looking at it. There are so many colors in your hair, chestnut and bronze, molten gold, even black."

Linc moved his head against Holly's fingers, caressing her in return.

She leaned over and inhaled deeply.

"Your hair smells good," she said, "like twilight rain with the heat of the desert welling up from beneath."

She closed her eyes for a moment, savoring the feel of his hair sliding over the sensitive skin between her fingers.

Linc felt the intensity of her concentration. He had to fight not to grab her and bury himself in her, seeking the hot, sensual oblivion where tomorrow never came.

"Holly," he said huskily.

"No. Not yet. Let me love you, just this once. Let me touch you. Promise me?"

A ripple of emotion went through Linc.

"All right," he said. "I'll try. But I've never . . ."

He shrugged and said nothing more.

Holly smiled almost sadly, for her heart heard what Linc had left unsaid.

He had never let a woman make love to him.

"I promise I won't hurt you," she said.

Linc would have laughed but for the shadows in her beautiful golden eyes.

Delicately, then with greater confidence, her fingertips rubbed over his scalp. She sought out and loosened tight muscles, hoping to ease the tension in him that had nothing to do with physical hunger.

Linc sighed and closed his eyes, giving himself over to the pleasure of Holly's knowing fingers.

After a time she kneaded down toward his neck, then back up, until he sighed again and relaxed even more.

Gently she traced the outer edge of his ears with her fingernails.

His breathing shortened.

With a soft laugh, Holly leaned down and nuzzled his ear.

"I wondered if you were as sensitive there as I am," she whispered.

Her breath was another kind of caress against his ear. The tip of her tongue touched lightly, searching and finding every sensitive point. Then, slowly, her tongue probed and retreated, probed and retreated in a rhythm he had taught her.

Suddenly Linc's arms pinned her against his body.

"Holly—"

His voice was too thick with hunger for him to say more.

Her teeth closed not quite gently on the rim of his ear.

"You're supposed to listen," she reminded him. "You can't listen if you're touching me."

"I don't know how much of this 'listening' I can take," he muttered.

"I've hardly started. Listen to me, Linc. Please, *listen*."

Reluctantly his arms loosened, allowing Holly the freedom of his body again.

"There's so much more I want to tell you," she said.

Holly's teeth moved down from Linc's ear to trace the strong tendons of his neck. Her palms massaged the swell of muscle where neck and shoulders joined.

He shifted against her touch like a cat.

"What are you telling me?" he asked huskily.

"That I love your neck and shoulders. The muscles fit so perfectly against my palms. It feels . . . complete . . . when my hands curve around you."

Linc closed his eyes, afraid to keep looking at Holly. He didn't know if he could keep from reaching for her again.

The aftershave he wore was so subtle she couldn't smell it until her lips rubbed over his neck. His freshly shaved skin was neither soft nor rough, simply very masculine in its texture.

She savored his skin with an unhurried kiss, then sighed and moved upward to nibble on his chin.

Linc opened his eyes, wanting to see the light in Holly's, hoping that there would be no shadows.

Her eyes had never looked more beautiful.

Or more shadowed.

"But I'm getting ahead of myself," she said.

"Ahead?" he asked, only half-teasing. "If you go any slower I'll be gnawing on my knuckles."

Holly put her fingers over his lips in a caress that also silenced him.

"I haven't even mentioned your eyes," she said. "They're whiskey with emerald glints, and those eyelashes . . ."

She kissed Linc's eyelids before she gently caught his eyelashes between her lips.

"Unfair," she breathed. "I've always thought it was unfair for a man to have such eyes. And your mouth."

Almost helplessly, her fingertip traced his lips again.

"When I was thirteen," she said, "I used to dream of what it would feel like to have those teasing, smiling lips kiss me. All those sensual curves and the hint of power beneath."

"Thirteen?" Linc asked, shocked.

"Umm," Holly agreed. "When I was sixteen I found out that my dreams weren't even a shadow of your kiss."

He started to say something, but she took his mouth with her own, making speech impossible. Her tongue explored his warmth with a thoroughness he had taught her.

She played with the rough surface of his tongue, savored the incredible smoothness beneath, and tested the hard serrations of his teeth. Then she tasted him deeply, rhythmically, repeatedly, while his body became hard and hot beneath her.

At last Holly lifted her head and sighed, letting the heat of her pleasure flow over his lips.

"You still taste like sage and rain and lightning," she said.

Blindly Linc's lips sought hers again. She laughed softly, eluding him.

"You promised," Holly said.

He took a ragged breath.

"Is it too late to plead insanity?" he asked almost roughly.

"Much too late."

Her mouth shifted to his shoulder. She put her teeth against the resilient muscles, biting with just enough force to arouse rather than to hurt.

It was another of the many things Holly had learned from Linc. It gave her intense pleasure to use what he had taught her, giving back the joy of his teaching.

Her hands smoothed down the line of his arms, cherishing each hard shift of muscle under his skin, the steel beneath the silk. In slow motion her hands moved over his chest.

"Your strength fascinates me," Holly said. "Things that I can't budge, you lift casually. Strength to make or break a world . . ."

Her eyes darkened, a shadow of her own vulnerability.

"So different from me," she whispered.

Linc heard the thread of fear in her voice and thought she was remembering their first time together.

"I would never have hurt you if I had known," he said.

"I know that."

"Do you really?" he asked urgently.

"Yes."

"But for a moment just now you looked almost . . . afraid."

"Yes."

"Why?"

"Listen to me, Linc," Holly whispered. "Listen to what my touch tells you."

Her fingertips found his flat nipples. She bent down and licked him with teasing strokes. His flesh gathered into tiny, hard points. When she caught one nipple between her teeth, his breath came in sharply.

"Different," she said huskily, "but alike again. You're sensitive there, too. Do you feel hot wires all the way to the pit of your stomach when I do this?"

She sucked on his nipple with lips and tongue, giving back the caresses he had given to her so many times before.

When Linc could bear it no more, his hands closed like a vise on her cheeks, forcing her to look at him. His eyes were smoky with desire. He searched her face for long moments.

Then he took her mouth in a kiss that was all the more overwhelming for its restraint.

"Does that answer your question?" he asked.

"Yes," she said. "But I have so many more questions. Will you let me ask them in my own way? And will you listen, really listen, with all of your heart?"

Holly saw uneasiness grow beneath the de-

sire in Linc's eyes. It was as though he had finally sensed just how much was at risk.

Body and mind and soul.

Breath held, she waited for his answer.

Twenty-four

Slowly Linc released his hold on Holly.

"If I had known what I was getting into," he said, "or rather, what I *wasn't* getting into, I'd never have promised."

She blinked, not understanding at first.

When she did, she laughed against his chest. Then she bit him with great care.

"You're killing me," he said hoarsely.

"I don't think so."

"I do!"

"Your heart is beating quite nicely," she said. "I can feel it beneath my tongue."

She slid down Linc's body, catching his chest hair between her fingers and lips.

He breathed a soft curse.

"I like your hair," Holly said huskily, "but I've already said that, haven't I? Rough and soft at the same time, springy, it tickles almost as nicely as your tongue."

Her fingertips traced the muscles of his torso to the edge of the towel.

Linc couldn't contain the shudder that went

through him any more than he could control
the blunt arousal that leaped subtly with each
heartbeat.

"Different again," Holly said. "So powerful . . ."

His breathing shortened as her tongue found
and teased his navel, stabbing lightly.

"But we're alike here," she murmured. "Sensitive."

She followed the line of dark hair from Linc's
navel to the edge of the towel.

He waited with breath held. Then he let out
a ragged sigh when Holly left the towel in
place.

The mattress shifted as she moved to the foot
of the bed.

"I'll get even, you know," Linc said huskily.
"I ache from head to heels."

"Ten toes," she said, laughter in her voice.
"That's the same for both of us."

She nibbled reflectively on his big toe.

"That tickles," he said. "Tickling definitely
wasn't part of my promise."

Smiling, Holly relented. She caught his foot
in her hand and rubbed up to his ankle, knowing that a firm touch wouldn't tickle him.

"I like your feet," she said. "Strong. But then,
all of you is strong. A strength you take for
granted."

Linc's calf flexed against her kneading fingers. He wasn't protesting her touch. He was
enjoying it. Looking at himself through her
eyes as she outlined and tested each muscle

made him understand his own strength for the
first time.

It also made Linc painfully aware of the precise area where he was most different from
Holly. It was the one difference she seemed to
be avoiding.

It was also the only difference that really
mattered to him at the moment.

Holly shifted again. Putting a knee on either
side of Linc's legs, she removed the clip that
held her hair in place.

"Do you like the feel of my hair on your bare
skin?" she asked, guessing the answer but
needing to hear it anyway.

"You know I do."

"You never told me, not in words."

*There are so many things we haven't said in
words,* Holly thought uneasily.

Shaking her head, she bent over and let the
silky black mass of her hair tumble across his
legs.

Linc drew in a swift, hissing breath.

"Now I really know how much you like it,"
she said, shivering in response. "I like knowing, Linc."

The towel barely covered half of his long,
muscular thighs. She turned her head and bit
him just above one knee. She liked the feel of
his strength beneath her teeth, against her
tongue.

He made a throttled sound.

"Another place where we're alike and yet
different," Holly said. "Your thighs are so hard

when you tense them, so powerful even when you're relaxed."

"I'm not relaxed now," Linc said through his teeth.

She looked at the towel tented over his blunt arousal and smiled slowly.

"I like that, too," she whispered.

Her hands moved upward, following the clean line of his legs beneath the towel. She separated the folds of cloth until he wore only the black fall of her hair across him.

Then she straightened slowly, letting her hair move over his changed flesh in a long, silky caress.

"God . . ." Linc said, his voice gritty.

"Different," Holly murmured.

She traced the outline of his arousal with a fingertip.

He shuddered heavily.

"Why are all the words to describe our differences either clinical or crude?" she asked softly. "Why aren't there any words to equal your beauty?"

His only answer was a groan that was also her name.

"You're beautiful to me," Holly said. "As beautiful as I am to you. But there are no words . . ."

Her hands moved up the hard curve of Linc's thighs until she surrounded him. Slowly, she bent down.

"Listen," she whispered.

With gentle care, she tasted all of his masculine textures as he had often tasted her own femininity.

Linc's breath came in with a harsh sound, caught in his throat, and stayed knotted there.

Holly sensed the elemental hunger that exploded through him. She felt it in the heat of his flesh, the violence of his pulse, and the shudders of raw need that tore through his strength.

Then she heard her name in the long rush of his breath.

"Am I hurting you?" she asked.

His answer was a groan and a movement of his hips that silently pleaded for more, not less, of her loving.

"Yes," she whispered. "I'd like that, too."

The differences that made Linc male fascinated and compelled Holly. She couldn't explore them enough. The soft heat of her mouth surrounded him with sultry, intimate caresses.

His body corded. He cried out wordlessly, telling her of the intense pleasure she was giving him.

An answering storm of desire broke over Holly, nearly overwhelming her. She moved up Linc's body like a cloud over a mountain, covering him with moist warmth.

With exquisite slowness, she began to join herself to him. Together they shared the fierce lightning that lanced through him when he was first kissed by flesh even hotter and more sultry than her mouth.

For a timeless moment Holly held both of them in that first instant of contact, unmoving, suspended in the still center of a passionate storm. Then she blended her body totally with Linc's, matching the urgent rhythms of his need with her own, letting the storm break over both of them until neither knew who was cloud and who was mountain, for both were fused by lightning into an ecstatic whole.

When the last, distant tremor of the sensual storm finally faded between them, Holly stirred against Linc's chest.

"I love you," she said softly.

She sought his luminous eyes beneath the dense shadows of his lashes.

"Do you finally believe that now?" she asked. "I love you."

His eyes shut. His fingers closed around her chin so tightly that she cried out in surprise and protest.

"Linc—"

"Don't talk about love."

His voice was low, deadly.

Fear engulfed Holly. Her fear was all the more terrible because she had allowed herself to believe that Linc had accepted her love in the passionate certainty of their storm.

She tried to speak, couldn't, and tried again. Finally she forced words through a throat that was tight with fear.

"That's like telling me not to breathe," she said.

Tears rained silently down her cheeks onto his hand.

"Loving you is the most—" She gasped and stopped speaking as Linc jerked his hand away.

Holly watched him lift his fingers to his lips, tasting her tears as though not able to believe in them, either.

"Why won't you believe me?" she asked despairingly. "If I were just plain Holly, would you let me talk about love?"

Linc's face changed. For the first time he showed the grief and regret that were like knives turning in his soul.

It was no less painful for her.

"That's it, isn't it?" she asked in a raw whisper. "I'm not Holly to you anymore. You never call me *niña*."

His eyelids flinched but he said not one word.

"What am I, Linc?" she continued relentlessly. "What horrible thing have I done that you won't even let me say the word love?"

Linc closed his eyes, shutting her out.

"There's no point in talking about it," he said. "You can't change what you are."

"And what is that?"

"A beautiful, selfish woman."

"Selfish? Because I won't shrug off my responsibilities and break my contract with Roger?"

"Yes."

Linc's tone was like his certainty, unshakable.

"No," Holly countered, her voice flattened by despair. "Quitting wouldn't change anything."

"The hell it—" he began.

"I'd still be beautiful," she said over his words. "And deep inside, you'd still distrust and hate me for that, wouldn't you?"

Beyond the window lightning arched invisibly and thunder muttered among clouds. The drapes swelled into the room, twisting sinuously in the wind.

Holly shivered, but it wasn't the tropical storm that chilled her.

Slowly Linc opened his eyes.

"I . . . don't hate you," he said.

"I don't believe you."

"Holly," he whispered.

"Just as you don't believe I love you." She laughed oddly. "In time, we may both be right."

"Quit your job."

"No."

"Does turning on every man in sight matter that much to you?" Linc asked roughly. "Isn't what we just had enough to satisfy you?"

"I don't give a damn about turning on any man but you."

Holly's voice was so soft, so absolutely certain, that even Linc had to admit she believed her words.

"Then quit modeling," he said.

"And prove how selfish I am."

Again her voice was soft, certain.

"What's that supposed to mean?" he demanded.

"Selfish people make others pay for their pleasures, right?"

Linc nodded curtly.

"Being with you is the greatest pleasure I've ever known," Holly said. "Replacing me would cost Roger a year of advertising time and millions of dollars. Why should he be the one to pay for my pleasures?"

Linc's face went cold.

"That's a lovely way of twisting words to suit your purposes," he said. "But I shouldn't complain if Roger gets the benefit of your talents. He's certainly given you—and me—the benefit of his."

"What do you mean?" she asked.

Linc smiled.

The bitter curve of his lips chilled her.

Suddenly she was certain that she didn't want to understand Linc's meaning. But it was too late.

He was already talking, breaking apart her world.

"It's quite simple," he said. "In the five days I wasn't with you, Roger taught you more about making love than most women learn in a lifetime."

Holly went white.

"Not that I'm complaining," Linc said with

a shrug. "You've stayed in my bed while I'm here. What more can I ask of a beautiful woman?"

Holly retreated from Linc until his hands caught her, held her with careless strength.

"Don't do this to me," she whispered, feeling herself breaking. "Let me go."

One of his eyebrows lifted in cool inquiry.

"Why?" he asked. "Is Roger finally getting impatient?"

"I've never been Roger's lover."

Holly's voice was thin, patient, as distant as an echo.

Linc can break my world, she told herself wildly, *but not me.*

Not me!

I won't break, not even for him.

"I said I wasn't complaining," he repeated.

"Damn you," she whispered savagely. "If I've pleased you in bed, congratulate yourself. You're one hell of a teacher."

She watched disbelief cross Linc's face and felt the same knives of regret and rage turning in her that she had sensed earlier in him.

"I came to you a virgin," she said, "something you didn't believe until too late. I can hardly come to you each time a virgin, and you won't believe in my love."

Her laugh sounded like a sob.

"You told me to trust you, Linc. And I did. Twice. You have yet to trust me, really trust me, once."

"Holly," he began.

No words followed, nothing but an agonizing silence.

"Tell me that you trust me," she coaxed. "Tell me that you love me. Just a little, Linc. Just a beginning."

Breath held, aching, she watched his eyes, his lips, the shadows of emotion tightening his face into harsh planes.

She heard all her worst fears confirmed in his silence. When she spoke, her voice was terribly controlled, almost gentle.

"Never mind, Linc. It doesn't matter anymore."

His hands tightened on her arms. He sensed her despair and anger as clearly as he felt the emotional storm seething just beneath his own control.

"Holly, don't do this," he said, echoing her earlier plea.

"Do what? Tell the truth?"

"What truth is that? Love?" he asked, his voice like a whip.

"This truth," Holly said. "Somewhere deep in your mind you're certain that loving a beautiful woman means destroying yourself. Given that, I can't blame you for not loving me. You're strong. You want to survive."

Again Linc's eyelids flinched, an involuntary reaction to his pain.

And to hers.

"But I do blame you," Holly said distinctly, "for taking revenge on me for something I never did, never would do, never *could* do to you."

She paused, listening to the thunder outside as though it was another voice.

Then she looked at Linc. A last flicker of hope moved in her eyes when she saw his turmoil.

"It isn't revenge," he said finally.

"You don't trust me, so you can't love me. It might as well be revenge."

"I don't blame you for what my mother and stepmother did."

"No, you simply think that I'm like them because I'm beautiful. I thought that I could change your feelings."

Linc looked away, unable to bear seeing his pain reflected in Holly's golden eyes.

She laughed sadly.

"I was very young, wasn't I?" she whispered. "I didn't realize that I might learn to hate before you learned to love. But I won't stay around that long, because hating you would destroy me. There would be nothing left."

Thunder curled through the room, sound without meaning.

Holly listened. Then she looked at Linc with eyes that no longer asked to be loved.

"I thought I could teach you about love," she said. "But you were the teacher. You taught me about hate."

"No," he said, his voice rough with pain.

His hands rubbed over her chilled flesh, trying to bring back warmth. She neither moved closer to him nor pulled away.

It was as though he didn't exist anymore.

"I don't hate you," Linc said. "I never meant to hurt you."

Holly moved to get off the bed.

"No," he said. "Let me hold you."

Like a shadow, she slid beyond his reach even though he was still holding her.

"You can't comfort me any more than I can erase the past for you," she said simply.

Holly looked at Linc for a long moment. Although tears burned somewhere deep inside her, she knew she wouldn't cry.

Tears were born of hope. She had none left.

Slowly his hands opened, releasing her.

Turning her back on him, she walked to the window and watched the clouds seethe with thunder and the rain that never came.

"Just chalk it up to a case of mistaken identity," Holly said. "You thought I was your sweet *niña*, and I thought you were the Linc I had always loved. We were both wrong."

She closed her eyes and waited.

Only silence answered her.

"Goodbye, Linc."

She didn't turn around again until she heard the door close behind the man she loved.

Twenty-five

Holly drove the Jeep with the leashed savagery that had become part of every movement she made during the last hundred days. Behind her a caravan of four-wheel-drive vehicles churned clouds of grit out of the dry, rutted road leading to Hidden Springs.

The time of summer thunder was over. It was as though the desert rains had been only a dream. The fragrant bloom of chaparral and flowers had come and gone as quickly as a blush. All that remained was the smell of heat and dust and drought.

The land was empty again, waiting in September's burning silence for the more enduring renewal of winter rains.

Holly looked up to the mountains just once. Then she didn't look again.

Barren, desolate, compelling in their power, immovable, unchanging, the mountains spoke far too eloquently of the man she had loved and lost.

She would not answer.

She would not even call his name in the silence of her own mind.

Behind Holly's fast-moving Jeep, the Royce caravan dropped back farther with each minute. She didn't notice that she was outrunning the rest of the crew.

If she had noticed, she wouldn't have slowed down one bit.

She had argued violently with Roger about returning to Hidden Springs at all. As far as she was concerned, there was no need to be within a thousand miles of the place.

The Royce Is Romance campaign was already wrapped up. The Desert Designs campaign didn't require a Hidden Springs location.

Any dry place would do.

Why not Egypt—history and pyramids and enigmas baking under the sun? she had asked Roger repeatedly.

He had insisted on the untouched, primitive splendor of Hidden Springs.

Holly had fought against it up to the point of breaking her contract. That she wouldn't do. Her work was all she had left.

And Roger had known it.

He had won. The Royce Reflection was on her way to the last place on earth she wanted to be.

But that was all that he had won from her. When he had realized that Linc was no longer part of her life, Roger had offered to fill the emptiness he saw.

Holly had refused with a polite, cool finality

that was totally unlike her earlier unease at his proposals.

I'm flattered, but no.

Why? Roger had asked. *You know I wouldn't hurt you. I don't have any bad habits and I'm certified free of anything more contagious than passion.*

No.

Shannon, we would be good together.

Listen to me, Roger. If the subject ever comes up again, I'll break my contract, leave Royce Designs, and never look back.

Shannon—

I've walked away from more in order to survive. Believe me.

He had.

The subject of an affair between Roger and the Royce Reflection had never come up again.

Nor was he the kind who held grudges. After a week of uncomfortable silence, he had resumed treating her with the easy, witty camaraderie they had enjoyed before.

The sands of Antelope Wash spun off the Jeep's tires in dry fountains that were as harsh as Holly's mood. Grit showered over the windshield, coating everything.

She ignored the sand and dust. She didn't slow the Jeep's hard-driving wheels by even a bit. She pushed the vehicle out to the edge of its performance and held it there with the same ruthless concentration she had used on everything in the last hundred days.

When she was in the grip of work or driving hard or pushing herself in some other way, she had at least momentary release from memories. It was as close to peace as she came.

But memories were always just beneath her Shannon mask, haunting Holly.

Linc had called her a week after Cabo San Lucas.

Holly, it doesn't have to be like this.

Do you have anything new to say to me, Linc?

And as she had asked, hope was a terrible ache in her.

I want you, Holly. I can't sleep for the hunger.

Want. Hunger. Those aren't new, Linc.

In silence, both of them had heard the words she would never ask again.

Do you love me?

In silence, both of them had heard Linc's answer.

No.

Then came the urgent words that were meant to fill that terrible silence.

Holly, don't do this to us. You want me. I know that as surely as I know I'm alive!

Softly she had hung up the phone. She couldn't bear to hear her own agony in Linc's voice.

Hunger wasn't enough.

If it were, she would never have left him.

Holly hadn't taken any more of his calls. The brief return of hope had hurt too much, reminding her of what it had been like to feel a dream come true, to love Linc.

To be alive, fully alive.

To believe that all things were possible, even

the love of a man who didn't believe beautiful women were worth loving.

In time, Linc had stopped calling.

In time, Holly prayed that she would stop caring.

Driven by her foot pressing heavily on the accelerator, the Jeep bucked and fishtailed up over the last ridge separating Holly from Hidden Springs.

The first thing she saw was three horses and riders at her former campsite. Abruptly she sent the Jeep into a controlled skid, stopping in a shower of stones and dirt well beyond the waiting riders.

Using every bit of her self-control, Holly fought her impulse to turn and hurtle the Jeep back the same way she had come.

No. That's something Holly would have done, she told herself bitterly. *Holly doesn't live here anymore.*

Only Shannon.

Because only Shannon could survive.

She sat unmoving behind the wheel of the Jeep, watching Linc as he sat on Sand Dancer not a hundred feet away from her.

Then he turned and looked at her, consuming her in a single glance.

For the first time Holly felt the relentless heat of the sun pushing her down, flattening her. There was nothing beneath, nothing to hold her upright. The world was falling away.

There was nothing supporting her but Linc's

intensity. And soon he would look away, leaving her to fall endlessly.

I can't let him do this to me.

Closing her eyes, Holly hung on to the steering wheel like a lifeline. She hadn't known until this instant how close to the edge of her world she had been living.

And how easy it would be to fall off.

The knowledge was terrifying.

"Holly?"

It was Beth's voice calling to her, not Linc's.

Holly gathered what was left of herself and opened her eyes.

Beth was on foot, walking quickly toward the Jeep, leaving the other two riders behind. A big yellow dog romped around the girl, all but tripping her with every other step.

Taking a deep breath, then another, Holly opened the Jeep's door and forced herself to get out as though she hadn't anything more on her mind than the heat of the day.

She ruffled Freedom's ears when he bounded up to greet her. Then she forced herself to smile, really smile, at the girl who was approaching so eagerly.

It's not Beth's fault that I loved the wrong man, Holly reminded herself. *She doesn't deserve the sharp edges and empty shell of Shannon's cynicism.*

She opened her arms and hugged Beth, saying to Linc's sister what she couldn't say to Linc himself.

"I've missed you so much," Holly murmured.

Her voice was thick with too many emotions. Too much Holly. Too little Shannon.

Beth's voice caught in a sob. She hung onto Holly for long moments before she could speak.

"Why—" Beth began. Then, quickly, she stopped. "No, I promised myself I wouldn't ask."

Holly tried to smile.

It almost worked.

"How are you?" Beth asked anxiously.

"Fine. Just fine."

"You look different. Like Linc. Older."

"I am."

Unable to bear hearing Linc's name again, Holly took off the western hat that all but concealed Beth's face.

The girl was exquisite.

"Talk about a change," Holly said. "Look at you!"

Beth's hair fell around her shoulders in a radiant tide, framing her face in smoldering honey curls. She wore just enough makeup to bring out the turquoise brilliance of her eyes. Beneath a transparent gloss, her lips were vulnerable, inviting, innocent.

"You've grown into your beauty," Holly said. "How does your brother feel abou—never mind. It's none of my business."

"Linc doesn't mind that I'm beautiful," she said. "Not anymore."

Holly made a sound that could have meant

anything. She didn't want to talk about Linc and beauty.

She didn't want to talk about Linc at all.

"Four weeks after he came back from Cabo San Lucas," Beth said, "he took me to Palm Springs. New clothes, new hairstyle, new makeup, everything I wanted except you for my sister."

Holly hoped her pain didn't show.

"You look happy," she said quietly. "I'm glad."

Beth blinked back tears.

"Linc wants me to be whatever I want to be," she said. "Beautiful or plain or anywhere in between. He loves me."

Holly felt the world falling away again.

"I'm happy for you," she whispered.

She was surprised that she could speak at all past the numbness gripping her soul.

At least he learned that much, she thought in helpless anguish. *The pain wasn't all for nothing.*

"Come back to the ranch with us," Beth said.

Automatically Holly shook her head.

"Please," Beth said. "Linc loves you."

Holly flinched as though she had been slapped.

"No," she said.

"But he does," Beth said quickly. "He hasn't seen Cyn or any other woman. All he's done is work like there's no tomorrow. He's awful to everyone except me. He's been so gentle with me that sometimes I just want to cry. Please come back. He loves—"

"Stop it," Holly interrupted savagely.

The girl's eyes widened with surprise and hurt.

Holly fought for self-control. After a few long breaths, it came. But it was fragile.

As fragile as Holly herself.

"Thank you, but no," she said carefully.

"I've missed you. I love you, Holly. I always have."

Holly's eyelids flinched.

"I feel the same way about you," she whispered.

"Then why—"

"Now that you and your brother understand each other," she interrupted quickly, "maybe he'll let you come with me. I'm going to Rio soon. Or maybe it's Tokyo and then Rio."

"Tokyo? Rio?" Beth asked breathlessly.

Holly shrugged. "I forget which comes first. Would you like to go with me?"

"Cool! I've never been anywhere but Palm Springs!"

Excitement made Beth look younger. Then her excitement faded. She sighed and looked over her shoulder.

"I don't know if Linc would let me miss school," Beth admitted, turning back to Holly. "I'm only here today because I threatened awful things if I didn't get the chance to see you."

Wistfully Holly smiled. She hadn't realized quite how lonely she had been until she thought of taking Beth with her, having someone to share her world with.

"Maybe during Thanksgiving or Christmas vacation," Holly began. Then she shook her head. "No, those are family times. Your brother will need you then."

Beth caught Holly's hand, shaken by what she had glimpsed for just a moment in the other woman's eyes.

"You could come here for Christmas and Thanksgiving," Beth said fiercely.

Holly forced a convincing professional smile onto her face. She had become very good at that in the last few months.

"Don't look so down in the mouth," she said, touching Beth's cheek lightly. "There's always next summer for us to travel together."

"It's not that. It's just—who will you spend those family times with?" Beth blurted.

Wishing that Beth were old enough not to ask such questions, Holly replaced the girl's hat with a firm tug.

"Who's the handsome man with you?" Holly asked.

"You mean Linc?" Beth asked, confused.

"No."

"Oh. Jack. I don't think of him as a man. Not like Linc, anyway."

Holly felt her smile slipping. She knew better than Beth ever would how few men like Linc there were in the world.

"Come on," Beth said. "I want to introduce you. You never really got to meet Jack last time."

Fervently Holly wished she hadn't driven so fast to Hidden Springs. If the others were here, she would have had an excuse to avoid Linc.

As it was, she could run like a scared child or she could walk over there and pretend there was no reason not to talk to him.

"Holly?"

"Coming," she said tightly.

Beth took Holly's hand and led her over to Jack. He saw them coming and dismounted.

Linc did not.

Holly felt a bittersweet relief that she wouldn't have to stand close to him. She smiled and shook Jack's hand, said polite, meaningless words, and wished that she had turned and run like the scared child she was.

I can't look at Linc, she realized too late. *So close. So far away.*

The pressure of his presence was like the sun, burning Holly's skin, melting her bones, making her dizzy for lack of cool air to breathe.

"Aren't you even going to say hello to Linc?" Beth asked.

Holly turned and glanced at him with unfocused eyes, looking without really seeing.

"Hello, Linc," she said casually.

There was a small silence.

"I've missed you, *niña.*"

The world dipped beneath her feet. Time fell away until she was nine again, standing on hot sand looking up at Linc, knowing somewhere deep inside herself that she would love this man and no other.

But he wasn't seventeen anymore, and she wasn't nine.

She stared up at him as though she had never seen him before. He was even more powerful than she had remembered. When his horse shifted restlessly, Linc's shoulders blocked out the sun.

Beneath the thick screen of lashes, his eyes searched Holly's, looking for something they both had lost. His face was harder, thinner, drawn with the inner tension that radiated from him. Like a caged lion, he waited for . . . something.

The saddle creaked as Sand Dancer shifted his weight.

Suddenly Holly realized she had been staring up at Linc for much too long. She turned to say something casual to Beth or Jack or even the dog.

No one was nearby.

Beth, Jack, and Freedom had withdrawn somewhere, leaving Holly to face the ruins of her dream with no support, no shield, no place to hide. She was shocked at the depth of pain she felt in Linc's presence. She had believed that she was beyond being hurt by Linc anymore.

Now Holly knew with terrible finality that her capacity to be hurt by Linc was as great as her love for him. There was no end to her vulnerability.

If he touched her, she would be destroyed. She didn't have the strength to leave him again.

He had called her *niña*.

In the distance she heard the sounds of ve-

hicles laboring over the last ridge to Hidden
Springs.

Holly didn't know that she had turned and
fled toward the caravan until she felt herself
gasping for air beneath the hammer blows of
the sun. She stopped abruptly, lungs aching as
she fought for breath.

The air was as harsh and dry as stone.

The first Jeep came over the hill far more cautiously than Holly had. When Roger saw her
standing in the road alone, breathing hard, he
signaled the driver to stop.

"What are you doing here?" he asked. "Did
your Jeep break down?"

"No."

"Climb aboard," he said, patting his lap.

Instead, Holly climbed into the cluttered
back seat and sat just behind him, ignoring his
offer of a softer place to sit.

"What's wrong?" Roger asked, turning
around.

"Just thought I'd see what was taking you so
long," Holly said casually.

He stared at her, then at the horse approaching the Jeep. And the rider.

Lincoln McKenzie.

"Did that cowboy—" Roger began harshly.

"No," she interrupted, her voice as hard as
his.

Roger said nothing more. He had learned
when she took that tone of voice, there was no
point in pursuing the subject.

Linc reined in his horse next to the idling Jeep.

"Hello, Roger," he said. "How's the rag trade?"

Chills chased over Holly's arms. Just the sound of his voice unnerved her. She refused to look higher than the stirrup that brushed against her side of the vehicle.

Yet she couldn't help noticing his sinuous power as he controlled the restless stallion. She couldn't help remembering what it had felt like to knead Linc's muscular leg, to test its resilience with teeth and tongue, to savor all the compelling differences of his masculinity.

With a small sound she closed her eyes and looked at nothing at all.

"Hello, McKenzie," Roger said. "Beautiful Arabian."

"Yes," Linc said.

"I should have taken Shannon's suggestion and arranged to use your horses for some shots."

"Holly suggested that?" Linc asked.

There was more intensity in his voice than such a simple question required.

Roger noticed it. He smiled slightly.

It wasn't a pretty smile.

"Yes," he said, "last year, when she first suggested using Hidden Springs."

"But not lately?" Linc asked, intensity fading.

"No. In fact, Shannon nearly broke her contract rather than come here this time."

Silently Holly wished that Roger would shut up.

"But she came," her boss continued. "She's a real pro."

"Yes," Linc said in a neutral voice. "I know that her work means more to her than . . . anything."

Holly caught herself shaking her head in a despairing negative. She stopped, but not before the others saw.

"Wrong," Roger said, his voice clipped. "Shannon told me that if I didn't behave, I could take my contract and tuck it where the sun doesn't shine."

Linc's smile was like lightning, white-hot and quick.

Roger's lips curled down.

"Yes, I thought that would please you," he said. "So I dragged Shannon back to you, though I doubt that you deserve her."

Holly gasped. Her eyes flew open.

Linc was no less surprised.

"Now," Roger continued briskly, "if you will kindly wave your magic wand and put the light and laughter back in the Royce Reflection, I will get on with my business of selling rags."

"That's enough," Holly said.

Her voice was brittle, balanced on the thin edge of breaking.

"Too bloody right," Roger retorted, turning to her. "Ever since you came back from Cabo

San Lucas, you've been a shell of the beautiful—"

"Just. Shut. Up!" Holly interrupted savagely.

Roger said something very inelegant beneath his breath, but offered no more comments.

She felt Linc's intense glance, but refused to look at him.

I knew coming back to Hidden Springs would be a mistake, she reminded herself.

But she hadn't realized how bad a mistake until now.

"Did Holly warn you about snakes?" Linc asked as though nothing had happened.

"Snakes?"

Roger turned and looked at her.

She shrugged impatiently.

"I warned the technicians," she said. "They'll be the ones barging about in the underbrush. They should scare off any snakes that might be around."

"Might?" Linc retorted sardonically. "You know damn well there are always rattlesnakes around the springs."

She shrugged again.

"I won't be the first one walking down any trail," she said tightly, "so there's no problem."

"What's all this about rattlesnakes?" Roger demanded.

Linc turned to the handsome designer.

"If Holly gets nailed by a rattler," Linc said coolly, "she's dead where she stands."

"The hell you say! I was told the beggars weren't that lethal."

"They aren't, unless a big one gets you on the neck or you're violently allergic to venom, like Holly. Then you are dead."

Linc spaced the last words carefully, so there could be no mistaking his meaning.

Roger tapped the driver's arm. "Turn around."

"Don't be ridiculous," Holly snapped. "I stand a better chance of getting killed in a car wreck."

"The way you drove in here," Linc said under his breath, "I believe it."

Roger looked doubtful.

"You're sure, Shannon?" he asked.

"Quite."

Her voice, like her mouth, was inflexible.

Roger hesitated, then sighed.

"Right," he said. "Let's get on with it, then."

"Not yet," Linc said flatly.

The blunt command startled Holly. She looked up—and froze, held by the hazel clarity of his eyes.

"After you're finished working, *niña*, we'll talk."

Holly's mouth went dry.

"No," she said. "We don't have anything new to say to each other."

But she was talking to herself.

Linc had spun his horse and cantered away before the first word was out of her mouth.

Twenty-six

Holly was perched on a pile of boulders that was bigger than a house. Hands spread on the rough, hot surface for balance, she leaned against one particularly massive stone.

Her fingernails gleamed with the color of a desert sunset. A matching color fired her lips. It was the cosmetics, not the clothes, that were being emphasized in this series of shots.

"Over your right shoulder this time," Jerry said.

Knowing what the photographer needed, Holly turned her head with a sinuous motion that made her hair fly. She challenged the camera with her tawny eyes, her unsmiling lips, the perfect black curves of her eyebrows.

"Catch Me If You Can" was the theme of the Desert Designs campaign. Holly was the essence of an elusive woman poised on the brink of flight.

"Fantastic!" Jerry said. "Again. Now right. Again. Again. Again!"

She responded to Jerry's commands with a

precision that always managed to look spontaneous, intimate.

That was Shannon's trademark. She had a flexible, unrehearsed beauty that made photographers fight for the opportunity to work with her.

"Okay. Break for reload."

Jerry looked up at Holly, perched precariously above him on a jumble of boulders.

"Not enough time to climb down, lovey," he said, "unless you need some more sunscreen."

She tossed back her hair so that it didn't cling to her hot cheeks. With unconscious grace she shifted to a more comfortable position.

"I'm all right for another half hour," she said.

"Water?" Roger called.

"Not yet," she said. "My back teeth are floating as it is."

The crew smiled and moved even more quickly.

From Holly's high perch, she could look beyond Jerry, past the technicians and their lights and reflectors, the makeup man and hair stylists, the colorful sultan's tent where she changed from one desert-inspired outfit to another.

The view was exquisite to someone who loved the desert as she did. The slanting light of late afternoon turned granite boulders into soft textures of gold and made even the smallest pebble leap out of its sandy background.

Beyond the hubbub of the set, desert animals were beginning to move cautiously out into the coolness of late afternoon, released from the sun's seamless prison.

Linc was off to the left, well out of the way of the technicians setting up more reflectors. He sat on the sorrel stallion, relaxed and powerful in his waiting, as patient as the desert itself.

Holly forced herself to look away. Jack was close to Linc, standing in the stirrups, peering behind the boulders where she was. Beth's horse stood near a large clump of brush, but she was not in the saddle.

On the far side of Holly's pile of boulders, Freedom suddenly started barking. Just as the sounds reached a frantic pitch, Beth's scream ripped through the afternoon silence.

Instantly Holly started for the girl. Heedless to the height and the danger of falling, Holly leaped from boulder to boulder. Out of the corner of her eye she saw Linc and Jack spur their horses into a dead run.

But they had a long way to go and Beth was still screaming, her voice raw with terror.

As Holly scrambled over the top of the boulder pile, she saw what Linc and Jack had already seen. Beth was frozen in terror, staring down at the ground where Freedom barked and made passes at a rattlesnake coiled in the sand.

The snake was trapped between the screaming girl and the snapping, snarling dog. It divided its reptilian attention between the two threats.

Beth stopped screaming as suddenly as she had begun. She swayed forward alarmingly, on the verge of fainting.

Holly leaped off the last rock and started running hard. If Beth fainted, she would fall on top of the snake. Then it would strike mindlessly, again and again, for that was the nature of a frightened snake.

The rattler could hardly miss Beth's face and her neck, the points of greatest vulnerability.

Freedom barked and started toward the snake.

Holly skidded to a stop, hoping that the dog would keep the snake's attention off the pale, terrified girl.

"It's all right, Beth," she said in a reassuring voice.

As she spoke, she eased forward, measuring the distance between girl and snake.

Not enough.

Any sudden movement could trigger the snake's strike.

I can't risk yanking Beth out of danger, Holly realized. *I'll have to get between her and the rattler.*

It was the only way to be certain that Beth wouldn't fall onto the snake if she fainted.

The girl moaned and swayed, drawing the snake's black-eyed attention.

Seeing an opening, Freedom rushed in, then leaped back as the rattler struck at him.

Holly slid between Beth and the snake just in time to catch the girl as her knees gave way.

She hadn't quite fainted, but she was no longer able to stand.

Bracing herself, she supported Beth, trying to hold both of them absolutely motionless.

Only then did Holly realize what she had done. She was standing in silk shorts and sandals less than three feet away from a coiled, buzzing rattler.

A snake can't strike more than its own length, she reminded herself firmly.

Unfortunately, she had no way of knowing how long the rattler was.

In blank fascination, Holly stared sideways at the snake, trying to guess its length from the thickness of its coils.

That's a damned big snake, she thought distantly.

Beth gave an odd moan.

Through stiff lips, Holly murmured reassurances and held the girl more tightly. Any movement from them would take the snake's attention off the snarling, leaping dog.

Out of the corner of her eye she saw Linc's Arabian race by and come to a rearing, plunging stop well behind Freedom. A hatchet blade flashed vividly in the sun as Linc leaped off.

"Freedom," he said coldly. "Heel."

Whining, obviously reluctant, the dog retreated and came to heel.

"Stay."

Linc's voice compelled obedience. The dog froze in place as though nailed to the ground.

With the odd, gliding grace of a stalking predator, Linc moved toward the rattlesnake from a direction opposite Beth and Holly. The steel head of the hatchet burned gold above his hand. His eyes were intent, focused on the deadly, poised head of the rattlesnake.

The reptile watched the man's approach with unblinking attention. The snake quivered along its thick length, making a sound like pine needles shaken in a paper bag.

Under normal conditions, when Linc met a rattlesnake he simply turned aside and let the snake go its way, as much a part of the desert as the sun itself.

But there was nothing normal about these conditions.

Slowly, Linc raised the hatchet above his head.

There was no warning before he struck. He simply surged forward and brought the hatchet down in the same swift, deadly motion.

The steel edge sliced through the rattlesnake and didn't stop until it grated on rock buried six inches beneath the sand.

Holly closed her eyes, shutting out the reflexive writhing of the dead snake. She heard Beth's choked cry as Jack lifted her into his arms. She heard him speaking broken words of fear and relief.

When she opened her eyes, Beth was wrapped in Jack's protective strength. They stood and held onto each other with silent intensity.

Watching them, Holly felt an instant of piercing envy. Since Cabo San Lucas her life had felt like the time before dawn, neither stars nor sunrise to grace the hollow arch of the sky, only a vast emptiness aching to be filled.

Hands closed harshly around Holly's arms, spinning her around, shaking her.

"That's the most stupid stunt I've ever seen anyone pull!" Linc said angrily. "Do you think you can't die? What the hell were you trying to prove?"

She simply stared at him. His face was like the stone she had touched earlier, harsh and unyielding. His eyes were narrowed, blazing with rage. His lips were thinned over his teeth as he yelled at her.

Behind her came Jack's low words of comfort to Beth.

Sudden laughter wrenched Holly, clawing to be free, a laughter as wild as Linc's eyes.

She clenched her teeth against the awful laughter. When she spoke, her voice belonged to someone else. Thin, calm.

Empty.

"Beth was going to faint," Holly said. "She was swaying forward. If she fell on the snake . . ."

Holly saw Linc's expression change as he realized how close his sister had come to dying.

"Good," she said distinctly. "I'm glad you can care about somebody."

Behind them came the sound of Beth's tears and Jack's continuing, gentle words of comfort.

Distantly Holly wondered what it would be like to cry again, *to have someone hold me, care about me, taste my tears and make them his own.*

Linc had done that for her the night her parents had died.

Linc held my world together with his strength and his caring. I drew on that night for six long years, my secret well of dreams and courage.

She had gone alone into an intensely competitive career in a world far removed from her childhood, and she had conquered it. Then she had come back to share her world with Linc, the world he had given her the strength to build.

But he doesn't want either my world or me.

And now Holly's secret well was dry, strength was draining out of her like night draining color and warmth from the day, *nothing left but darkness.*

God, I'm tired. So tired. Nothing left. Nothing . . .

Holly heard her voice at a great distance and realized too late that she had been thinking aloud.

It doesn't matter. Nothing matters.

She had lost her balance and fallen off the edge of the world, spinning into the darkness below.

She didn't even know that Linc caught her, breaking her fall, or that he carried her into the dressing tent, cursing her boss every step of the way.

Linc laid Holly carefully on a pile of colorful satin sheets that had been used for earlier shots. He touched her pale, still face with fingers that shook.

Then he stood up swiftly and went to tear a strip off of Roger's elegant hide for working her so hard.

Holly came back to consciousness with all the colors of sunset blazing and rippling overhead.

That's wrong, she thought vaguely. *Sunset is hours away.*

Outside men's voices were arguing.

Roger and Linc.

"—taking her with me," Roger said.

"Like hell you are," Linc snarled. "You've been working Holly so hard she can barely hold up her head!"

"It's not the work, you bloody idiot, it's—"

She put her fingers in her ears, stopping the sound of voices. She hadn't the strength to face Linc yet.

She could barely face herself.

A few minutes later she cautiously took her fingers out of her ears.

The arguing had stopped, replaced by the familiar sounds of the crew packing up equipment.

They'll have to wait for the tent, she thought. *I'm too tired to leave right now.*

With a long sigh, Holly pulled a flame-colored satin sheet over her head and let herself sink into sleep.

The next time she awoke, the brilliant colors of sunset were still flaring and rippling overhead. This time she recognized them for what they were.

The sultan's tent, she thought, dazed. *Why am I here? I thought we were finished with that part of Desert Designs.*

Restlessly, Holly turned her head and looked around.

I'm wearing the wrong costume for the interior script. Shorts, not harem pants.

And why am I underneath one of the satin backdrops?

Abruptly, memory returned.

I fainted.

The realization stunned Holly. She had never even come close to fainting before in her life.

How did I get here?

No memory came to her but that of hearing an argument. She had shut it out.

And then she had slept from sheer nervous exhaustion.

Linc. He was arguing with Roger.

Even as Holly thought Linc's name, she knew he was nearby, alone with her in the desert. She sensed him watching her, a presence as powerful as the mountains.

And as unyielding.

Gentle fingertips stroked Holly's cheek. She flinched away, not able to endure being hurt again. Suddenly she wished that she had not awakened at all.

The quiet surrounding the tent was absolute, telling her that Linc had won the argument. Roger and the rest of the Royce Designs crew had left.

Linc had not.

The warmth of his body flowed along her side as he lay down next to her. Protest rippled through her, a spasm of stiffness that passed quickly because she hadn't the strength to sustain it.

She felt the thick weight of her hair lifted off her neck, only to be replaced by Linc's kiss burning against her skin in a caress that was all the more consuming for its gentleness.

"No," Holly whispered. "Don't."

Linc heard the pleading in her voice, and the fear beneath it.

"Why?" he asked.

"Nothing's changed," she said. Then she laughed brokenly. "Bad to worse. That's a change, isn't it?"

"Everything has changed, *niña*. I love you."

Holly put her hand against her mouth and bit into her own skin to keep from crying out in protest.

Too late, she thought in anguish.

I can't believe him.

I can't let myself believe him, because if I'm wrong, if I let myself hope and love and live again . . .

And lose again.

"No," she said starkly.

"Look at me," Linc said.

His voice was as gentle as his fingertips, his kiss.

She closed her eyes and fought against hope.

He kissed her eyelids. Very gently he took her hand away from her mouth. He kissed the livid marks her teeth had left on her skin.

"I knew I would love the girl called Holly from the first time I saw her staring up at me on the trail with her heart in her eyes," he said. "But I was seventeen and she was only nine."

His voice was soft, as though he was talking to himself.

"I watched Holly grow up until one night she ran out of my parents' house and threw herself into my arms. I wanted to kill my parents for frightening her."

She tried not listen.

It was impossible.

His fingertips were touching her face as though she was a beautiful, fragile dream he was afraid of awakening.

"I took Holly home," Linc said, "kissed her, kissed her again and again, wanting her until I shook with it . . ."

She tried to say something, to make him stop retelling her own dream in his words.

But he kept talking in a voice that was husky with desire and regret and an emotion she was afraid to name, much less believe in.

"The next night I held my sweet Holly again, but differently. Her parents were dying, and she wept in my arms and I learned that shared grief was as binding as shared desire. She let me hold her, cry with her, love her. And then she was gone."

Linc paused, remembering. His eyes were dark with pain.

"I never wanted a woman as much as I wanted Holly," he said, "until six years later in Palm Springs, when a cat-eyed, black-haired model held out her arms to me and promised me . . . everything."

Holly moved restlessly.

"Don't," she said. "I can't live through it all again. Not now, knowing how it ends."

Gently, irresistibly, Linc continued.

"Suddenly I understood what had happened to my father," he said simply. "I no longer hated him, but I knew I would hate myself if I gave in to what I felt."

She made a small sound and shivered.

"I didn't see Holly beneath Shannon's fire," Linc said. "I didn't realize that I wanted Shannon *because* she was Holly. All I saw was a woman beautiful enough to destroy a man's soul."

"Linc—no."

His lips brushed over hers, silencing her with a tenderness that was like a razor slicing through her soul.

"I lashed out at what I saw," he said. "I was trying to protect myself from the kind of hunger I thought I'd never feel again. But I felt it. God, how I felt it."

Linc paused, touched Holly's lips gently, and kept talking, trying to make her understand what he had only just begun to understand himself in the last hundred days.

"I couldn't sleep," he said. "I saddled Sand Dancer and set out on the roughest trail I could find. It was a wild night and a damn fool thing to do."

His sad smile tore at her heart.

"But people who love sometimes do foolish things," he said, "like stand in front of rattlesnakes to save someone else's life."

Linc put his fingers beneath Holly's chin and turned her to face him.

"Thank you for Beth," he said quietly. "I already had figured out that you weren't the selfish woman of my nightmares, but I didn't know just how unselfish you truly were."

His fingers radiated warmth through her cold body. Her own hand moved, covering his. His hand turned and his fingers laced through hers.

Holly watched him, her eyes tawny in the dying light.

"I had better luck than I deserved the night I rode into the storm," Linc said. "I woke up next to the woman I loved and thought I'd lost. She fitted against me so perfectly, melting in my hands . . ."

His voice caught and for a moment there was only the sound of the wind teasing the brilliant canopy.

"Then I found out that Holly was Shannon," he said. "I felt betrayed. Caught like my father.

A fool. I took the only revenge I could and proved what an utter fool I really was. I'll never forgive myself for that, *niña*."

She said nothing, only laced her fingers more deeply with his and watched him with something close to hope in her eyes.

"Yet you forgave me," Linc whispered. "You came to me like a cloud to a mountain, sinking into me like desert rain, giving life to me. But you were Shannon, too, and I was . . . afraid of you."

A tremor went through Holly at the thought that he had feared her.

"Each time we made love," he said, "you sank more deeply into me. And then you said goodbye because I couldn't say the simple truth. I love you. I want you for my wife. I want children with you, a family. A lifetime."

"Linc," she whispered.

It was all she could say. Her throat was tight, aching with all the tears that she hadn't allowed herself to cry since Cabo San Lucas.

Linc looked at Holly's pale, drawn face and was afraid he had understood himself too late.

"Don't look so frightened," he said heavily. "I'm not asking you to stop being Shannon. I want to add to your life, not take away from it. I'll travel with you when I can, stay home when I have to. Just let me have part of you again. I love you so much. . . ."

His voice caught and his eyes searched hers.

"Tell me I'm not too late," Linc whispered. "Tell me that living without me is like dying every day. Tell me that you still love me."

Holly put her fingers on his lips to stop his words. She couldn't bear his pain any longer.

It was too like her own had been.

Like dying every day.

"I love you," she whispered.

She felt him tremble beneath her fingers, felt the heat of his breath expelled in a long rush.

His strong arms tightened, starting to pull her close. Then he stopped as though he had been shot.

She knew that he was remembering the moment when she had awakened. She had flinched at his touch.

She drew his mouth down to hers, breathing her warmth into him, her life, her dreams.

Her love.

Slowly their bodies flowed together, healing each other with a touch and a sigh, melting into each other until neither could say whose lips were kissed, whose tears were tasted, who spoke first of the life they would share, children and laughter, dreams as strong as the people who dreamed them.

And then there was only silence and need, cloud and mountain, the season of rain and life renewing.

Enjoy an excerpt from DEATH ECHO by

ELIZABETH
LOWELL

```
Manhattan
Monday
9:00 AM
```

Prologue

Y ou must believe me. St. Kilda Consulting is our best hope."
Former Ambassador Steele pinched the bridge of his
nose and wished he'd never met the woman who now sat opposite his desk. "Alara…"

"I'm no longer called that."

Steele blew out a hard breath and wheeled his chair back from
his desk. Very few people on earth could make him uncomfortable. The woman no longer called Alara was one of them.

And one of the most dangerous.

"Just as I no longer work for the government," Steele said.

"We established that years ago." Alara smiled almost sadly. Her
silver hair gleamed, hair that once had been as black as her eyes. "In
the shadow world, St. Kilda Consulting has made quite a reputation
for itself. Trust is rare in any world. Even more so in the shadows."

"You're asking him to break that trust," Emma Cross said,
speaking up for the first time in fifteen minutes.

Steele and Alara turned sharply toward Emma, telling her what she'd already guessed—they had forgotten they weren't alone.

All emotion faded from Alara's expression. It was replaced by the frightening intelligence that had made her a legend within the nameless, anonymously funded government agencies whose initials changed frequently but whose purpose never did.

"I came in soft," Alara said coolly, "requesting not threatening. I don't have time for games with disillusioned children." She looked at Steele. "America could lose a major population center in less than ten days. We need St. Kilda to prevent that. We will have what we need."

Without looking away from Alara, Steele said, "Emma, summarize the facts as they were presented to us."

Emma's light green eyes watched her boss for a moment. Then she began speaking quickly, without emotion. "As given to us, no questions asked or qualifications offered. Ms. Alara's department or departments have been following various overseas entities. One of those entities is suspected—"

"Known, not suspected," Alara cut in.

"—of stealing and reselling yachts," Emma continued without pause. "One of the stolen yachts was specially modified to hold contraband—chemical, biological, and/or radioactive. Motives, whether the actors are state or non-state, weren't part of Alara's presentation, which is going to make finding and stopping who or whatever is the enemy before time runs out is just this side of impossible." She looked at Alara. "No surprise the bureaucrats and politicians want to dump this steaming pile on St. Kilda's doorstep."

Steele almost smiled. Emma Cross had a pretty face and a bottom-line mind.

"The excuse for said dumping," Emma continued, turning back to Steele, "is that St. Kilda has an agent who has been investigating missing yachts for an international insurer. The yacht, *Blackbird*, which I have been tracing, is a dead ringer for the refitted and purportedly dangerous yacht pursued by Alara's department. Or departments. The person, group, or entity responsible for theft of the nameless yacht wasn't identified. At all."

Alara's still-black eyebrows rose, but she said nothing about Emma's coolly mocking summary. The older agent simply sat in her crisp business suit and pumps, looking like an employee of a middle-management team, back when women were called secretaries rather than administrative assistants.

"Satellite tracking and other intel confirm that a yacht believed to be the *Blackbird* will be offloaded from the containership *Shinhua Lotus* at approximately fifteen hundred hours Pacific Coast time," Emma continued. "According to St. Kilda's investigation, an unknown transit captain will pick up the boat in Port of Seattle. We have no assurance that the yacht aboard the containership is the same one that originally was loaded aboard the *Lotus*. We won't have that assurance until someone finds a way to get aboard either the containership or the yacht. I'm sure our would-be 'client' has the resources to covertly conduct that search."

"Had," Alara said. "Past tense."

"You have a leak," Emma said bluntly.

"Always probable," Alara said. "St. Kilda has carefully and repeatedly distanced itself from any traceable connection with any U.S. intel agency. The targets won't be looking for you. They sure as bloody hell are looking for us. We don't have anyone on the ground who isn't being followed."

Emma kept her mouth shut because she hated agreeing with the other woman. Nothing personal. Just past experience. The officers and agents she had worked with all over the world had been decent people, at the lower levels. The farther she went up the food chain, the less trustworthy the bosses were. Again, nothing personal. Just the Darwinian facts of survival in a highly politicized workplace whose rules changed with every headline.

"Do you have anything else you can tell St. Kilda?" Steele asked.

"Not at the present time," Alara said.

Emma made a rude sound.

Steele didn't bother.

"You aren't required to help," Alara pointed out.

"But it sure is hard to do business in the U.S. when everyone who works for St. Kilda is audited quarterly," Emma said, "when St. Kilda personnel are stopped at the border, or their passports are jerked, or their driver's licenses are revoked, their spouses fired, and every business that approaches St. Kilda is warned not—"

Steele held up his hand.

Emma swallowed the rest of her argument and waited. Steele knew how harassment worked. Good old Uncle's bureaucrats could hound St. Kilda to death. Literally.

"That's the price of living in a society you can't fit around a campfire," Alara said to Emma. "Cooperation is required in reality if not in law. Ambassador Steele knows this. Why don't you?"

Emma hoped her teeth weren't leaving skid marks on her tongue. She really wanted to unload on the older woman.

Because Alara was right.

"Reality is a bitch," Alara said. "When all else fails, you can count on that." She glanced at her watch. "In or out?"

Steele rolled his chair to face Emma. "You're off the hook on this one. Be prepared to brief another St. Kilda employee in less than an hour."

"No," Emma said. "I'm in."

"I don't want someone whose head isn't in the game," Alara said.

"No worries." Emma's smile was thin as a knife. "I've learned to use my head, not my heart. I'm in unless Steele says otherwise."

"You're in," Steele said,

"Nine days, which began counting down at midnight," Alara said, coming to her feet. "When the time is up, civilians die. If we're lucky, the number will be under a hundred thousand." She looked at Emma with cold black eyes. "Be smarter than your mouth."

1

E mma Cross gripped the round chromed bars of the pitching Zodiac's radar bridge as it raced over the Puget Sound, twenty miles beyond Elliott Bay. St. Kilda Consulting had assured her that the boat driver was capable. But Joe Faroe hadn't mentioned that the dude called Josh didn't look old enough to drink.

Was I that young once?

Yeah, I must have been. Scary thought. You can make some shockingly dumb, entirely legal decisions at that age.

I sure did.

Josh must have, too. His eyes are a lot older than his body.

She had seen too many men like him while she worked as a case officer in places where local wars made headlines half a world away, innocents were blown to bloody rags, and nothing really changed.

Except her. She'd finally gotten out. Tribal wars had been burning before she joined the CIA. The wars were still burning along just fine without her. World without end, amen.

Until Alara had dropped into St. Kilda's life.

She has to be wrong, Emma told herself. *God knows it wouldn't be the first time intel was bad.*

But if she's right...

The thought sent a chill through Emma that had nothing do with the cold water just inches away.

Nine days.

Automatically she hung on as the Zodiac bounced and skidded on the wake of a ship that was already miles behind them, headed for Elliott Bay's muscular waterfront. She pulled her thoughts away from what she couldn't change to what she might change.

Emma tapped the driver and shouted over the roar of the huge outboard engines. "Shut it down."

He eased off the throttle. The boat slid down off plane and settled deeply in the steel-colored water. Like a skittish cat, the inflatable moved without warning in unexpected directions.

"You okay?" Josh asked.

"As in not wanting to hurl?"

He smiled crookedly. "Yeah. As in."

"I'm good."

He gave her a slow once-over and nodded. "Sure are."

"Faroe told me about you, darlin', so thanks but no thanks."

Josh looked at her eyes for a moment, nodded, and waited for his next order. No harm, no foul.

Emma wished she could say the same about her job.

Shading her eyes against the bright afternoon overcast, she looked west, toward the Strait of Juan de Fuca. Swells from the distant Pacific Ocean, plus choppy wind waves, batted at the twenty-foot-long Zodiac, lifting and dropping the rubber boat without warning. Some of the waves had white crests that streaked the gray water.

"We good?" she asked. "That wind's kicking up."

"No worries. We can take three times the blow, easy."

Land looked real far away to her, but she'd learned to trust expert judgment. For all the pilot's fresh-faced looks, he was utterly at home with the inflatable and Puget Sound.

"Let me know if that changes," she said.

Even as Josh nodded, she switched her attention back to the western horizon. Ten minutes earlier, she'd spotted her target when it was only a dark blob squeezed between the shimmering gray sky and the darker gray sound.

Now the target was a huge ship plowing toward them like a falling mountain. Dark engine smoke boiled up from funnels behind the bridge deck. The deck cargo was a colorful collage of steel shipping containers stacked seven high. The boat was close enough that she could make out the white bow wave it pushed up before it.

"That her?" Josh asked.

She lifted binoculars, spun the focus wheel, and scanned quickly. On the Zodiac's shifting, uncertain platform, staring through unstabilized binoculars was a fast way to get seasick.

The collage leaped forward and became a random checkerboard of colors, a toy for giants playing an unknown game.

"Meet the container ship known as the *Shinhua Lotus*," Emma said, lowering the glasses. "Standard cruising speed close to thirty knots. One hundred and eighty thousand horsepower. Her hull is steel, a thousand feet long. She's stacked with more than fifteen thousand steel freight containers. One hundred and sixty thousand tons of international commerce at work."

"Gotta be the most boring job in the world."

She glanced quickly at him. "What?"

"Driving that pig between ports. Tugs do all the fun stuff close in. The ship's captain mostly talks on the radio."

She looked at the little boat that had carried her out to meet the *Lotus*. Twenty feet long, six feet wide and powered by two outboard engines. She touched the fabric of the Zodiac's inflated side tube. It was only slightly thicker than the rubberized off-shore suit she wore. All that supported the boat was the breath of life, twenty pounds-per-square-inch of air pressure.

And one of the biggest ships ever built was bearing down on them, bearing bad news in the shape of a yacht called *Blackbird*.

She lifted the binoculars again. The huge ship overwhelmed her field of view. Everything was a fast-forward slide show.

Stacks of shipping containers in various company colors. The windshield of the bridge deck. The hammerhead crane next to the forward mast.

The black-hulled yacht perched in a cradle on top of stacks of steel boxes.

Hello, Blackbird. *So you made it.*

If that's really you.

"How close can you get to the *Lotus*?" she asked.

"How close do you need?"

She pulled a camera from the waterproof bag at her feet. Unlike the binoculars, the camera had a computerized system to keep the field of view from dancing with every motion of the boat.

"I have to be able to see detail on a yacht on top of the containers. A two-hundred-millimeter lens is the longest I have."

That and intel satellite photos, courtesy of Uncle Sam. Too bad I don't really trust Alara.

For all Emma could prove, the photos St. Kilda had been given could have been taken on the other side of the world a year ago. Or three years. Or twelve. Not that she was paranoid. It was just that she preferred facts that she'd checked out herself. Thoroughly.

"Two-hundred-millimeter lens." Josh whistled through his teeth and narrowed his eyes. "And the lady wants details."

"What's the problem?"

He held up one finger. "That great pig up ahead is throwing a ten-foot bow wave." A second finger uncurled. "The Coast Guard patrol boats would be on us like stink on shit. After Nine Eleven, they lost their sense of humor about bending the rules."

No news there for Emma. "You saying it can't be done?"

"Depends. How bad do you want to swim or go to jail?"

"Not so much, thanks." She let out a long breath and reminded herself that impatience was a quick way to die, and she was chasing nothing more dangerous than luxury yachts.

At least she had been, until Alara appeared like a puff of darkness. "I can wait until the tugs are nudging that 'great pig' against a dock."

"If you're working on a really short clock," Josh said, "I'll be glad to take a run at the *Lotus* right now." He grinned suddenly. "It beats my usual gig—hauling seasick tourists out to chase whales."

She thought about it, then shook her head. "It's not life or death."

You wish.

She laughed silently, bitterly. That was why she'd quit the CIA and taken an assignment from St. Kilda to investigate yacht thefts. No alarms with this job. No adrenaline exploding through her body.

No blood.

No guilt.

And best of all, no corrupt politics.

Guess again, she told herself. *Then get over it.*

"Back to shore?" Josh asked.

"Not yet. Keep the *Lotus* in sight while you give me a sightseeing tour of the famous and beautiful Elliott Bay."

"Legal distance maintained at all times?"

"Until I say otherwise."

2

Standing on top of seventy-foot high stacks of containers, with only the unforgiving steel deck below to catch
him, Mackenzie Durand wrestled with the cargo sling that
would lift the yacht off the *Shinhua Lotus.* He looked up to
the glassed-in cab of the deck crane, where the operator was
waiting for directions.

Hope he knows what he's doing, Mac thought as he held up
his right hand and made a small circle in the air. Sign-language
for giving more slack to the cable that held the lifting frame.

The operator dropped the frame six inches at a time until
Mackenzie's hand clenched into a fist.

The cable stopped instantly.

Damn, but it's sweet to work with professionals, Mac
thought as he began positioning the sling on the yacht's black,
salt-streaked hull. The man in the cab might be a miserable
son of a bitch who beat his wife and was an officer in the most
corrupt labor union on the waterfront, but when he was at the
controls of his pet hammerhead crane, he could be as sure and
gentle as a mother cradling a nursing baby.

Mac manhandled a wide strap into position just ahead of the
spot on the hull where twin prop housings on the *Blackbird*
thrust out like eggbeaters. Lift points were crucial in control-
ling a vessel that weighed almost thirty tons.

Besides, if anything went wrong, he was going to be splat on ground zero. He'd been there, done that, and vowed never to be there again. He'd been the lucky one who survived.

At least he'd told himself he was the lucky one. After a few years, he even believed it. During daylight.

At night, well, night was always there, waiting with the kind of dreams he woke from cold, sweating, biting back howls of fury and betrayal.

Long ago and far away, Mac told himself savagely. *Pay attention to what's happening now.*

When he was satisfied with the position of the lifting strap, he signaled the crane operator to pick up cable. The frame went from slack to loaded. The aft strap was in front of the propellers and the forward strap was even with the front windshield. Both straps visibly stretched as the overhead cable tightened.

Just before *Blackbird* lifted out of its cradle, Mac clenched his fist overhead. Instantly the crane operator stopped bringing in cable.

Mac checked everything again before he scrambled up the ten-foot ladder that stood against the swim step at the stern of the yacht. When he was aboard the *Blackbird*, he gave the crane operator a palm-out hand signal with fingers spread.

Take a break, five minutes.

The operator nodded and reached for a cigarette.

A *Lotus* deckhand appeared and took the ladder away from the yacht's swim step.

Mac popped the hatch in the rear cockpit and went down below. He had been a professional transport skipper for five years. He was regularly dropped on the deck of a boat he had never seen before and was expected to take command of it immediately. Since he didn't plan on going down with any ship, he had developed a mental checklist as rigorous and detailed as an airline captain's.

He liked the idea that if he died, it was his own screw-up, not someone else's.

The first thing Mac did was snap on the battery switches. Each of the eight batteries was big enough to power a hybrid automobile. A quick check of their status showed they had retained enough charge on the ten-day trip from Singapore to start the yacht's engines and operate its various systems.

Next, he opened the seacocks that supplied saltwater to the cooling systems of the two shiny new Caterpillar engines that drove the boat. Oversized engines, a special order that made for a cramped engine room.

Gotta love those yachties with more money than sense, Mac told himself.

Quickly but thoroughly, he checked the hose clamps on the through-hull fittings to make sure none had vibrated loose at sea. Cooling water was good. Gushers of saltwater in the bilge weren't.

The through-hull fitting that normally supplied cooling water to the generator had been left open to drain rainwater or ocean spray out of the yacht during the voyage. Mac closed the seacock so the small ship wouldn't sink minutes after it touched the waters of Elliott Bay.

He checked the through-hull fittings for the septic and water maker systems, then the fuel lines that fed the two six-cylinder diesel engines. He had been assured there was enough fuel aboard to make Rosario, sixty miles to the north, but he was suspicious by nature.

It had saved his life more than once.

A shipping crew in Singapore, where the yacht had begun its voyage, could make hundreds of dollars by shorting the fuel tanks. Mac didn't want to come into the Rosario rigging yard at the end of a tow line.

The sight gauges for both fuel tanks showed less than an inch of fuel.

Ah, human nature. All for me and screw you.

His first stop would be the fuel dock on the Elliott Bay

waterfront. The good news was that the diesel fuel in the feed lines from the tanks looked clear. With quick, economical motions he checked both fuel filter housings for water.

All good. At least the greedy sucks put in clean fuel.

What there was of it.

He looked carefully around the engine room. Salt water was as corrosive as acid to metal parts and systems. Even with the best of care and maintenance, time and use and the sea would mark the yacht. But right now, she was bright and clean, shining with promise.

Mac loved taking a new boat on its first real cruise. It was like meeting a really interesting woman. Challenging. That was where the reward came—getting the best out of himself and an unknown boat. Or a woman.

No one else at risk, no one else to die, no one else to survive alone and sweat through nightmares the same way.

When Mac had finished his checklist, he climbed back up out of the engine compartment and went inside the salon to the helm. Plastic covered the upholstered furnishings. The teak dining table and polished granite of the galley counter were protected beneath cardboard and shipping blankets, as was everything else except the wheel. But the opulence of the yacht's fittings was evident in the bright brass lamps and the oriental style carpeting on the salon floor.

Mac opened the teak panel that concealed two ranks of electrical circuit breakers and meters. He noted a scratch on the inside of the door. Cosmetic, not a problem. He checked each carefully labeled meter and breaker, going down the ranks, engaging breakers and energizing the circuits he expected to need.

The last two breakers he threw were marked Port and Starboard Engine START/STOP. When he engaged them, two loud buzzers signaled that the Caterpillars in the engine room were ready to go.

With a final check of the batteries, he went back through the salon, into the well, and up the narrow six-step stairway to the flying bridge. He checked the switch settings on bridge controls, then lifted his hand and twirled his fingers in a tight circle.

The overhead crane operator smoothly picked up five feet of cable, lifting the yacht up and out of its cradle. The fresh afternoon breeze off Puget Sound tried to turn the boat perpendicular to the container ship, but the operator had anticipated the wind and corrected for it. The overhead crane arm swung the yacht toward the huge ship's outside rail.

For a second Mac felt like the boat was adrift, flying. This was the part of the job he didn't like, when he had to trust his life to the crane operator's skill.

He looked out over the waterfront toward the Seattle skyline beyond. The restless sound, the rain-washed city, the evergreen islands. The beautiful silver chaos of intersecting wakes—container ships, freighters, ferries, tugs, pleasure boats zipping about like water bugs.

One of the water bugs seemed to be fascinated by the process of unloading the yacht. Mac had seen the Zodiac while he waited for the *Lotus* to be nudged into its berth. The little rubber boat had weaved through the commercial traffic, circling ferries and tugs, taking pictures of everything, even the Harbor Patrol boat that had barked at it for getting too close to the *Lotus*.

Sightseers, Mac thought, grateful he no longer lived a life where the little inflatable would have been an instant threat. *Sweet, innocent civilians.*

He did a quick check of the water near the container ship, where he would soon be dropped into the busy bay. A small coastal freighter, freshly loaded with two dozen containers destined for local delivery, steamed west toward the San Juan Islands. Two Washington State ferries, one inbound to Seattle and the other headed across to Bainbridge Island, were passing one another a few hundred yards to the north. A City of Seattle fireboat was making way toward its station at Pier 48, and a dozen pleasure craft of varying sizes were crisscrossing the riffled waters in the afternoon sunshine.

The black rubber Zodiac with two people aboard lay about a hundred yards offshore, bobbing and jerking in the wakes and chop. The open craft had a shiny stainless steel radar arch and the logo of a local water tour outfit. The captain and single passenger wore standard offshore gear to protect them from wind and spray. The passenger was busy with the camera again.

The round black eye of the long-distance lens made the fine hairs on Mac's neck lift.

Too many memories of sniper scopes.

He shook off his past and watched as the crane operator delicately lowered the yacht into the water until Mac signaled for a stop. The operator held the boat in place in the cradle, afloat but not adrift. Mac checked his instruments once more, then touched the switch that locked the batteries into series and hit the port start button on the console.

Beneath him, he felt as much as heard one 550-horsepower engine rattle and cough. He held the switch closed while he glanced over his left shoulder toward the stern quarter of the boat.

Black smoke belched, then cleared and belched again. The stuttering sound of engine ignition suddenly smoothed out into a comforting, throaty rumble.

The starboard engine started more easily and leveled out instantly. He went to the stainless steel rail aft of the bridge and checked. Both exhaust ports were trailing diesel smoke. Beneath it, he could see the steady flow of cooling water.

Good to go.

He signaled thumbs-up to the crane operator. The yacht slipped down a few more inches until the water held the boat. Moments later the slings went slack. Then the operator let out enough cable to ease the lifting frame far enough aft that the yacht was free.

The big power pods took over as Mac put the engine controls

into forward. She felt solid. Clean. Good. A grand yacht doing what it had been designed to do.

Mac idled away from the container docks. He purely loved the first instants of freedom, of being responsible only for himself. Grinning, he glanced over his shoulder to check the wake.

The black Zodiac was moving with him. No faster. No slower. Same direction. Same angle.

The hair on Mac's neck stirred again in silent warning.

This time he didn't ignore it. He went below, got his binoculars, and took a good, long look from the cover of the cabin.

You're being paranoid, the civilian part of himself said.

The part of him that had been honed to a killing edge ten years ago just kept memorizing faces, features, and boat registration numbers.